ALMAS

ALMAS

VICTOR F. PALETTA

www.victorpaletta.com

ISBN 978-1-793-86182-5

Published in the United States of America

For Thomas, Estelle, Josephine, and Robert

1

An overcast night obstructed a pale moon, while along the shoreline crashing waves sent inland a white mist. On this bleak, isolated piece of land, survival of the fittest and biggest played out every day. Daily competition, particularly when food dropped from the sky, whipped the island up into a frenzy, enticing those out of hiding from all corners. Everything was deceptive and harsh, especially the erratic and often grim climate.

With genetically enhanced senses to match that of other prey, they found their way in the cover of night. The leader of the pack pointed directly ahead, grunting in a stomach-wrenching tone. With a dwindling limp one Cult lingered behind, remaining a couple paces back. Running and sprinting for hours in search of cover, the terrain offered little, if nothing. But at last, they found a promising narrow slit inside a tall mound of rock—what they thought was rock. Once cramming inside the stench was obvious; it was a mound of excrement, most likely from the one who was tracking them. Everything prior to the mound was a dead end, either in the form of steep cliffs or salivating teeth. Silence was now their best ally. No one spoke. The next roar was ear-splitting; whatever hunted them drew nearer, approaching from somewhere behind the blinding fog. Those hiding in the crevice could only wait, listening to the encroaching snarls, patient and hungry.

"You! Face him!" a Cult panicked from behind. Nearest to the crevice entrance was the last Cult to enter, the one with a handicapped leg. The beast was moments away. The one called upon was shoved out—an offering. Standing naked and alone, his spiny claws and jagged teeth were his only defenses. Sticking out his serpentine tongue, he measured the warm air, sensing his adversary's quick approach. Turning in the direction of his impending doom, he appeared calm. After seconds of meditation, unexpectedly, the exhausted Cult fell headlong into the earth; his body began twisting and contorting. From what little the others could see, they may have thought he was having a panic attack until he haltingly turned stiff as a corpse.

Upon its arrival, the predator discovered its prey lying peacefully on the ground. Clamping violently on its closest extremity, it next proceeded to toss the carcass back and forth, scaled flesh shredding between its teeth. The others were horrified, listening to crunching and tearing of tissue and bone, every so often glimpsing predator and prey. Like vermin embedded in their dark lairs, they knew that they were next, but it was to be expected, for where they had been taken nobody left in one piece. Peering out, their breathing resumed. They were run down and trapped. There was no point in being quiet anymore, as their heartbeats alone gave away their positions. Dying at the bottom of the food chain never entered the mind of a Cult, until now. The creature lowered its head; its searchlight eyes were substantial. It appeared that Ether Island had a way of driving even Cults mad with fear.

The glimmer in the beast's eyes was soon accompanied by another pair just as ominous, but smaller. The creature picked up its head, and both its lantern eyes went blank, perhaps closing them; yet snarls and growls could not cover up its discomfort. A short struggle ensued until everything went silent.

A cool, icy voice spoke out, clouding the head of every hidden Cult.

"You cowards," rippled the voice. "If I didn't need fresh legs, I would extinguish every last one of you," the voice declared.

"A Supreme! It can't be," mumbled one Cult before choking to death. The others could only watch. Seconds after, he rose to his feet displaying an expression of certitude and calmness.

"Now, everyone, listen closely" were the words of the newly risen Cult.

"Drake," said one alarmed Cult. Uncertainty was all that the others felt, for the question on everyone's mind was, *Why would Drake be present on Ether Island?*

"Yes," revealed Drake. Drake turned toward his subjects, careful not to give any eye contact. Every one of them was aghast. "I don't care why any of you were sent here. That does not concern me. If your will to survive is strong, some of you will make it out." The crevice was narrow enough for them to stand in single file, and the opening above rose many feet. Thick cloud cover broke apart in the night sky, and a brief glimpse of moonlight shined down. In the dim light, Drake tilted his head skyward.

"Do any of you know why this place is called Ether Island?" Drake asked the huddled bunch, inhaling. "It brings about loss of sensation, loss of consciousness. Most taken here die a peaceful death—lack of awareness and sensitivity. Ether, once thought to fill the upper heavenly regions of space, now fills the empty space of this island, plainly resulting in anesthesia." Drake was about to continue before a frozen Cult intervened, seemingly thawing out before his eyes.

"Why are we frightened? Can't we have a peaceful death?" the tremulous Cult spoke, craving more than ever the desensitizing effect of anesthesia. Tiny prey such as themselves easily succumbed to the gas, whereas bigger predators were better equipped; even though they, too, became numb and lethargic, they did not become paralyzed.

"This, I'm afraid, is my fault. My father's anger must have hardened his heart. He must have reversed the ether inhibiting gas. His ignorance will lead to our escape. For now, we have able bodies with sound minds, and can work together. You will turn your terror inside out. You will rise above your fears. My friends, you must now take advantage of your terror occulta."

They felt relieved and hopeful being in the presence of Drake, but each was puzzled.

"You're probably wondering if you have this gift. Every one of you has it, and I can assure you, you will need it. As you can see, I have already put it to use." Drake put both hands to his face. "There are many stages, but for now, all you need to know is the first." Shrieking and crunching sounded off in the woods nearby. Something else now trampled down trees like toothpicks in search of them. Drake looked skyward once again, but this time with his eyes closed.

"What shall we do, Master?" asked a worried body, unable to hide his fear. Others voiced the same concern through frightened stares of their own. Seconds later, Drake awoke from his unruly state of mind.

"With my crippled leg, he must've thought I wouldn't last five minutes. He also didn't count on me finding others," said Drake with a little mirth. He gave neither reply nor showed concern for the one soon to arrive. *Why would he send me here with others?* Drake asked himself. *Must he have known what I would do? Why would he rid the island of its mind-altering gas, the only thing capable of keeping me subdued?*

Drake's first impression upon landing on Ether Island was one of cruelty, of his father wanting him conscious before death, but perhaps, Drake thought, *There was another reason.*

The trembling was getting closer, and the rumble of hunger could no longer go unnoticed. Drake turned to the others, standing adjacent to the Cult farthest in the back.

"Aaaahhhh, yes, perhaps," uttered Drake to himself, and then went on, "Lesson number one: close your eyes, rid your fears, and welcome death." His words were hypnotic.

It's hard to imagine taking such an order on demand without much time to prepare, but every Cult obeyed and willingly closed their eyes. After blocking out the shaking waste in circumference, the Cults began seeing death as a reward and not as a punishment, and soon cherishing what might come after. Their fears dissipated. This was all Drake needed to encourage them deeper into the unknown. The energy stirring the air around them was radiant. It came quick, as their leader was there to deliver it at its cataclysmic peak. What the others could not see was the final ingredient to their alternate states. With their eyes still closed, Drake bit his own arm. Green pus oozed out from between his dark scales. Raising his arm to his mouth, he slurped his own fluid, sucking and chewing crudely. Spitting it out in form of a spray, the green mist covered all. Their eyes cracked open, revealing a white membrane glaze.

"Now, everyone out," Drake calmly ordered. Upon command, each came out of hiding. All were possessed and now pawns in a dangerous game of chess, completely under their master's control.

2

Dray eagerly hooked Jamie beneath her legs and carried her to bed. Anxiously laying her down, they joined in an intense kiss. Exchanging silent stares, their fingertips, legs and arms hooked. These were special days and nights for both, especially awakening to the sound of one another's peaceful breathing. Kissing her softly on the forehead, her fine, straight nose rubbed up against his bottom lip.

"What shall we do today?" Jamie asked, hugging Dray close.

Dray tiredly responded, "Stay in bed."

"But we must leave sometime. Won't you miss being followed by all your fans?" asked Jamie, coyly. Her piercing almond eyes drew out another kiss.

"Ah, yes, my beloved fans," Dray said as he unfolded his arms from around Jamie, folding them behind his head.

"When will you accept that you're their hero?" Jamie turned toward Dray. Dray looked up at the plush drapes hanging carelessly from the ceiling.

"We should move those drapes by the window."

"Who cares about the drapes? Why do you always change the subject?" Jamie sternly replied, but not upset. She looked more concerned.

"Wouldn't you?" answered Dray as they both now gazed above.

It was the everyday, menial things Dray loved best, but he kept this to himself. Up until a month ago, his entire life had been comprised of challenging routines and always getting up alone. Now everything was fine; every day he awoke with a warm, fragrant body next to him. He inspected his room and thought back to his old one in corporal training; though it was now buried beneath heaps of rubble, it was hard to forget. He often compared his old lifestyle to the present. He enjoyed his new living quarters among other amenities. His old room was for sleeping and recovering from his day's objectives, but this one was for living; something he was growing accustomed to—which often accounted for him wanting to stay in. Dray and Jamie seldom discussed his upbringing in corporal training; instead, he often asked her questions about her youth. Discovering more with each passing day, he never seemed to get enough. Their bed faced a ten-by-twenty-foot window overlooking the city. Gazing out, he and Jamie could see hovering vehicles carrying Endeavors and Survivors and robots going about their business. This also helped contribute to his desire to stay in; he could see a whole lot from where he sat. Entertainment in Endeavor society was never scarce. Since their last military victory, celebrations were held nearly every night; though over the past few weeks fewer Endeavors and Survivors attended. The reason being that they were still at war, and every able body contributed wealth and manpower to their overall prosperity. Scientists were also hard at work, constantly improving on their latest technology.

"My mom wants to see me today," Jamie announced after a long pause. Dray shifted his attention from the disorderly mess in the corner. On the sofa nearby, clothes and shoes were scattered about, as he realized how much his wardrobe had grown. His closet was full on account of Jamie moving in more of her things, yet she left much behind with her mother, Madge.

"Yeah, sounds like a good idea," Dray sighed, almost sad to hear that they would be apart for the day. "I think I'll go see John and Al, see how they're doing." It never occurred to Dray how much time he and Jamie had been spending together; he enjoyed every minute of it. They did see family and friends as much as possible but mostly together.

Sunlight crept deeper into the room as Jamie sat up and rose out of bed. Outside and above the city, the Stargaze proved its worth day in and day out; their protective windshield to the outside never failed. Dray recalled the Survivor's Skyscape in Compound 40 and the beauty it once projected, but nothing could compare to the natural rays of sunlight. He stayed in bed while Jamie went about getting ready; her slender and regal physique always stirred something within him. He learned to control his lingering Morphic Formula whenever his heart rate picked up. Jamie suspected he could control it but never asked how. Observing his formula's lasting side effects was a fascinating task for her.

"All right, so I'll see you later," whispered Jamie, kneeling over Dray.

"Yeah, I'll meet up with you this afternoon."

"Don't you want to know where I'll be?" Jamie asked with a cringed brow.

"I'm sure I'll find you."

"Good, because I'm not even sure. ... Be good," Jamie said softly before kissing him good-bye. Dray sat up and got out of bed. He felt unusually well today, because for one reason or another being apart from her always bothered him. Something awful happening to her was a constant worry of his, but strangely he now felt the more vulnerable of the two, and he did not know why. Since entering the Endeavor City, nothing but hospitality was given, but every so often his biological radar told him to be on alert.

Maybe I'm just being paranoid, Dray thought as he picked some clothes off his sofa and tossed them inside his closet, but the clothes slowly tumbled back out. He shoved them in deeper, this time, shutting his closet door behind. He put on some gray pants with a white long sleeve shirt, and over his long sleeve he wore his black vest. Jamie insisted he try the newest Endeavor styles. Next to his door was an intercom. He dialed John's number and discovered he was not at home. He tried Al next and got the same result. He next thought about calling Jason but remembered his new position as an instructor. Dray was asked to become an instructor himself but decided when he was not getting military updates, Jamie was the only one he wanted to be with. Since he could not contact John or Al, he decided to surprise Jason.

Dray followed his corridor out to the elevator and went down, toward the deepest reaches of the Endeavor compound. He could have taken the slide, but the view on the way down did not compare. Before reaching the bottom, he spotted Al in one of the many side shops circling the great expanse. A smile always popped up when he saw Al haggling with one of the shopkeepers. In fact, since he gave Al the idea of opening his own shop, Al's been nagging him ever since to retrieve his memorabilia back at Compound 40. But the Endeavors reminded Al it was still too dangerous. Dray did not mind the challenge but agreed with the others that it was still too soon.

After passing the Hanging Gardens at ground level, the elevator light came on. Like Compound 40, there was a whole network of tunnels beneath the Endeavor City. *It shouldn't be long until Bruce is finished*, Dray suddenly thought, recalling his meeting with Dr. Roberts the day before. The doctor reported progress with Bruce but did not give a finishing date. This encouraged Dray. His scout was most likely that extra sense of security he was lacking. He counted on Bruce the most. His robotic canine had proven his worth in battle.

Dray always felt like he was being watched. He often wondered if his Morphic Formula was the reason for any surveillance, but he certainly did not think he was dangerous. Something else was also bothersome, maybe another reason why they might be keeping a close watch. *But what do they know? Dr. Roberts told me my tests were fine.* Dray could only wonder why they would lie to him. Remembering Varo's last dying words and his ability to leave his body never escaped him. Dray never imagined he himself was a Cult or could possibly turn into one. *How would they react?* He feared how the Endeavors and Survivors would respond. The thought of their hero turning into a Cult would be the worst thing imaginable. He would be the first to admit not wanting anyone around who might change into such a repugnant creature. Clearly, if this were to ever occur, the subject in question would be locked up and experimented on like a lab rat.

The elevator came to a smooth, descending halt and out stepped Dray. As he turned the corner, a lot was still on his mind, distracting him from the person he was about to run into. With his head tilted forward, looking more at the floor than ahead, he dwelled on the possibility of becoming a Cult.

"Oh!" reacted Dray, running into the unsuspecting body. "Sorry." Before contact, she too was oblivious of Dray, looking down at some papers. She managed to cling to her folder as her fall placed her sitting upright on the cold floor. She looked annoyed and upset. Her body language hid nothing.

She wore a stylish two-piece uniform, all black and few markings. She looked like someone with authority. From what Dray could also see, she looked young and in shape. As he helped her up, he scanned her sandy blonde hair down to her black leather shoes.

Her recognition of Dray came quick. She had seen him once before. He carried himself well, and his confident demeanor was unmistakable. But today, he looked troubled. Being up close for the first time, she peered back into his commanding eyes.

"Hi, you're Dray," she said.

"Yes, and you are?"

"Grace, nice to meet you." They shook hands.

"Are you an instructor?" Dray suspected but asked anyway.

"I am. I teach in a room next to your friend, Jason. He talks about you all the time."

"I'm on my way to see him right now. I thought I'd pop in and surprise him. Is he still in class?"

"He is."

After a brief pause, Dray carried on.

"Well, it was nice meeting you."

"Same here," replied Grace, stepping around Dray and boarding the elevator. *He sure doesn't seem very happy*, Grace pondered, standing inside the elevator, unable to take her eyes off him. Before the doors closed, Dray, too, had a hard time looking away, turning for one last glimpse at the lady in uniform. As he made his way down the hall, his thoughts were no longer on turning into a Cult.

I wonder what she teaches.

3

Night covered the eyesore of blood and limbs, but the spoiled scent did not go unnoticed for too long. More notably, though, night could not cover up the cries of Cults fighting with bare claws and teeth. Their ferocity matched that of the beast swatting at them, sometimes swatting them in half with just one swipe. Yet the Cults were unafraid and continued fighting while their own carnage lay scatted about. The beast's eyes were prime targets, but they were situated high above as he stood tall, except for when he bent low to take a bite. His gaping jaw hung low and wide and finished what little else his claws could not.

The Cults were tenacious prey, for when one of them was wounded, they backed off, until a gaping slash or cut revitalized, quickly putting them back into the fray. The ones whose limbs were entirely hacked off took longer to reenter. Chaos ensued and was what soon attracted others prowling in the dark.

Drake ran from the fight with three others at his side; they were ready to do his bidding at any moment. He knew the commotion was bound to attract others and knew it would not be long until something picked up their trail. The trees nearby were thin and tall, a sad source of evasion should anyone decide to climb. *No one escapes Ether Island without transport*, Drake thought. The vehicle that dropped him off jetted away soon after, so there was no point in retracing his steps. Even though he lacked a solid plan, he felt confident now that he had fresh legs. *We will run until we hit water*, decided Drake, but the water was just as dangerous, perhaps even more so than the island. And Drake knew it.

"Stay back!" Drake ordered a Cult at his side. "Up ahead!" he grunted to another. "You! With me!" For now, this was his plan: to have his last three pawns picked off before him. The last Cult remained at his side. The others did as they were told. One slowed his pace, remaining far behind, the other sprinted ahead. His orders were swift and given between short bursts of breath. To an unfamiliar eye, and in the light of day, the Cults would have looked unusual running the way they did. They could have easily been mistaken for other inhabitants on the island, their upper bodies bending freakishly close to the ground.

Back at the bloodbath, four more beasts arrived; the last Cult lay helplessly on the ground. He had been used as a decoy, but he would not have known or cared. He writhed and squirmed, absent of one arm and one leg, but this did not help rejuvenate either limb. Glaring up at ten circling eyes, and being lightly dripped on by drool and blood, he looked furious as they were about to lower their necks and feast. His companions were already consumed, minus a few limbs here and there. *Close your eyes, redirect your fears, and welcome death* was all the Cult could think. It was a flashback to moments ago when he was promised another way out. Since this was the last thing on his mind, he did just that as he closed his eyes. He simmered his rage, which had replaced his fear, and with no other choice, he welcomed death. Upon opening his eyes, in his ultra state, he found himself floating above a frenzy. No longer did he crave the numbing gas, as he had become an invisible vapor himself. Looking down, it was evident he had joined the other damned souls wandering for eternity on Ether Island. In his ghostly state, he decided to follow the others. *May as well be witness to their fate.* He was in control of his actions and no longer a slave to his master. Vengeance was not on his mind, for what could he do? Upon catching up with the first fleeing Cult, he enjoyed the view, and most of all, the chase he had now become a part of.

A convoy of predators picked up Drake's trail. Creatures not already on the hunt were now joining up; the stampede alone indicated prey. The Cult farthest back decided to turn and make a stand. It was a valiant attempt to head them off, or at least slow them down, but proved futile as he was effortlessly swept aside. He was flung up and over the first charging head, and after coming down many mouths were there to greet him. Drake smelled water up ahead as fog became moist on his skin. The onslaught in pursuit was gaining with every stride; it appeared the whole of Ether Island had come alive.

They were yards away from the coast, about to breach the tree line, when the lead Cult got picked off. Now down to himself and another, Drake was running out of options. Glancing to his left and right, trees were being flattened by an avalanche of claws and teeth. They were closing the gap, but amidst the sea of death, gloom was not etched on Drake's face—he came up with a plan. Although he had never tried it before, he remembered the secret passed down by his father. *What better time than now?* thought Drake. He had already had success converting his helpers, and anything at this point was worth a shot. A fleeting moment gave Drake a glimpse into his past.

=

"Come, son, let me show you how. But you must remember, Drake, it can be dangerous," Varo cautioned as he walked toward the edge of a cliff, with Drake and another at his side. The Cult next to Varo was already brainwashed and would have jumped off had he been ordered. After removing his cape and handing it to Drake, Varo wore little else underneath. "We have very dense skin, as you can see," said Varo as he stroked the back of the helpless Cult, inching his fingers up and down. With one serrated nail, he made an incision from the Cult's head to his lower back. "Nature has given us a great advantage over our enemies. When sliced in the right spot, it comes off with ease." The one being

19

harvested for skin stood motionless, having felt nothing from Varo's slithering fingers. His scaled flesh stretched and pulled, coming clean off his muscle beneath. Varo continued to tear and slice away, saying, "The more the better, son, the more the better." Drake was young, but vividly recalled that even he winced at the display. His father stood with an outstretched hand, holding another Cult's bare flesh.

"Our skin can replenish itself, and if we want, we can combine it with another's," Varo said as he threw the skin around his neck and back, molding flaps between his arms and lower body. "Now, watch, see how it works." As he had indicated, the other's flesh rejuvenated, as Varo's own flesh mended itself with the new. Flesh was expanding and growing oddly around Varo, as an additional layer now covered his old. Deciding enough time had elapsed, Varo jumped without saying a word. Drake exulted at his father's courageous leap but gloried more at his miraculous ascent out of the great abyss. A flesh hang glider sprouted from all corners of his father's body. He soared like a crane! Drake was in complete awe of his father. He vowed never attempting it himself unless he absolutely had to.

=

Presently, Drake's cape would have been welcome, for falling and gliding with grace was one thing he could do, and what he had done not long ago in a deep canyon. But an eventual landing in the sea was not an option. What his father had done had taken him far under his own volition. It was madness, but if it meant madness, then madness it must be.

Only feet away, Drake saw an escape route and ordered his last follower up a tight squeeze of an embankment. On their way up, they plowed into loose rock with bare feet and hands, crumbling what little they could to cause a landslide. Corking the narrow entrance was more than Drake had hoped. After reaching the top, he could see waves crashing down below. All along the coast, the water met the sea at a steep incline. Also, down below, splashing off to the side just as the waves, beasts collided and fought for positioning.

Drake began the ritual of removing flesh, and after imitating his father, he now held out layers of scaly flesh. With little enthusiasm as to his next course of action, he was almost in disbelief as he swung the warm, slimy hide around his back. The Cult standing before him was unaware and could not have cared less. His master could have strung his organs in a pearl necklace for all he cared.

Drake now had to take a leap of faith, the same leap his father had taken. Should his leap fail, crashing into the sea was the least of his problems; those patrolling the waters presented just as many teeth. Meanwhile, his flesh felt sensational, delivering an odd sense of security. With the help of Mother Nature and his scientific forefathers, his body chemistry read his mind, like a caterpillar instinctively morphing into a butterfly.

The clawing and scratching behind grew louder as the hunters bulldozed their way to the top. After giving his final order, Drake turned toward the sea. Scanning the dark horizon beyond, apprehension was unmistakable—once he jumped, there was no turning back. However ready he was, though, he waited, until there was no other choice but to jump.

The time had come, as Drake turned to see his loyal guard attempt to defend their position. Taking a final deep breath, he jumped, avoiding an outstretched claw. Like dominoes, those behind spilled over the edge and into the water. They tried desperately climbing back up, but the wall lining the sea was too steep. Drake fell like a rock before a coastal wind caught hold of his huge batlike wings. They flung out wide just like his father's had, and with every muscle, he pivoted and banked his monstrous frame. Flapping seemed impossible, as his parasail limbs were taken by the wind. As he gained in altitude, his anatomy took hold, carrying him away. Glancing back and below for the last time, Drake said good-bye to Ether Island. Between each crashing wave, he watched as glittering eyes extinguished. His hunters had become the hunted.

4

"Hello!" said Jason upon opening the door. "What a surprise. Class, this is Dray. Dray meet my class," Jason introduced as they shook hands. Dray regally entered the room, looking over attentive students. The kids knew Dray well as he was practically a legend, a leader to follow and live up to. Not only did he lead the charge in the rescue of his people, but he also removed the head of the snake, Varo.

"Hey, everyone, I didn't mean to interrupt, but I'd enjoy sitting in and listening for a while," Dray revealed.

"I'm sure my class won't mind. Have a seat." Dray spotted an open seat in the back and proceeded toward it.

"Well, let me just wrap this up," Jason informed, turning back to the subject at hand.

The room was plain and simple, like the ones Dray and Jason were accustomed to growing up. In Compound 40, reporting to Academic Hall, apart from their sleeping quarters, was a brief break from everything else. Dray wondered if it was the same for these young ones as well. Jason stood in front and continued with his lecture. Dray listened as every student. He was eager to learn more about the Endeavor curriculum. Although they appeared to be listening as attentively as Dray, many were still too distracted by his presence. They were young students.

"So, no matter what their numbers, the last vehicle next to you is your best chance. Your shield can give you crucial minutes in planning ahead. If you know the basic boundaries, you'll have a better idea of how to deploy it." Jason pointed to a hologram of an Endeavor vehicle. Dray spotted the spear ray in front and knew right away what he meant. "I wish I could speak from experience, but when I was on the front line, we weren't equipped with spear rays. But I can tell you one thing, when activated, nothing would've been able to knock out our power." Jason glanced over at Dray, thinking he would agree.

Dray remembered a similar lecture not long ago, but the discussion was on why unmanned vehicles weren't equipped with spear rays. Dray assumed a manned vehicle would be appropriate but still felt uneasy about it.

"The blazer switch is our latest upgrade. It allows more time in holding beneath the light. I know this stuff is a little advanced, but Jeremy asked why chemistry and physics were so important. Having some knowledge in this area will help you better understand the development of such weapons. I'll see everyone back here tomorrow. Dismissed." Jason wrapped up his lecture.

"Dray, I'm glad you came," said Jason, patting students on their backs as they left.

"I'm feeling pretty restless these days," Dray started to explain, as they stepped out of the room. Walking down the hall, Dray could see students entering and exiting other rooms nearby.

"You could always come give lectures. I'm sure the students would like it."

"I'm sure they would, and I'd be happy to someday. ... Chemistry and physics?"

"Yeah, my two favorite subjects," replied Jason with a smile. "I know they're young, but I can't help talking about combat. They don't know how easy they have it. Our program didn't compare."

"How so?" queried Dray.

"They're raised differently. They get a choice after they finish first year. They learn everything the average citizen soldier knows, girls and boys alike. After they pass their courses, they choose whether to further their rank. Which most do. That's where the real testing begins."

"So, they get to decide if they want to be put through hell," concluded Dray.

"Precisely."

"Any news from Michael and Peter?" Dray asked, changing topics, looking down the hall.

"No, no news. I think they were crazy to leave."

"Why's that?"

"I admired their decision to go, but I couldn't imagine getting captured again. Give me a few more months and then ask me to go on a mission."

"I wish I had gone with them," Dray responded sorrowfully.

"It's not like they're on their own. And with Archimedes I'm sure they'll be fine. I agreed with Commander Tarpin, Dray, we need you here."

A few moments of silence passed until a group of students rounded the corner into Jason's room.

"What're you doing later?" asked Jason, turning from his students.

"Meeting up with Jamie at some point. Later tonight, I'm thinking the Great Mantle."

"Sounds good, I'll see you there. By the way, how are you two doing?"

"Things couldn't be better."

"I want you to meet someone tonight," announced Jason. "Look at those youngsters. I got to go."

5

Drake felt more alive than ever before, looking down at the dark sea below. In the pitch-black, minus brief passages of moonlight, how far up and down seemed impossible to gauge. Drake drifted as high as he could. The wind was cool and crisp before the red sun slowly rose over the horizon. Now, with warm light helping guide his way, his confidence grew more by the minute. His bone structure was still an anomaly; how it helped his wings expand from his body was miraculous. He figured the extra flesh had acted as a catalyst, not fulfilling the exact ingredients itself, but rather spawning the necessary changes within. The longer he stayed airborne, the stronger his limbs grew. As he soared through the early morning sky, he wondered how his father had removed his wings. Varo never mentioned what happened to them but did reveal that his flight time depended on the flesh harvested. Presently, how long his wings remained was the least of his concerns.

The wind calmed, and it became harder to produce his own updraft. He ascended as high as he could when the wind picked back up. After flying for quite some time, his energy was beginning to wane. He did not not know how much longer he could stay airborne.

In the distance, something came into view. Drake was becoming light-headed from exhaustion but knew what it was that he saw. The Great Dome was magnificent, a sparkling oasis out in the middle of the ocean. Constructed out of an ice-like substance and other material, it had considerable buoyancy and strength. It resembled a glacier He had known that the monstrous dome lingered somewhere out in the great expanse of blue, but it was pure luck that he happened to cross its path. It was constantly on the move. The last he remembered, Captain Leach was in command, and still loyal to his father, no doubt. Drake was losing altitude fast and wondered if he would reach the ship before hitting the water. Little specks came into view. As he imagined, many would be there to greet him.

Standing watch, several Cults saw something in the distance. Only a select few in the world had ever seen the likes of another in Drake's form; his appearance alone startled the bravest among them. Little did they know was just how exhausted the winged creature was. They sounded the alarm, drawing the attention of the entire crew, including Captain Leach, standing with two warriors on the Great Dome's highest level.

"Stand firm!" Leach ordered one of his warriors.

"Sir, who could it be?" asked one warrior. A few anxious minutes passed before the Captain's scope homed in on the unidentified foe.

"Ready battle stations!" Leach shouted. He was aware of Drake's sentence to Ether Island, and by now had received word of Master Varo's fate. No one knew Drake's intentions. No chances were to be taken. Leach did not recognize Drake but knew that there were few out there with his capability.

The Cults on deck received word to stand firm. Their eyes widened when they saw their fellow warrior come down from the sky.

Drake gained more strength once seeing the commotion on deck. After clearing the Great Dome's perimeter, he came down like a skydiver, smoothly, until losing wind ten feet above the surface; in the final seconds he dropped fast. His landing was felt by those nearest to him—the added weight on his back equaled two warriors combined. As he flexed his monstrous wings, their nervous stares gave Drake a little ease. Taking one step forward, they all moved back. Drake knew they could have blasted him where he stood.

"At ease," said an authoritative voice from behind. Leach walked through the crowd gathering on the south sector of the Great Dome. Others were taking up positions high above and all around. There must have been tens of thousands; the Great Dome appeared to be a floating city. "State your intentions and be careful with your actions. I do not want to give the order, but if I must, I will. I'm in command here," Leach announced, halting thirty feet from Drake.

They might not know who I am, thought Drake. But he suspected Captain Leach had a guess. After catching his breath, Drake reached behind him and caressed his wing. He did not answer the captain. The closer he came to each warrior, the more he seemed able to feed off their energy. He grew stronger by the second and felt as though he could take flight again.

"I am Drake," Drake finally revealed, deciding to be up front with the captain. "I was unjustly sent to Ether Island. Everyone here should know. I have few desires. First, I want protection until I reach land. Second, I want to speak with my father. And third, I want something to eat." His requests were reasonable and wishing to speak with his father would have given Leach a break.

"Master Varo was killed twenty days ago," Leach began. Drake looked at him with dagger eyes. "Since his demise and your sentence, a vacuum in the Far East has caused infighting. And our enemy in the west has grown bolder ever since. My orders were to hold the Great Dome, which I have done so honorably. Whether your sentence was just or not does not erase your rightful place to rule after your father. ... Commander Spiels has taken control on land. Your timely arrival is most welcome. Now get our Supreme something to eat" were the final words of the captain. Upon hearing the latest news, Drake felt unmoved, turning toward the ocean. He no longer had to face his father. Commander Spiels was now his concern. He would be a formidable adversary should he decide to fight.

"How did he die?" asked Drake, turning toward the captain.

"One of our warriors reported an ambush at prison 680."

"How could this happen?" Drake questioned further. Seconds after being offered safe harbor, his wings began folding, or rather crumbling, until finally shriveling up into his back. It appeared the more relaxed he felt, the faster his wings dissipated. All around, inquisitive eyes watched the spectacle, wondering if they, too, were capable of doing the same. Even Captain Leach seemed impressed. Drake took little notice.

The morning ritual had begun, whether upon Drake's arrival or not, all Cults come out when the sun comes up. Drake also soaked in the sun's rays; revitalizing for a Cult.

"I don't know," replied Leach. "The humans have developed a new weapon. We don't know what it could be," he added after a considerable pause.

"I think I may have faced this weapon. This weapon sent me to Ether Island, and now, if what you say is true, it sent my father into the hereafter."

For the first time in Drake's life an icy chill ran up his spine, separate from the chill always circling throughout. Whatever fears he had faced on Ether Island could not compare to the one capable of bringing down his father.

"Let me show you to your quarters, Master Drake," said Leach, motioning toward the dome's entrance. Drake followed the captain as all others watched in silence. The

Cult sent earlier to retrieve some food approached with smelly fish and a red cloak. After devouring the fish and putting on the cloak, Drake carried out an inspection, continuing alongside the captain.

"Where are all the strikers?" asked Drake, knowing the Great Dome's capability of delivering devastating attacks abroad.

"Commander Spiels has taken them all out. All we have left are our air defenses."

"What other aircraft do you have?

"We are working on a new fleet, sir, but it's going to take some time."

"Captain, tell your men to get back to their posts." Drake was beginning to take command after hearing how vulnerable to attack they were. He was not taking any chances.

"Back to your posts!" yelled Captain Leach. They scattered like flies.

"Speed up production on fewer aircraft. I must find my division as soon as possible," Drake said, beginning to think out loud. He was back into war mode.

"Master Drake, your division was decimated by Commander Spiels. After your imprisonment, his orders were to take out any still loyal to you. Your father wanted to send a message, but after his death, Spiels went even further—he killed everyone who ever fought for you." Drake was startled, even more so now than when he had heard of his father's fate. Commander Spiels was not going down without a fight.

Many minutes passed before Drake and Leach reached the Great Dome's main entrance. A massive archway stood before the entrance, and inside was a bastion of warmth and light. Cults, young and old, went about their business. Heads turned toward Drake and Leach as they made their way through the city. The captain veered left, steering them toward another massive archway. Drake's red cloak distinguished him from others; only those with the utmost power could wear red in its entirety. Leach wore a black cloak with red stripes.

An angry Cult was standing over a female, yelling furiously and swinging his fists. Drake felt this would be a good opportunity to give a speech.

"Captain, I wish to address your people," stated Drake, reaching out and grabbing the head of the ill-tempered Cult. His jagged nails dug deep into his flesh. The Cult had little time to react as he stood upright and stared blankly ahead. Drake effortlessly drug him alongside the captain. The female being abused was bewildered and frightened. The Cult beneath Drake's fingertips began withering away, giving off a stench that soon attracted those behind closed doors. Deciding he had walked far enough, Drake halted as close to the dome's center as he could.

"Attention! Master Drake wishes to speak!" Captain Leach made the announcement.

"As you all are aware, I have very little patience for those pretending to have power when they don't. I will not tolerate aggression unless ordered by me," said Drake. His words were spoken with care, and if what he was saying was true, he was altering every male Cult's way of life.

"From now on, both genders will coexist equally on this great carrier. I want every ounce of energy spent contributing to production, not beatings. We are going to war and I need your cooperation. Anyone who wishes otherwise—will end up like this," warned Drake, releasing the limp body between his fingers. The putrid Cult slumped to the floor with a thud.

"Captain Leach will continue at the helm while I draw up plans for future operations. This is all I have to say at this time. Captain, show me to my quarters."

6

Dray went for a walk in the Hanging Gardens. The scent in the air was euphoric. It was the combination of flowers, vegetables, and fruits. And not many people were out and about, making him feel even more at ease. The morning was still young, giving him plenty of time before meeting up with Jamie. He looked up at the Stargaze. Viewing the massive window had become a ritual, especially in the morning. He wished more than ever to deploy back out into the wild; whether it was because of the unknown or the danger, it had given him the feeling of being more than just alive, but rather unrestrained. His short time in the wild was enough to get him hooked to the sights and sounds of Mother Nature.

Amidst all the diverse sensations one suddenly stood out. Dray's nostrils flared as he whiffed what approached. What he detected was mechanical in nature, distinct from other robots and machines. Machines, too, had different components that made them tick, and this one had something the others did not.

Dray smiled from ear to ear before turning toward his scout. It was what he had long been waiting for. It was Bruce! He had tracked down his master in a city full of people. Sparkling new, he looked magnificent. Bruce halted, tucked in his back two legs and sat. Dray touched the top of his head, and as programmed Bruce stood up, turned to his side, and let his master carryout an inspection.

"Bruce, I thought I lost you," admitted Dray, kneeling beside him. Bruce's eyes were on fire, a melting pot of orange and yellow. Dray noticed newer features, perhaps upgrades.

"Ah, I see you two have found one another," Dr. Roberts said as he came up the path.

"Dr. Roberts, what a surprise," Dray replied, still smiling at Bruce. "How on earth did he find me?" Dray asked as he turned toward the doctor.

"His sensors were reconfigured, but your scent code remained intact. He's been tracking you since this morning. It's part of his final testing."

"He looks bigger. What's this?" queried Dray, running his fingertips over Bruce's lower frame.

"When we took him apart, we examined his inner casing and discovered he was hit with something devastating. Whatever it was, it ate through his frame and weakened his Olithium coating. What you're touching has been upgraded to not only scan his entire body but also act as a protective shield. So far, he's been impervious to everything we've put him up against. Before, he could barrel through much, but now we surmise nothing can stop him." Dray grinned.

36

"Is there anything else?" asked Dray, looking side to side to see if he could find anything more.

"Yes, there is," replied Dr. Roberts with a smirk. "When Bruce was in the Endeavor lab, I thought of an additional upgrade. I recalled that early morning when we first arrived, when you and Bruce rocketed out from the gorge. I thought, 'Wouldn't it be something if Bruce could carry Dray without harming him'—that is, if something like that should ever occur again." Dr. Roberts paused before explaining further. Dray looked perplexed. "Bruce, show Dray what I'm talking about," the doctor said as he looked from Dray to Bruce.

Upon Dr. Roberts' request, Bruce trotted ten feet away. Two fins popped out from each of his two sides, and below his neck a tiny motor majestically appeared; a blue flare fired out from one end. Below his tailfin, a motor four times as big came online. Next, a saddle formed on his back—two hand grips slid out from his shoulder blades.

"The design is not what I first had in mind, but their workflow was able to analyze the data and compute the best solution. The two fins on either side are larger than the old, for more stability of course. And instead of the two rockets below his underside and on his back, we put one in front and one in his rear, able to counter faster speeds. His outer metal alloy is like that of Archimedes', in that it can bend autonomously to better fit one's circumstance, adjusting for whatever Morphic Formula stage you may be in."

Bruce looked ready to go, and after his final adjustment, he turned toward Dray and Dr. Roberts.

"Well, he's waiting," said Dr. Roberts as he, too, turned toward Dray.

"What're you crazy? I'm not even wearing my bio-suit," Dray cautioned.

"That's what the front motor is for, Dray, so he can cruise at slower speeds." Dr. Roberts waved his arm toward Bruce. In turn, Dray's wild, innate curiosity took hold as he stepped closer to his scout. "This is his final test," added Dr. Roberts. Too concentrated on Bruce, Dray ignored the doctor's last words of advice.

"This must explain why you're bigger. Don't do anything till I say, Bruce," Dray warned, not yet fully comfortable with what he was about to do. He remembered his last ride with his scout, particularly his landing, or rather fall—cocooned in his bio-suit. Dray swung one leg over, hunkering down on top; Bruce's outer frame bent to match his rear. Dray turned toward Dr. Roberts, but not much was left to say. His hands were sweaty, making him even more uncomfortable as he held the metal grips tight. As his heart thumped and adrenaline picked up, his body began changing. His forearms stretched longer, adding more bulk, matching the strength of his legs. And his hands grew stronger, now practically cemented to the bars. Nothing could tear him away from Bruce.

Dr. Roberts acknowledged, *If not for his special condition, flying at a rocket's pace would be impossible.*

"Okay, Bruce, show me what you can do," Dray commanded under his breath, still unsure. He bent low, chest pressed flat on Bruce's back. Right on cue, Bruce tilted his head skyward. He opened his mouth and shrieked a wild sound. It was Dray's first time hearing his scout's callsign. They blasted off, gaining altitude faster than Dray imagined they would; he figured they would take it slow on their first flight.

Endeavors and Survivors were settling down for lunch when a missile launched from the gardens. Bruce had pulled in all four limbs and no longer resembled a canine. They circled the city and picked up speed. Dray's skin color altered, and his heart pounded. They circled higher and higher until reaching the opening Stargaze. As fast as a bullet, they shot straight out.

In a flash, Dray and Bruce disappeared beyond the mountain's peak. Dray tried glancing back, but the force was too great. Within seconds, they had risen thousands of feet, and Dray realized that without his bio-suit he could not handle the altitude.

"Bruce!" shouted Dray. "Go—back—down!" Dray yelled but was not sure if Bruce could hear him. Bruce spun around, pulling a 180, gaining more thrust with his rear rocket. Dray's legs flapped free and clear behind; his only contact now was with his two clenched fists. Bruce leveled out, giving his master time to straddle back on. Underneath, Dray's muscles flexed and his skin hardened. The only inspection he could get was of his hands and wrists. His skin, which had now hardened into scales, looked metallic. Dray was blending in with Bruce. Careening toward the earth, the wind tortured his eyes until covered over by a filmy, protective membrane. Through his every pore he soaked in his surroundings, literally, beginning to detect airborne particles seeping through sensory glands on his body. Flying in Archimedes was great, and gliding with Icarus wings was hard to forget, but now he may as well have been experiencing teleportation—moving from one point to another was happening in a blink of an eye.

Dray and Bruce must have done four laps around the mountain until they went headlong into the canyon. Nosediving toward the earth, Dray's legs once again lifted back up and fluttered behind Bruce's rear. But with his firm hold he had grown confident. The wind howled as Dray attempted to give Bruce a command.

"Bruce!" Dray shouted, but this time his words were deeper in tone. His voice had changed. "Go back!" he ordered as close to Bruce's right ear as he could. To pull up and forward was nearly impossible, but in his excited state he found the strength.

Bruce made it back to the Stargaze in no time at all, hovering nearby before it opened. They rotated 360 degrees, Bruce's two rockets countering the blistering wind. Dray looked out toward the horizon—he felt unstoppable. Upon entering the Stargaze, Bruce shut down his two engines. They dropped like a stone! Dray panicked until his scout fired back up, slowing their descent back into the gardens. Dray's forearms shrunk, and hardened flesh receded.

Endeavors watched Dray and Bruce's descent. Jason and his students were also present.

"Look, kids, look at them go" was all Jason could think to say. By the looks of it, all the students appeared to want a Bruce of their own.

7

A small team of Endeavors hustled over the barren plain in pursuit of a much faster enemy. Each soldier ran at an arm's length; leading the charge was Commander Wolf, with Michael and Peter running behind him. Above, a feint shadow was cast down by Archimedes. The Cults were running like cowards, but very fast cowards. The hotter it grew by midafternoon, the faster the Cults seemed capable of running.

"Archimedes! Stop them before they reach their drones!" Wolf shouted toward the sky. In the distance, praying mantis drones rapidly approached. Wolf spotted Archimedes coming out of a cloud. He looked like the rest with a silvery blue tint only visible to those wearing bio-suits.

"Detected," Archimedes reported back, zeroing in on the paint he had marked the enemy with earlier. One Cult sensed him and veered off course, dodging the triangular aircraft's outstretched limb. Another nearby was plucked up, unaware, and severed in four different places. The lead Cult turned and fired his melting micro waves. Archimedes swung wide and shot back into the sky. Another Cult went mad, blasting in every direction.

2

One drone went for the Endeavors with a giant leap, but was snatched up, split apart, and dropped by Archimedes. The other two accompanied the fleeing Cults.

"They're getting away!" yelled Wolf, still protected beneath their force-field of blinding light.

"We have no choice!" replied Michael. He broke formation and hurled his spear. Following his lead, the twelve others carried out the same. Even in the intense light of day, their rays glowed bright, as some traveled close enough to make their own protective shields high above. Michael's ray was the first to land, splitting the ground behind one Cult, deactivating. The next twelve rained down at once, some overshot but others hit their mark; two spears caught a drone and Cult, melting both through and through. Like a vulture, Archimedes circled high above, signaling where death lie below.

"Cults and drones eliminated," reported Archimedes.

"Retrieve!" ordered Wolf. Their spears were eerily sticking up from the ground, having obliterated all that they had come for. Wolf spotted movement. He reached down and grabbed the twitching head of one drone. Reactivating his spear, he cut through its metal casing with blowtorch efficiency. Holding it up like a trophy, he did not have much to say—his men knew how he felt. Having the Cults on the run was refreshing, and successfully destroying them gave hope for future missions.

Something caught the corner of each Endeavor's eye. Returning home alive would be their next mission.

8

His room was dark, but it provided a sense of clarity that only a Cult could appreciate. Drake sat quietly staring up at his wall, and with his hands coupled across his lap, he seemed at peace. He contemplated the latest from Captain Leach. After searching for answers that would not come, he turned to his door—two knocks sounded.

"Enter," said Drake quietly. In walked the most foul-looking creature. The four-foot tall humpback would be painful for any human to watch, but Cults took pleasure in the ugly side of nature. These creatures did not do much physically in Cult society but could sometimes explain the unexplainable.

"To whom do I owe this great honor?" Drake asked the mystical specimen entering the dark room. He slouched against the wall like a drunkard until clumsily sitting in a chair.

"I was called upon by nobles," his words were throaty, difficult to hear and understand. He looked and sounded exhausted, but what he lacked in physical strength he made up for in intelligence.

"Can you give me answers? Will you tell me everything I must know?" Drake questioned. Their bodies were cold, but with their spectrum of vision feint traces of body heat were detected. Drake hit a switch and emitted an orange light. He smiled once seeing more distinct features of the Meggido.

"Yes," the Meggido finally replied, shifting positions in his chair. "Ask what you will, but remember, Master, I cannot answer all in the manner that you seek. Certain things—must occur in the natural order, as you are aware."

"Did my father want me to escape Ether Island?" asked Drake, hoping to get some closure.

"He did. He wanted to test you, see if you were ready—preparing you to eventually take his place. Another, like I, gave council weeks prior, telling of a perfect window on the horizon. That window was your failure in Death Valley," revealed the Meggido, unraveling a sliver of his cloak. His flesh beneath was identical to a Cult's, except deformed in every way possible. Boney lumps protruded in areas that would otherwise be flat, and his head was big and lopsided, a perfect match to the rest of his unnatural body. His hands and feet were crusty and old, with brown nails freakishly long. Normal Cults felt superior in every way, but all respected the Meggido's unseen qualities.

"How exactly was my father killed?" was Drake's next question.

"His neck was broken by two fangs. He, and the one who delivered the blow were in occulta states," the Meggido sounded sad.

"A Cult did this?" Drake said uncertainly.

"Yes. In time, you will meet him." Drake patiently waited for more detail, but nothing came. He had power over the little slouch yet was restrained in how much he could glean from him.

"This is absurd. How can I prepare for battle not knowing what I'm up against?"

"There are powers in this world much greater than you."

"What?"

"In nature, one can find secrets and unlock them. Some secrets are inconsequential for the average soul, but others have greater meaning." Drake sat still, waiting for additional information.

"Before you entered this room, I thought I was sure of at least one thing. Now, I am utterly upset, Meggido. I have one final question before I let you go. How strong is my one, true enemy?"

"You do not have one true enemy, you have two. They are very powerful," the Meggido finished, sluggishly rising from his chair.

"Good-bye, Master," said the Meggido, hobbling out.

"Wait," said Drake, but he was too late. The door closed. Drake lowered the light. *Rubbish. Meggidos, what do they know?* Drake thought to himself. The products of failed experiments long ago, Meggidos were mostly entertainment for Cult society. *Two enemies?* pondered Drake, once again covered in complete darkness.

9

Dr. Roberts stood motionless and silent as he awaited Dray and Bruce's return. The gardens could have been a maze with its intricate quadrant rows of vegetation, if not for the sign posts at every corner. Over one's head, in complete circumference hung wire mesh, suspending vines nearly three stories high. Toward the center, directly opposite the Stargaze, the netting ended, leaving a large round opening. Dr. Roberts stood below this opening, and when he finally saw the two descending, he took a couple steps back. Bruce dropped rapidly through the opening before reigniting and extending his legs. Dray, Dr. Roberts noticed, looked excited—his grayish skin tone was also noteworthy. Dray held tight until the rocket between his legs shut down, and only then did he loosen his grip.

"How was it?" asked Dr. Roberts.

"Fantastic," answered Dray, deciding it was safe to dismount. Bruce slid back his left and right fins and simultaneously put away his front and rear motors. "I wouldn't recommend it for anyone else, though," Dray added, turning from Dr. Roberts back to Bruce. Watching him flex and recede back into canine form was quite remarkable. His back crumpled up and out as if an invisible suction cup were present, mending a dent the size of a saddle.

"Dray, I've been meaning to ask you, how are you feeling?" Dr. Roberts posed.

"I feel fine. As you said weeks ago, my Morphic Formula still lingers, but other than that—"

"The real reason I ask, Dray, is because I think your formula exists due to your unique blood type."

"My unique blood type?"

"Yes. I've done further studies on your test results, and the only conclusion I've come to is your ability to retain formula because of your condition. Dray, you and I both suspect what's happening. I can see what you're experiencing. We need to take a good look at this before it is too late. Your Cult phenomenon needs to be traced back to its source," Dr. Roberts finally revealed what he had long known, simultaneously relieving Dray of a heavy weight. Dray was finally going to get some answers, or better yet some help.

"I've suspected this for some time," answered Dray. "I just didn't know how or when to bring it up. I wanted to believe that it was only my formula acting up, but I'm able to do things outside of what the formula should allow." Dray put his head down and slightly turned toward Bruce. Bruce looked at Dray with fiery eyes, sensing his master's pain and disappointment.

"It's going to be okay. We're going to do everything we can. No one needs to know about this, Dray. Come, how about you and I go to the lab and talk about this some more?" Dr. Roberts suggested as others approached. Dray's answer was a head nod, also signaling to Bruce. The three set off down the path, turning at a bend with an arrow pointing toward the elevator.

Dr. Roberts sat in front of a bio-tank's computer screen. Dray sat next to Bruce near the other end of the lab.

"Human genome experimentation; it's been going on for centuries. I'm sure you've been briefed on some of the history behind your Morphic Formula. I was a big part of its earliest development. However, other scientists, way before my time, had been doing the same experimentation with different species. What I'm about to tell you has been kept secret since the beginning—since the Great Divide. We were our own creators of doom and destruction. The Cults had to be seen as a misfortune, an incurable disease, brought about by Mother Nature alone and not humankind. Our ancestors couldn't resist developing a super weapon—the ultimate weapon. We're responsible for the rise of Cults," Dr. Roberts admitted, glancing every so often at his screen and then back at Dray.

"So, what was meant to help us in war nearly wiped us out," Dray concluded.

"Yes," replied the doctor. Dray could see that Dr. Roberts was tired, more sad than exhausted, seemingly. But Dray knew it was not his fault. This happened a long time ago. Dr. Roberts was not responsible.

"We developed a weapon to fight against our own kind, nation against nation, but the test subjects turned on us," Dr. Roberts continued. "From what I've been told the first formula acted much like the present, the one in you, only activating in short intervals. But something went wrong, and over a short time the soldiers began changing permanently. More critical though was their thinking process, remembering who their loyalties lie with. Our compound was the first—the first to spawn the Cult. Their gradual mutation took years to finally set all the way. During this time, it was safe to go above. There once was a city close by, not far from the depths of Compound 40. After the divide, the city came under attack. Only a handful of survivors escaped and found refuge in Compound 40. I was told only a select few could seek shelter. The compound couldn't support the entire population, so only enough were chosen to keep us alive. This was the beginning of the early expansion of the compound. The labs were already there, but a whole network of sectors went up in the decades after. What I'm telling you was first told to me by my father. He had taken a vow to never speak of it, but he wanted me to know the truth. All my research led me to believe that the only way to fight the Cults was to develop a new formula. I studied test samples that had been saved, even though some had wanted to destroy them. I learned from my predecessors' mistakes, the biggest one being the type of specie they selected. Years of testing was done before I felt it was time. We were taking too many losses on the battlefield." Dr. Roberts said sorrowfully.

"Dr. Roberts, it's not your fault—you're probably the only reason why any of us have survived at all. We both know you wouldn't have made it, here, without the Morphic Formula. But you're leaving one thing out—me. Why am I turning into a Cult?"

"Well, we don't know that for sure. Your formula seems to be counteracting with the Cult in you. I don't know how it's doing it, but it must be. We can be thankful for the counterbalance. As to why you have Cult in you in the first place, I don't know. You may somehow be connected to the first Elites who became Cults," speculated Dr. Roberts. His theory made sense, but Dray still needed to learn how.

"So, I'm a descendant of a Cult? And a cross between the two formulas?"

"It would seem so, but don't be discouraged, Dray. Use it to your advantage. My only concern, and that of Commander Tarpin's, is your ability to think clearly and not get blinded by the evil that the first formula instilled."

"Who all knows about this?" asked Dray, more suspicious now than before. If Commander Tarpin knew, then who else knew?

"Commander Tarpin and I are the only ones who know. A few other scientists suspect something but didn't get to thoroughly analyze your tests. Dray, as you probably already suspect, you're being watched. Commander Tarpin sees you as a potential risk to his peoples' security. Some of what you were told when you first arrived was true, about Cults and humankind, and the Great Divide. Although the story has been altered somewhat, there was some truth to it. When the first humans began changing into Cults, without any threat or panic from war, they were treated harshly and became pariahs. Instead of going to war with our adversaries, they attacked us, spreading their evil seed like wildfire. Dray, I don't want anything to happen to you, but I'm afraid I don't have much control around here. All I can do, and what I was warned not to do, was give you a heads-up." Dr. Roberts knew the risk, not for disobeying Tarpin, but for warning someone who could become a full-fledged Cult. But he trusted Dray. More importantly, now, Dray had complete trust in Dr. Roberts. As reassuring as this was, though, Dr. Roberts was only one man. He could defend him with words all day, but in the end Tarpin's actions would speak louder.

"It looks like it's just you and I, Bruce," said Dray, looking toward his scout. Bruce's reaction was like that of most canines, powerful yet docile, as he looked up at his master.

"I'm afraid that's not entirely true," replied Dr. Roberts, a little unsure how to navigate through his next words.

"What do mean?" asked Dray, surprised.

"Jamie is also being watched. You both are, every second of the day—who you two also come into contact with. I told you, Dray, they're not taking any chances. People you talk with are not all considered for quarantine, but those with direct contact are."

Deep down in Dray something stirred, momentarily showing in his eyes. His worst fear had come back, the fear he had experienced nearly a month ago—the fear he felt for others. He worried for Jamie more than himself.

"Jamie doesn't have anything to do with this," Dray responded, upset as ever, but knew his plea would make no difference with Tarpin.

"For now, go about your business, and act as though everything is fine. Don't worry. If worse comes to worse, I'll help you and Jamie as much as I can," assured Dr. Roberts, preparing to leave.

"Are we being watched right now? Can they hear us?" asked Dray.

"Most likely. Who knows if they can hear us. Your movements are more important to them. What you or I say is not going to make a difference. Tarpin knows I'm loyal to you," Dr. Roberts answered as he rose from his chair. "One last thing," said Dr. Roberts before turning the corner and exiting the lab. "I'd like to run some more tests on you. You can trust me, Dray. You know where to find me." Dray thanked the doctor before he left.

When he's ready, Dr. Roberts concluded. The doctor and Tarpin both agreed to keep Dray close and not box him in a corner.

10

"How are you doing there, sir, can I have a word?" Al greeted the busy man. The shop owner was hoisting heavy boxes with an unusual device. When he turned and stomped toward Al, Al had an incredulous look.

"I used to have a shop like yours," Al stated, comparing his own shop to the one before him.

"What kind of shop?" asked the man.

"I sold ancient weapons and memorabilia," Al enthusiastically replied, scanning over the contraption strapped behind the man's arms and legs helping him lift heavy equipment. His arms extended with a simple reflex of his wrist, and there were metal grips acting in place of his hands. He greeted Al with a cold metal hand, as his real hand simulated the gesture behind.

"My name's Sam. I specialize in gadgetry." Al now had a better understanding of the store sign out front that read: *Easy Does It.*

"I'm Al, it's a pleasure to meet you." Al shook the surprisingly gentle hand.

"So, where's your shop now?" Sam asked as he went back to lifting boxes. The shelf behind him was tall and wide, but his nifty gadget allowed for easy reaching. The metal frame encasing his back was performing like a forklift.

"It was destroyed in Compound 40," Al told him as he watched him continue stocking his latest merchandise.

"Oh, you're from Compound 40! A Survivor?" Sam turned to Al with renewed curiosity.

"Yeah, luckily for me, though, my nephew told me much of my stuff was left intact, which came as a surprise, considering the destruction of everything else. I've been trying to convince someone to help me go retrieve my things, but they say it's too dangerous. It wasn't my idea in the first place—to start my own business again. I loved having something to do every day. I wish Dray had never mentioned it," explained Al, his eyes wandering from Sam toward the rest of his shop. The shelves were filled with alien-looking equipment. Some stuff looked old, Al recognized, but much appeared new, perhaps improvements to their original designs.

"Your nephew's Dray? Incredible! I've wanted to meet him. I can't believe it."

"Well, he's not exactly my biological nephew, but I treat him as such. If you don't mind me asking, Sam, how much would one of those cost?" Al asked, pointing toward Sam's additional four mechanical limbs.

"This Strongarm is expensive because I haven't made many of them. I intended it to be for the elderly, to help them get around, you know, and lift things. But it's been a huge success with all ages. It's made from a metallic alloy that I like to call Droxititan, my own special concoction. It's extremely light and durable. Only weighs fifty pounds, but once turned on it's like being reborn. Here, why don't you give it a try," Sam offered, unhooking himself and stepping out. Al's eyes lit up as he walked over.

"Yeah, my shop was kind of like this one. I collected old things. I guess you could call some of them gadgets. I improved and fixed them, much like you do here," Al said as he strapped himself in, comparing apples to oranges as he mostly cleaned and polished his things. Sam did not suspect any embellishment and appeared interested in what Al had to say. Al was a gifted scientist, but his mechanical creativity did not compare with what surrounded him.

"I probably can't afford this," said Al as he took two steps forward, nearly falling over. Recovering, Al picked up where Sam left off. Lifting merchandise suddenly became fun.

"How does it feel?" asked Sam, seeing Al enjoy the pleasure of working with a Strongarm. In fact, Al looked a little too comfortable as he was about to lift his forth box.

"Boy, I sure do miss working," Al admitted. In those few minutes, Al's satisfaction went through the roof, wearing the Strongarm and stocking shelves. Sam could tell that Al missed his shop and made him an unexpected offer.

"I'll tell you what, Al, until you're able to retrieve your things and get enough funds to open up your own shop, I'll let you help me out around here. I'll even loan you the Strongarm, so you can show it off to your fellow Survivors." With his heart shining out of his eyes, Al stood awkward and silent encased by the Strongarm. Forgetting his multiplied strength, he rushed over and gave Sam a hug.

"Okay, put me down!" Sam shouted, but his muffled plea went unheard. Al was too overwhelmed and distracted with delight.

"Sorry!" said Al, opening his eyes and seeing Sam's pained expression. Sam fell to the floor holding his ribs.

"That's okay," groaned Sam. "You forgot what you were wearing. It could happen to anyone." Al took off the Strongarm and helped Sam get up.

"I'm all right, you can let go. I'll be fine," uttered Sam, recovering with short breaths.

"I don't know what I was thinking. I guess I wasn't thinking. I'm so sorry." Al looked sadder than ever. One might have thought he lost his chance to work at *Easy Does It*.

After a moment of silence, Sam responded, "If I still let you borrow the Strongarm, promise me you won't do that to anyone else."

"Certainly, I wouldn't dream of it," Al replied. "So, I can still come back? Your offer still stands?" Al added. Sam's brief hesitation worried Al.

"Don't worry about it. Sure, come by tomorrow," Sam confirmed, taking his hand from his side and grudgingly extended it toward Al.

"You sure you want me to borrow this? You don't need it to finish up?" asked Al, shaking Sam's hand.

"I have others. Just be careful. I'll see you tomorrow." Al put the Strongarm back on, and with two strides and a smile, he walked out of the shop.

I can't believe I haven't seen others in one of these, Al thought, covering many feet with each stride. Endeavors smiled and chuckled.

11

"So, what do you think of this place?" John asked Eric. The two were strolling around the highest level of the city. There were few people nearby, and it was quiet, unlike down below in the busier parts.

"I like it. But I still miss my home—and my hydro pod," Eric honestly replied.

"It's hard starting over again, isn't it?" John said as he stopped to look over the railing.

"Yes, it is. But what can we do? We survived. That's all that matters." Eric also looked over the railing. The city spiraled up like a corkscrew in the shape of a beehive, with its bottom half cut off at the Hanging Gardens. Fifty feet above them sat the Stargaze. Every stone archway and steel platform were decorated with intricate patterns and designs. The Endeavors greatly cherished their city. Daytime's last rays of light crept away, and interior lamps lit up. Walls and steel beams glistened spectacularly.

"Do you remember when we were young, and you said to me, 'I can't wait to get older'? Eric spoke to the empty space beyond.

"Yes. I thought we would have more freedom," recalled John.

"I agreed with you," Eric responded and went on to say, "I, too, felt we would have more choices. But what choice did we have in escaping our home?" Eric turned toward his longtime friend.

"What are you saying? Of course we didn't have to escape. We could have chosen to stay and fight—and die. Sometimes you just need to do what makes sense," said John, looking back over the railing.

"What are we going to do here?" asked Eric.

"Live, join the Endeavors, help in any way we can," John thoughtfully replied.

"No, what are you and I going to do? Dray and Dr. Roberts are helping in any way they can. I was retired before arriving here."

"We have to start new lives, maybe start a family," John suggested hesitantly, recalling Eric's son and wife experiencing horrible deaths.

"I never wanted to bring a child into this world after Ted left me Dray," John revealed after thinking it over. "The sorrow I felt when they took Dray away—and he wasn't even my own child. ... The war has turned in our favor, Eric. A family here will have a better life," reasoned John. He struck a chord in Eric.

After a long pause, Eric finally spoke, "You don't think we're too old?"

"Of course not. I knew a man in his seventies who had a kid. You know, we're living longer these days when we're not being hunted down."

"I guess there's only one thing left to do," said Eric with a sigh.

"What's that?"

"We have to find a couple of women who think we're good looking."

12

The earth shook as numerous tornadoes appeared on the horizon. Thousands of storm mites began popping up from the soil, gyrating heads full of teeth leading the charge. The Endeavors identified them right away, known to dig up from their lairs before a storm. Once excavating to the surface, they used the powerful wind to go on the hunt. Their lightweight, spongy bodies allowed for easy liftoff.

Through the hailstorm of wind Wolf shouted, "Back to the vehicles!" as the storm advanced.

Engulfed in a swirling black cloud, Archimedes flew at top speed but was taken by the wind.

"We're not going to make it!" Peter yelled.

"Huddle!" Wolf ordered, before their vision was completely obstructed by debris. "Spears!" Their force-field incinerated flying rocks but could not shield them from the wind. They were swept up like pebbles.

Archimedes encountered the first wave of storm mites. Using the harsh winds to his advantage, he began rotating like a giant throwing star. The storm mites stood little chance. Some deflected off his fuselage while others hit the edge of his wing frame, severing in half.

Michael made his way through the twisting and tearing gauntlet, praying for a gentle landing. A storm mite barreled toward him but was speared through and through by someone's loose spear ray.

A rock smacked Peter's spear ray from his grip. He worried for the others as he watched it tearing through the clouds, killing storm mites by the hundreds. It would remain active until hitting the ground.

"Watch out!" warned Peter. His spear ray struck one Endeavor. The explosion from the impact was enormous.

Wolf swung left and right, swinging at just about everything could. He spotted Peter's spear spinning toward him. Timing was everything. He took a swing and struck its center, causing it to deactivate. Orbs of light blinked on and off in the distance—signs that others were still alive.

13

Commander Spiels' eyes were serpentine, and his entire body was hairless.

"Is this a joke? Drake is alive?" the commander dryly responded, but the rider did not reply. Riders tongues were removed. It made them less of target on their journey; no point in torturing them if they could not speak. Their hands also lacked two fingers necessary to write. "I must reply. Take him outside. I need time to think," Spiels ordered, turning back to his desk. His guards took the rider outside.

Drake's message mentioned something about cooperation and peace. But Spiels knew better. There could be no peace after what he had done to Drake's army. He wrote something down on a piece of parchment and sealed it with a purple gel. Calling back in his guards, he gave them instructions.

"I'm going to make this simple. I must locate Drake. After he leaves, I want our best tracker to follow him," ordered Spiels, handing over his letter.

=

A *ratatat* sounded on Drake's door. He granted access and in walked a Cult holding another Cult by the arm.

"A slave girl wishes to speak with you, Master," the Cult announced as he let loose her arm. She was a Cult but did not look like one. Female Cults were immune from turning completely and permanently retched. Her legs were long, slender, and fleshy, human-like. A tunic hung loosely around her waist and shoulders, tied together with a thin silk strap. She was beautiful. But female Cults could alter their appearance — she could turn ugly at the drop of a hat.

"Come forward," said Drake, closing his screen on his desk. She elegantly walked in, holding her head high as if modeling what she wore.

"I did not mean to disturb you, Master, but I wish to have a word," she said softly, bowing her head obsequiously.

"What is it you want?" Drake asked, taking pleasure in not seeing her beauty but lifting his mind from other matters. Her eyes were green and accompanied by rosy lips. She had dark brown hair.

"I want to thank you for your kindness and wish to give you comfort in any way I can," her words spilled off her tongue, seeming to linger well after they were said. Before Drake could speak, she added, "My name is Echo, and I was the one being beaten upon your arrival. The male you killed was my caretaker."

"I'm sorry for your loss. Please, have a seat. What a lovely name — Echo. Tell me, what makes you so sure I am kind?" he asked, deciding her comforting him would be his toying with her. As she sat, she revealed her bare feet. On her two pinky toes she wore two snakelike rings, spiraling around the length of each toe. Her fingernails and toenails were painted green.

"I expect whatever answer I give may not be the one you want," Echo replied after some thought.

"No, please, what makes you think I am kind and desire comfort in these troubling times?" Drake questioned further, sounding annoyed. How could anyone think he needed comforting?

"You are strong, Master, but even the strongest need comfort." Echo paused briefly before going any further. "These are troubling times, and in these troubling times we must all work together. And your kindness has been your new order. No one has ever banned the harsh treatment we experience daily. This has lifted many spirits," she reasoned. Drake looked at her with admiration. To suggest that she could offer him comfort was bold, but to imply that his kindness was out of respect for her gender was even bolder.

"As generous as it may seem, it was not my intent. I do not rule to please. I rule to keep order," Drake admitted, staring at her until feeling the need to look away.

"Why do you not have a queen?" asked Echo, choosing to be even bolder. Drake looked insulted.

"An honest question from a deceptive female. One must have complete rule before having a queen." But they both knew there was no such thing as a queen. There were only kings. Echo didn't reply, but her body language spoke for her. Drake's attention turned to a flashing light on his desk.

"Thank you for your visit, Echo. In a way, you've reaffirmed my wisdom. I guess that is comforting," Drake concluded, observing what he'd been keeping a close eye on before she entered.

"Thank you, Master," said Echo, standing. But before she left Drake had one last thing to say.

"Echo, after we dock at Coarse Bay, I'll have a special task for you. Now leave," he informed her.

Their talk was all that she needed; Echo grinned walking out.

=

The rider stepped outside and looked up. As he opened his mouth, he sighed, deeply exhaling and inhaling; it would be some time before his next breath of fresh air. It was a sunny day but cold, and after securing his message on his belt, he approached his ceres. The best all-terrain vehicle was still the four-legged creature. It had big, round eyes, muscular legs, and was nearly four times the size of a horse. Its mouth was monstrous, but the creature did not appear threatening. On its left and right flanks, crude armor was surgically implanted. These beasts never appeared happy but performed well for their riders. Food and protection were their reward; and though they were big animals, carnivorous predators, half their size, hunted them. The unnatural way in which a rider was transported accounted for their half dead look. The beast lifted him up into its mouth; its teeth and tongue securing him in. The journey back to Drake was going to be challenging, but like a pigeon a ceres and rider always found their way back home. The rider's ceres darted left to right with gazelle-like agility, yet with every leap Spiels' drone doggedly kept up. Careening around trees and, sometimes knocking them over, the rider felt every jolt. He battled the constant shifting sending him into solid teeth and grainy tongue.

With each giant leap Spiels' drone flew above the trees, tailing his zigzagging target below. Landing in wiry undergrowth, the drone cut through tree limbs with its scythe-like limbs. The chase never slowed as the daylight hours ticked away.

14

Dray found it hard to breathe as he and Bruce left the lab. *I must run away. I'll take Jamie with me,* Dray thought but reconsidered. *I must go on my own.* He turned to Bruce. "I don't know what to do." Dray leaned up against the wall. Bruce tucked in his back two legs and sat. "I can't just pretend everything is fine. It's only a matter of time before they lock me up. I'm worried about you, too, Bruce. You're their first barrier." Bruce glanced up at Dray.

Dray and Bruce walked down a pathway, Bruce leading the way. Head nods and smiles were given as they halted in front of an elevator.

"It's going to be dangerous out there," Dray said to Bruce, boarding the elevator to the Great Mantle.

Jamie sat next to Madge and Tulip, and over by the railing stood John and Al. Al was showing off his Strongarm. Commander Tarpin was talking with his Endeavor soldiers.

"Dray! How was it?" Eric startled Dray, swatting him on the back. Dray, caught off guard, promptly turned. Bruce stopped dead in his tracks, scanned Eric, and recognized his face and voice.

"How was what?" Dray replied.

"Your little excursion," answered Eric.

"Oh, it was excellent," Dray admitted. Everyone turned toward Dray as he entered with Bruce.

"Come sit next to me," said Jamie, patting the back of an empty seat, looking Dray's way. Dray walked over and gave her a hug, an unusually long one. He also hugged her mother, Madge. Tulip, Jamie's dog, sniffed and whimpered wildly near Bruce; the scout remembered her well, being licked all over.

"So, what's up?" asked Jamie, as other conversations near and far resumed. She looked as happy as ever.

"Will you marry me?" Dray proposed. His words hung in the air. He appeared just as bewildered as Jamie. Moments ago, his primary focus was on leaving the city.

"Dray, yes, of course," replied Jamie, hugging and giving him a kiss. Madge stood up and expressed her own joy.

"Dray and Jamie are getting married!" Madge announced.

John and Eric gave one another surprised looks.

"When?" asked Jamie.

"The sooner the better," answered Dray.

"Well, then, how about tomorrow night?" offered Tarpin, adding, "I'll send word to our holy man."

"Holy man?" John queried.

"He's the holiest man we have."

"Is that okay with you?" Dray placed his arm around Jamie.

"That would be wonderful," she replied, giving him a kiss on the cheek. Jason stepped out of the elevator with Grace, unaware of the news.

"What's going on? Why is everyone so happy?" Jason asked.

"Dray and Jamie are getting married," Al said, trouncing over in his Strongarm.

"Congratulations. Dray, meet Grace," introduced Jason.

"Hi," greeted Dray, extending his hand.

"Congratulations," expressed Grace.

John and Eric were taking it easy over by the railing.

"It seems everyone's getting hitched, aye, Eric," John said, leaning against the railing. Eric sighed before turning back around. Smirking, he scanned the city below.

Al walked up from behind Bruce, extended one Strongarm arm, and attempted to pet the scout on the back. Bruce spontaneously turned, chomped Al's arm off, and trotted away.

"Bruce! What the heck was that?" Al's voice was shaky. Bruce sat holding his arm. "Can I have my arm back, please?" Al asked, attempting to reach out and grab it. Bruce turned to the side, dodging Al. The spectacle had now gained everyone's attention. Al chased Bruce, Tulip immediately joining in. "Sam's going to kill me," yelled Al, remembering his promise to take care of the Strongarm. Everyone laughed. Dray finally called off Bruce.

"Bruce, give him back his arm," ordered Dray. Bruce halted, turned, and tossed Al's arm back.

"Are you sure he passed all his final tests? I think a wire must still be loose," Al complained. He stomped out of the Great Mantle holding his broken arm. He was the first person to ever sneak up on Bruce.

"I don't think Bruce is the one with a loose wire," Eric chuckled.

"Sir, we've lost contact with Team Ten," an Endeavor interrupted. Everyone heard the message over the intercom.

"Where was their last location?" Tarpin replied, palms planted flat on the table.

"We lost their signal in a storm. Their vehicles haven't moved since they left them on foot," the Endeavor informed.

"What about Archimedes?"

"We haven't received a signal from him either."

"All right," said Tarpin, turning from the intercom.

"They could be anywhere by now," said an Endeavor nearby.

"We must send out a search party," Jason announced.

"And lose another team? Need I remind you that they were a search party themselves? They knew the risk. Commander Wolf was one of my best," revealed Tarpin gloomily, rubbing his eyes and forehead.

An Endeavor stepped forward, saying, "They're on their own now. All we can do is hope for the best. Let's give Archimedes a chance. I'm sure they'll make it back."

"I'm sick and tired of this," Jason spoke up angrily. "We've gotten soft. We need to take the fight to them in greater numbers. Why can't anyone else see that? If we keep sending out small teams this is going to keep happening. This is war," he reminded.

"Jason's right. We should rally the troops," Dray joined his friend in agreement.

"These are my troops and I'll decide when to use them," Tarpin said, agitated.

"For all we know, it's only the weather that's separated them," intervened another Endeavor. Dray turned toward Jamie and then looked down at Bruce. Dray's eyes revealed something he could not say in words—there was nothing he could do.

"Dray, it's okay," Jamie uttered softly. She held his hand. The uncomfortable silence ended when Jason decided to leave.

"Congratulations, guys," Jason said to Dray and Jamie. Grace also said good-bye. Dray knew how close Michael and Peter were to Jason.

"Let's go," Dray said to Jamie. "Commander Tarpin, so we'll see you tomorrow night, then?" Dray confirmed. Jamie stood up from the table.

"Yeah, but first, go meet Bill Hagen, the holy man. He lives in the Hanging Gardens. His number is seventy-nine. He'll like to meet you beforehand."

"Bye, everyone," announced Dray. Madge came up and gave Jamie a hug.

"I'm so happy for you, dear," said Madge.

"Thanks, Mom. I'll see you tomorrow."

15

Michael picked up his aching head as he lay flat on the ground. He was in a daze. He did not know how far he had been taken, and his spear ray was nowhere in sight; and neither Peter nor a single Endeavor were anywhere to be seen. Day soon turned into night. Sounds in the distance gave him chills. Staying low to the ground, he crawled over to a tree. He scanned his environment, discovering he was in an open clearing surrounded by trees. He took a moment to catch his breath, but before long, his threat detector beeped. Against the tree, his bio-suit reflected its bark.

The big cat had lengthy fangs, and its eyes were a yellowish white, practically lighting up the ground beneath its paws. With one leg still raised, the beast froze in midstride. Its whiskers twitched, and its nostrils flared, it turned toward Michael. Colliding, the two tumbled in the grass. The cat's fangs slammed into Michael's chest. His bio-suit sent the cat ablaze.

Michael rose to his feet inspecting his kill. The cat's twelve-inch fangs looked useful. A stone nearby made a great tool. He crushed its skull, loosening its fangs, and tearing them out. Weighing both, he determined that they needed more weight. Whittling two notches at both ends, he fastened two rocks with the tall grass. His fang daggers were impressive.

=

Commander Wolf groaned, but his bio-suit's mask muffled his discomfort. Next to his right hand lay his spear ray; miraculously, it had remained at his side. Not too far away was a patch of scorched earth; the final resting place of one of his men. *His bio-suit must have imploded from the impact,* Wolf guessed, glancing up at the broken tree limbs. With his spear ray in hand, he looked for the others. His bio-suit told him his environment was a humid eighty degrees Fahrenheit. The jungle was overwhelming.

A mosquito the size of man's torso buzzed Wolf's way, and others soon joined it. It was not too long before the commander's bio-suit detected the attack, electrocuting each mosquito upon contact. He became a human bug zapper as he made his way deeper into the jungle. His threat detector beeped on and off as the mosquitos came and went; but beeped louder when a greater threat arrived. Twirling his fiery spear rapidly, their heads and limbs fell at his feet. Their beaks were long and sharp. More raptor-like birds soon arrived. Wolf stood firm, breathing heavily. They circled like vultures. Once deciding to feast on their own, they cleared a path for Wolf. Their meal looked appetizing, Wolf observed, especially the cooked parts.

=

Static scrambled and is what eventually woke Peter. His mask malfunctioned, leaving him blind. At first, he panicked, moving frantically side to side, imagining he had experienced a severe head wound, the reason for his loss of sight. Hitting his chest, he deactivated his mask; he could see again. His black hair was drenched in sweat, and his bloodshot eyes showed fear. His fall had placed him on a steep ledge above a cliff. A small crack appeared before the entire cliff broke apart. Before falling, Peter struck his chest, masking back up. His left wrist crunched when he came to a stop. The pain shot up his arm. He could hardly move, crawling toward a small cave. He drank some water trickling off the wall. His breathing slowed, and nerves calmed. Peter passed out.

16

The rider's ceres jumped skyward, toward a gray sky and a massive raven. The big bird swooped down, banking near, encouraging the ceres to regurgitate; out came its rider. Freefalling, the black bird speared him like a fish. Hanging limp and defenseless, the rider's scroll hung visibly on his side. With one talon securing the rider, the bird's other one snatched up the scroll. The raven rose hundreds of feet before releasing its prey, then majestically soared away. Closing his eyes and folding his hands across his chest, the rider took one last breath before crashing into the forest.

Spiels' drone approached the rider lying dead on the ground. Hooking him by the neck, it rotated him 360 degrees. His scroll was missing. Flinging the mangled body off to the side, the springy drone sprung from the forest.

17

"You look upset," said Jamie. Dray looked as somber as Bruce, standing in the elevator.

"No, I'm just concerned, that's all," Dray replied as the elevator door opened to their floor.

"Concerned about the wedding?" Jamie now looked a little worried herself.

"No. I'm worried about something else," Dray answered as they entered their room.

"So, what's wrong?" Jamie sat down on a couch. Bruce looked toward Dray.

"I spoke with Dr. Roberts earlier this morning. He knows something about me that has him concerned. We don't know how to explain it." Dray sat down across from Jamie and Bruce. She waited for him to explain further, but either he didn't know how to or did not want to.

"Dray, can I ask you a question?"

"Yeah, sure."

"That day we first kissed you said you were in your bio-suit. But the bio-tank hadn't been brought to you yet. It's been bothering me."

"That's kind of what I wanted to talk to you about. Something is happening to me. We're being watched. They think I'm a Cult." Jamie felt sick on the inside. Dray studied her reaction. She wished for another answer, anything that could explain his invisible nature over a month ago.

"He thinks there's still a chance I might not turn. My Morphic Formula appears to be counteracting with the Cult Formula. And—"

"Cult Formula?" queried Jamie, frightened.

"Yes. The first Morphic Formula was Cult Formula."

"How can this be?" Jamie turned away, seemingly asking herself it appeared.

"None of the soldiers spoke of it. By the time they knew what was going on, it was too late. I guess our ancestors tolerated them for some time, until seeing them as threats. The Cult Elites became outcasts—they became our enemy."

"Dray, I still don't understand. How could this be possible?" Jamie's eyes welled up. Dray stood up and moved closer. Kneeling before her, he tried to explain. Bruce did not move.

"Look, everything's going to be fine. There's still a lot we don't know, but Dr. Roberts is going to help me find the answer. I may have to leave, though, Jamie" Dray lowered his head across her lap, facing sideways toward Bruce.

"Leave? But why? You don't have to leave. Where would you go?" Jamie caressed the top of his head.

"I don't know yet, but until then, I need you at my side. After I'm gone, they'll see that nothing is wrong with you." Dray looked up.

"How can you step outside your own body? Scientifically speaking, it just not possible." Jamie hungered to know, wanting him to do it again.

"It would seem. But I'm sure, at some point, morphing into an animal was thought to be impossible. Playing God has cursed us all. What version of the curse am I? My outside appearance may change soon, Jamie. But I can assure you that my heart will remain the same."

"What do want me to do?" Jamie asked, wrapping her arms around his shoulders, his around hers.

"There is one thing you can do," Dray replied.

"Yes."

"Marry me tomorrow night, then wait for my return. Can you wait for me?"

"Oh, Dray," said Jamie, giving him a kiss. Speaking softly next to his ear, she replied, "I will wait for you—as long as it takes."

Tears rolled down her face. Dray did not have to see them to know they were there.

18

Dray and Jamie woke early the next morning. After their last talk every second of the day seemed more precious. For their wedding, Jamie wanted something nice to wear, perhaps a flowing white dress. For Dray, something in black.

"They say you're not supposed to see the bride's dress before the wedding," Jamie said with a grin.

"I'll wait for you outside, then," Dray smiled back, adding, "I'd like to also go see this Bill Hagen."

"Let's go."

"After you." Dray turned to Bruce, poised to go. Dray opened the door. John was about to knock.

"Good morning," John happily greeted.

"Hi, John," said Dray.

"Hey," greeted Jamie, giving John a hug.

"Is there anything I can do? I mean, for this evening?" John looked eager to do anything it appeared.

"Ah, I don't really know what you could do, John. But you can come with us right now? We're going to see Bill Hagen and then go shopping."

"I'd be delighted," answered John.

As they boarded the elevator, Dray said, "The Hanging Gardens first?"

"Fine with me," responded John.

"Can't wait," said Jamie, holding Dray's hand. Bruce stood like a sentinel. With his cool, calculating eyes, he never missed a beat. He zoomed in on Jamie and Dray holding hands. Without any contact, he measured their heart rates and body temperatures; he detected the rise in both. Tilting his back, he let loose a roar. It shook the elevator and cracked the window.

"What is it, Bruce?" Dray knelt in front of his scout. John and Jamie exchanged puzzled looks. Dray got back up as the elevator door opened. Bruce led the way into the Hanging Gardens. After winding down different paths, they came to an entrance. The hallway led deep into the base of the mountain. Bruce came to a halt at its very end.

"What do you people want?" a gray-haired, green-eyed man asked. His wiry hair stood tall, adding more inches to his height. He answered the door before they even knocked; he must have been looking through the peephole. The man looked overwrought, adjusting his black robe.

He's supposed to marry us? Dray wondered.

"Commander Tarpin said to come see you. We're getting married tonight. I think you're supposed to marry us?" said Dray, turning to Jamie, and then looking back at the man.

"Oh! Sorry. Come in. Yes, now I remember."

"I'm John," John introduced himself.

"My name's Limbo. I'm sorry about that. I've been hounded all week. More and more people are seeking me

85

out these days. It appears I'm only useful when they're in despair."

"I didn't realize so many were in despair," said Dray, asking, "What could be so concerning? Things seem to be going well from what I see."

"This city is a marvelous place, a sanctuary from evil. But after living in one place for so long, walls can eventually close in on you." Limbo walked over to a chair. He noticed Bruce standing behind the others. "Well, look at you," he said, sitting. Bruce stepped forward, nearly eye level with their host. Limbo touched the top of Bruce's head. He mumbled something to Bruce and then turned his attention back to his other guests.

"Mr. Limbo, I'm curious, in our city, we felt safe inside our compound. The walls of protection were comforting," replied Dray. Limbo rose and walked over to an archaic-looking altar. A ray of light cast through a decorative window above it.

"Sometimes, walls can feel restricting. The average Endeavor doesn't feel they are at war. Most have never witnessed the terror on the outside—in particular, the young. They take for granted this city and the protection it offers. They feel imprisoned, however. No one can leave. But it's for their own good—I constantly remind them." Dray looked over the luxurious room. It had red carpet and lavish furniture, and on the walls hung large paintings depicting beautiful landscapes. Other pictures were of mystic figures sitting beside pools of water. Pine incense filled the air. Dray wondered where the light from the window came from. They were far from the Stargaze. Distracting him from that thought was something Limbo said. He never thought of the city as one big holding cell. He knew now why his request to go with Michael and Peter was denied; it was not for his protection but rather to keep the compound's location secret.

They've never trusted me, thought Dray. *I guess leaving won't be so easy.* This was uplifting for Jamie; the thought of Dray not being able to leave. John vividly recalled what life was like on the outside.

I'll choose being locked down any day of the week, John concluded, looking around the room.

"Anyway, so you wish to get married, splendid. Congratulations. It's been quite some time since my last ceremony. I'll meet you tonight on the platform beneath the stars. Any questions?" Dray and Jamie shook their heads, indicating neither had anything to say. "Well, then, it was nice meeting you. I'll see you tonight." Limbo walked them to the door and shook Dray's hand. After saying good-bye and watching them leave, he took a deep breath.

In the back of Limbo's place was a door to another room. A dark liquid seeped through its bottom. The incense had covered up the scent of blood.

19

"Your aircraft is ready, Master," Captain Leach reported.

"Good. Continue to Coarse Bay. Send scouts in advance to begin recruiting," Drake ordered, standing up from his desk.

"What then?" the captain asked.

"Wait for my instructions. I must leave. Someone has intercepted my communication. I must find those responsible," Drake stated, standing over the shorter captain. The captain stared directly ahead. In a cold voice, Drake added, "The Meggido was right. Double our patrol and alert the city, we are being watched," Drake practically whispered.

"We've been infiltrated? Who could it be?" the captain softly asked. Drake wrapped a black cape over his red cloak.

"I intend to find out."

"I will do as ordered," replied Leach.

Drake walked toward the center of the Great Dome, his cloak and cape dragging behind. Male Cults stood on either side, bowing. Females dropped to their knees. Echo stood out among the crowd, taking a knee. Paying little attention, Drake advanced toward his aircraft. Beside his aircraft stood a warrior holding a pillow, and on it were two microbands.

The warrior Cult presented the pillow, bowing. Drake strapped them on, turned toward the crowd, and raised his arms. The dome grew hot. Lowering his fists, the devilish heat vanished. When his minions raised their heads, he was gone.

20

"Can anyone out there hear me?" repeated Michael as he crept along, but too far out of reach. He moved slowly like a sniper, surveying in every direction. His scope was his imaging screen, and his bullets were his daggers at his side. Kneeling, he flicked some dirt with one dagger and decided to darken both. Staying camouflaged meant staying alive, yet after his last encounter his confidence was shaken—his stealthy bio-suit could not hide him from everything. Being alone was tough—dying alone was even tougher. He envisioned death one day fighting alongside fellow warriors.

Michael's itinerant path finally came to a halt. To his right a sturdy tree beckoned him to climb. Reaching its highest branch, he positioned against a sturdy limb. Taking precaution, he slammed each dagger behind him; he now had two safety bars keeping him secure. *Today's my birthday* thought Michael, looking up. The stars flickered bright like candles; he figured he'd make a wish. Zooming out as far as his imaging screen would permit, he zoomed in on orbiting satellites; to his surprise one exploded. *Too close to the atmosphere,* he determined, refocusing. Seconds later, another went up in flames. Something shot it down. More explosions followed the first. Before closing his eyes and falling asleep, he sighed relief—the Cults now had fewer eyes looking down. His unknown helping hand gave him a nice birthday gift.

=

Peter awoke with a mind-numbing chill and he began coughing up water. A flashflood had carried him down through the winding rocks. Frightened, he hit his chest and activated his mask, warming. After the rain let up, he deactivated; his vision slowly adjusted. He looked up and decided climbing would be impossible. It was not long before he sensed danger. He found a dark crevice and crawled in. Outside heavy rocks tumbled past him, and in every direction loose rubble kicked up. *What on earth could it be?* Peter wondered. Warm air swept past his neck, following behind it was an awful stench. Directly behind him sat cold, gray eyes. Peter attempted to strike his chest but was too late. The crevice shut! Teeth came down! White flashes flared from his bio-suit, shedding more light on his slimy grave. The hungry rock mouth was not deterred. Tiny droplets of blood trickled down Peter's neck and cheek. In the end, his bio-suit's implosion ruined his earthy predator's meal.

=

With his spear ray glowing bright, Wolf plowed through leafy walls. Tree branches caught fire, sending up orange flames in his wake. His vision turned, alerting him to the early morning; he had been running all night. The jungle was alive, caving in on him from all sides. Vines swung down and whole trees jumped out in front of him. Giant spiderweb vines appeared, tangling any part of the him they could reach. But the aggressive limbs would have to do more, for the commander was just as tenacious.

Spinner blades would be great, Wolf dreamed, recalling the day he first saw them with Dray. His energy drained with every swing of his spear; it grew heavier the faster he moved. The more he incinerated, the more the jungle tried to eat him alive. His last swing was sluggish, yet by just holding his spear level and running, both ends destroyed everything in their path. Two interloping nooses snagged him, picking him up beneath each arm. His spear ray fell to the ground, deactivating. Once tightly bound, his invisible nature was gone. He wondered how long it would be before he died of dehydration.

It must have been an hour before Wolf heard something; though he could not see, he could still hear. *Strange,* the commander thought. The voices sounded human. The language was foreign to him; he wondered if he was hallucinating. It sounded like an aerosol can, but as the sound came near it sounded more like a fire extinguisher. Unbeknown to him, he was being doused on the outside; whatever filled the air was not a fire-retardant chemical. The vines holding him captive receded back into the jungle. Wolf fell to the ground and looked up, discovering a group of frightened, half-dressed people. They stood over him holding big cylindrical tanks with large nozzles.

"¿Quién es?" asked a man stepping forward. Wolf recognized the language and was lucky enough to know some. Another man inspected Wolf's spear ray. Wolf slowly stood up. They all moved back.

"Be careful with that," said the commander, addressing the man with his spear. Wolf reached out his hand but was quickly denied. They outnumbered him thirty to one, but he did not believe them to be hostile. *I need that repellent to make it out anyway — whatever it is,* Wolf concluded.

"El Diablo," a woman's voice echoed from behind. Wolf's appearance and voice were alien.

Do I really sound like the devil? Wolf thought to himself, certainly aware of the meaning of "Diablo."

"No, I am not el Diablo," Wolf said slowly so they all could hear. The word "no" in front of "el Diablo" was universally understood, but they still stood ready to attack. *How on earth have these people survived?* Wolf wondered. They looked like ancient Mayans, minus the tanks strapped on their bare backs. The commander hesitated before striking his chest, figuring that if their chemical spray did not harm them, then it should not do him any. They gasped, seeing the commander's face.

"¡Usted es un hombre! ¡Increíble!" an excited man proclaimed.

"*Sí, soy hombre. Bueno,*" replied Wolf, happy to see the nozzle lowering away. The more Spanish he heard, the more he remembered.

"*Por favor—déme...*" Wolf looked to the gentlemen holding his spear.

"*Sí, déselo,*" ordered the first man to speak. Wolf now knew who was in charge.

"*Mi nombre es Wolf. Gracias,*" the commander took back his spear.

"*Mucho gusto. Soy Bracken.*" Bracken reached out his hand, eyes widening once Wolf shook it. If not for his bare face, he could have easily blended back into the trees.

"*Vámonos!*" Bracken yelled, waving his hand. As Wolf followed, he noticed Bracken ejecting tiny spurts from his tank. They were in control of the jungle—at the very least holding it back. He began piecing it all together, how they've been able to stay hidden.

Even drones stood little chance, surmised Wolf, having just experienced the futility of entering this place. *Nothing can move without that spray.*

Bracken fit every description of a warrior. From head to toe he was covered with tattooed muscle. His face was painted green and black, and his ears were pierced. They all had machetes strapped to their waists.

"Wolf, *¿dónde vives?*" Bracken asked, interrupting the commander's thoughts. Wolf gave the only answer that he could.

"*El norte,*" answered Wolf, adding, "*Y tú, ¿dónde vives?*" Bracken tilted his head back and nodded.

"*Estamos cerca,*" said Bracken, which the commander interpreted to mean that they were close. The group moved on, accompanied by a floating head—Wolf's head. At least now his unfiltered words were less foreign. Over the sound of their spray Wolf heard water.

"Bracken, *necesito agua,*" the commander informed. Bracken halted and turned toward his people.

"Wolf *necesita agua. Vámonos por allí,*" Bracken gave the order as they changed course. They headed back toward the sound of water. Wolf licked his parched lips; he could smell the water. Having reversed directions, he was now at the head of the column, Bracken pointing the way. A river with a waterfall came into view.

"Ah, thank you," uttered Wolf, rushing toward the water. He jumped in, drinking. The others kept watch, their tank nozzles poised. Bracken was happy to see the commander's face rejuvenate.

"*¿Estás listo?*" asked Bracken, giving him a friendly smile.

"*Sí, muy bien,*" Wolf replied, climbing out of the water.

How could they trust me so quickly? Wolf pondered, but knew his life depended on their protection, and he knew that they knew it.

They reached the top of a hill, and below them was a sight like no other. Wolf paused to take it all in. There was a village, or rather a city among tree tops. Above and below was a massive clearing, spreading wide the jungle growth; and in each tree, as far as his eyes could see, sat houses. Villagers went about their business, some cooked over fires, while others tended to chickens and goats. Children played, chasing one another with sticks.

"Wolf, *bienvenido a mi ciudad,*" Bracken welcomed, raising an arm toward the city. Wolf cautiously made his way down, the entire time keeping watch on the vibrant people. The others accompanying him were quick to spread word of his arrival. The kids' laughter hushed while the cooking meat sizzled. Everyone turned to have a look at the floating head; the commander guessed he was their first visitor. The boys and girls followed him, whispering to one another inaudible words. Wolf figured he would lighten the mood, rapidly turning his head. The kids screamed and ran away. Wolf and Bracken both chuckled. Others eased up a bit, but some were not as trusting.

"*Aquí,* Wolf. *Pónte esto,*" Bracken said to the commander. The others unstrapped their tanks and dunked their heads in large, wooden barrels. Bracken proceeded to do the same, covering his entire body with the oily fluid. The wooden barrels were all over the place.

It could be a custom of theirs, thought Wolf, but he had to ask before doing the same.

"*¿Por qué?*" he asked, receiving a grave look from Bracken. He interpreted the look to mean, "Just do it." And without further delay, the commander spread the slimy liquid all over his face, neck and hands—every limb. The substance trickled down and off his bio-suit, but after a few more coats it stuck on. His entire form was now visible. Villagers stepped closer once they could see the rest of him. The village elder approached.

"Welcome," the man spoke in English.

"You speak English?" Wolf replied in wonderment.

"Yes. Not much. Some." From behind his back, the man took out a leather-bound book with a red tassel hanging loosely down the center. There were no words or descriptions from what the commander could see. Not even a title. "Name, Jaxifer," said the old man, greeting him with a handshake.

"Nice to meet you, Jaxifer," said the bewildered commander. Wolf had so many questions to ask yet found himself speechless.

"*Milagro, es* what you wear now. What you put on," Jaxifer said as he pointed toward the commander's yellowish stained body, adding, "So jungle won't eat. ... Good, yes." Jaxifer smiled. Wolf tried returning the same look of glee, but instead, gave a halfhearted grin.

"Yes, very good—*milagro*," Wolf finally replied. He knew "*milagro*" meant "miracle," and that's exactly what his still being alive was—a miracle.

"Here, take. Look," Jaxifer handed him his book. It was old and written by hand in English, but as the commander thumbed through the pages, he noticed the second half was in Spanish. Every chapter title was in Latin. As Wolf further inspected, he noticed the first and last pages were torn out; he did not have a clue.

"What is this?" the commander asked.

"Same book, two halves—that's all," replied Jaxifer. Wolf attempted handing back his book.

I guess the second half is a translation of the first, Wolf concluded, still holding out the book.

"No, you read now," Jaxifer pushed the book back into commander's hands. Wolf kept the book.

"I'll read it at once, thank you, Jaxifer," said the commander, now turning toward Bracken. "Have you read it?" he asked Bracken.

"No ha llegado su hora," Jaxifer responded instead.

Not his time, translated Wolf, guessing who else might have read it, but decided to change the topic to more pressing matters.

"I will need your help getting through the jungle. Can you help me?" Wolf inquired. He needed to find out if they were going to help him leave.

"You stay with us now, good," Jaxifer's smile faded, and the commander recognized it right away. A few uneasy seconds passed. Wolf decided using tougher words but paused mid-sentence. He determined that the best course of action was just being grateful for their hospitality. Forcing their help might backfire, and the last thing he wanted, tired and hungry, was to take on a whole village.

"Okay, I will stay," said Wolf, nodding.

21

"He seemed like a nice guy," Jamie said to Dray and John, stepping out into the Hanging Gardens.

"He seemed quick to get us out of there, but other than that, sure, Mr. Limbo seemed fine," Dray admitted, but his thoughts were on having to leave the city. Jamie was also distracted, too focused on getting married.

"I liked the guy, minus our initial welcome. My only question is, and I probably should have asked him—" John halted, appearing as though he had forgotten his question.

"What, John?" Jamie asked.

"Who is he? Didn't Commander Tarpin say to go meet Bill Hagen?" John finished saying.

"Limbo could be his nickname" was Dray's answer.

"Yeah, it could be what he goes by around here. Maybe it's his middle name," Jamie offered a possible explanation. Bruce had never met Bill Hagen; nothing seemed unusual. They continued toward the elevator, putting Limbo behind.

"Where to next?" John wanted to know. They all looked out the elevator window.

"We're looking for a place that sells nice clothes, John," Dray informed.

=

100

"Every cat gene has a human equivalent—the sequence of DNA in our two species is so similar. We can determine which gene is which by comparing DNA sequences," Dr. Roberts explained to the scientist standing next to him. They were going over charts in a bio-tank lab.

"Can we still use Dray's sample to make another formula?" a scientist asked Dr. Roberts.

"No, Dray's sample is compromised. It's still unclear what will happen to him."

"Why cats, Dr. Roberts? I still don't get it," Tarpin interrupted, turning the corner to the lab's entrance; he appeared to have been eavesdropping. Tarpin crossed his arms and leaned up against a wall.

"Our initial intent was to determine the genetic basis of hereditary defects in cats. Ones that appeared identical to human illnesses, such as hemophilia, were of interest. Like people, cats suffer from some of the same cancers and viral infections."

"So, what happened then?" asked Tarpin, looking as though Dr. Roberts was just filling his head with nonsense.

"Well, because cats, both wild and domestic, have evolved genetic solutions to various diseases, understanding them can provide important clues about our own responses to those diseases. By unlocking the secrets in their genes, we were hoping to find better treatments and even cures for fatal diseases."

"Please, Dr. Roberts, tell me more," Tarpin said with a taunting look.

"Jeffrey, try to explain it to the commander. I want to see how much you've learned," Dr. Roberts asked Jeffrey, giving an uneasy look the commander's way.

"We have many diseases in common with cats, and over millions of years of evolution members of the cat family have stayed closer, genetically speaking, to humans, than let's say our best friend, the dog, and all other mammals—except apes and monkeys, I guess." Jeffrey looked confused, adding, "Advancements in the field of molecular genetics has made it possible to locate individual genes on chromosomes—"

"That's good enough, Jeffrey. I think the commander gets the point."

"I still don't get the transformation and how the Morphic Formula in Dray remains potent. ... And his Cult phenomenon, which worries me more every day," Tarpin stated, uncrossing his arms and taking a seat.

"Man, cat, or mouse, it's the assemblage of genes, encrypted as a string of DNA molecules that dictates how we look and even behave," was Dr. Roberts' answer, sensing the commander knew more than he was letting on.

"Ah, I see. So, you've uncovered these evolutionary strategies that will not only enable us to further improve our lives, transforming us, but also provide us with innate resistance to viral genes? Am I right?" Tarpin grinned sullenly.

"Yes, something like that," replied Dr. Roberts. Tarpin stood up from his chair.

"The next time you see Dray, Dr. Roberts, have him meet me in the Great Mantle. I want to ask him what it feels like to be the next stage in human evolution. Good day, gentlemen," the commander finished saying before exiting the lab.

=

"Good afternoon, Sam," greeted Al as he took two strides into *Easy Does it*.

"Hey, Al," replied Sam, looking up from his counter and seeing Al holding a free mechanical arm.

"Did it break?" asked Sam, knowing full well that something powerful had to help it split apart. *What could he have done?* Sam wondered.

"It was the strangest thing, you'll never believe it," Al began to explain. Sam, meanwhile, walked around the counter, giving Al a quizzical look.

"Try me," said Sam, grabbing the arm from Al and inspecting it thoroughly. He noticed strange dents on one end, which was about to confirm the rest of Al's story.

"Dray's scout dog, Bruce, I don't know if you're familiar with him, but he got startled and bit my arm off. I probably shouldn't have snuck up on him, but how was I supposed to know what he'd do. You should have a look at him when you get a chance. I told Dray that I thought something was wrong with him," Al took some blame for the incident, but not much.

"Fascinating, Al. I hope you've learned your lesson. ... Is it really true that he flew down into a gorge and saved Dray?" Sam asked, no longer concerned about his damaged Strongarm. Al looked surprised by the question.

"Why, yes, it is true," Al replied as Sam put the arm down on his counter.

"Since Bruce entered this city, it gave me the idea to design my own personal companion. I'm still months away from finishing. The only problem is getting authorization," Sam was sad to admit, suspecting he would never see his creation come to life.

"You need authorization?" asked Al, undoing his straps on the Strongarm.

"They don't want anyone in the civilian sector owning anything too powerful. They feel it could disrupt the chain of command," Sam informed, looking past Al. A customer entered his shop.

"How are you doing today?" Sam warmly greeted.

"Very well, thank you," the lady replied. She looked to be in her late fifties. She looked like she was on a mission, eagerly searching for something in the shop. Al thought to impress Sam on his first day, even though he had no idea where anything was.

"Can I help you find something?" Al offer some assistance.

Well this should be amusing, thought Sam, leaning against the counter.

"Yeah, I'm looking for—wait a second, who are you? Who is this, Sam?"

"My name's Al, I'm the new guy. I just started today," Al was happy to say.

"Well that's great. I don't think Sam has ever had anybody work for him, mostly because he doesn't want anyone meddling with anything. He's afraid they might break something," the lady whispered the last part to Al.

"That's not true, Eve. I let customers touch my things all the time," interjected Sam.

"Customers need to test what they're buying. They need to know how to use it—or see if it works," said Eve smiling at Al. Al smiled back, agreeing.

"Is he at least paying you to work?" asked Eve, turning toward Sam.

"Oh, well, I'm not doing this for money," replied Al, taking a firm stand, adding, "I just like working," he honestly stated. Sam and Eve both looked impressed.

"Al used to have his own shop. Store owners know how to handle their merchandise..." Al glanced at the damaged Strongarm, then quickly looked away.

"So, what're you looking for, Eve?" asked Sam.

"I need a laser. Mine mysteriously disappeared, and I need one for tonight. I'm going hunting with my daughter in the Flat Basin."

"The Flat Basin? Hunting?" queried Al.

"Yes, we go once a month. It's extraordinary. You should join us."

"I'm not sure Al would like that," responded Sam.

"Most men enjoy going. I think he would have a great time," Eve argued.

"I would be delighted. Just tell me when and where," Al excitedly accepted the invitation.

"I guess this means two lasers," replied Sam, procuring two lasers from a metal container. "I've made a few improvements, mainly giving them a better handle. Other than that, they're still just as powerful. Al, this is how you adjust the power. The higher the power, the longer you have to wait between each shot." Sam pointed out two different settings, switching off the safety. Next, he pointed the laser toward one corner of his shop; a piece of metal went up in smoke. Al was intrigued.

"Light amplification by stimulated emission of radiation," said Sam, adding, "these could actually be classified as illegal. But Eve and I go way back—I trust her."

"We're going to shoot living things?" asked Al, inspecting the smoldering metal.

"Rats," replied Eve, grinning.

"What do you mean—rats?" said Al, turning.

"Big, nasty ones," answered Eve.

"Now, Al, I have to warn you to be careful with this. Don't use the highest setting to bring one down. When this light blinks it means you can shoot again. On this setting, it takes about five seconds between each shot. Eve will tell you more when you get there," informed Sam, handing Eve one laser, the other to Al.

"Good," Al said, inspecting the laser. Glancing back up, he asked, "Now, where shall we meet, Eve?"

"How about the Hanging Gardens—right in the center. Say, seven o'clock?"

"Sounds great!" answered Al, holstering his laser on his belt. Eve placed fifty coins on Sam's counter, more than enough to cover both.

"Thanks, Eve, let me know how they do," said Sam, placing the money in his drawer.

22

Saucer-shaped wings extended from Drake's striker as he flew close above the waves. White mist covered his window, yet he kept descending closer. He taunted whatever lurked beneath the surface.

"There will be no truce. There will never be peace," Drake grumbled to himself. He felt a presence, something his naked eye could not detect. He wanted to call out to it and see if it would respond or appear; its closeness was tantalizing. After an unseen power took control of his striker, Drake added, "The battle of your time has been fought—and you lost." The only sound came from the thrashing sea below; then there was a voice. Reclining, Drake listened with arcane obedience.

"Why do you question my ways, son? Was it not I who set you free, giving you the power to fly? My battle has not been fought and lost. This war is on three playing fields. Not all earthly creatures have taken his side. Show them your power—deceive them—give them a taste of what they can have. Embarrass our enemy. He ruined my occulta bliss and spoiled our original flesh. ... He must die," finished the ebullient voice.

"Who, Father, who is he?" questioned Drake, evil spreading darker on his face.

"He calls himself Dray!" yelled Varo in a godawful tone. Drake's dark eyes cleared. Varo vanished.

But first—Spiels' flesh is mine, determined Drake, pulling up from the perilous water.

Not long after reaching land, Drake's biological radar went off. His fleshy scales turned savage red. Down below he saw why; the earth was covered in a sea of crimson. From high above, minerals from rock and scorched earth explained the dark iron color. But Drake knew better—it was blood. The time had come to test his striker. Streaking across the daytime sky, he zeroed in on the hordes delivering their bloodletting. It was on a scale he had never seen before. He unleashed ant fragments.

The centurions wrestled the powerful beasts to the ground before falling on them to feast—their victims' weakened state made this fun for them. Centurions looked human but lacked the intelligence of one. They defended their Cult masters against beasts growing stronger and stealthier by the day. Their masters encouraged the competition. The only predator they sought to eliminate was man—the only beast they truly feared. Drake smiled as he watched them bathe in blood. Covered in meat and fat, the giant men were taken by surprise. The hairy centurions, each in command of a hundred trained lions, stood twenty feet tall. They shot their heavy weapons skyward. They were furious. How dare someone threaten them and their cattle. With horns like Spanish bulls, their cattle were massive creatures, each the size of a short bus. They bucked their horns madly as blood filled their eyes; some even goring their own. Drake recognized their insignia—Spiels' centurions. He would reach the commander sooner than anticipated. A centurion's bacteria-infested projectile shot past Drake, missing. Ant fragments split into millions, and upon contact they dug in like hungry tics. Their objective was to seek vital parts and destroy. Centurions fell by the masses, joining their cattle, succumbing to an unnatural death. Their massive rocket-propelled grenades did not compete with what now devoured them from within.

Cherub, a centurion, was standing watch on the farthest edge of the slaughter. He felt the ground shake beneath his feet as his men frantically ran. The antlike critters eating his soldiers spread fast; even with their massive strides, the centurions could not outpace what plagued them. Tactically dispersed, Drake's weapon cornered them in on all sides. Luckily for Cherub, he had arrived late to the feast, giving him time to decide, the most basic instinct of any creature— fight or flight. Gripped with fear, he mounted his tree-sized weapon on his back and fled.

"Why, Master? Why?" wailed Cherub, tossing a watermelon-sized grenade behind him. Shouts quieted into groans, then all went silent. Cherub was alone.

"Payback for my troops," bragged Drake, unleashing another round.

23

The morning sun woke Michael the next day, still sitting in the tree; his dagger handlebars succeeded in keeping him put. Dislodging them, he now used them like ice axes, clawing his way back down the tree. He hit the ground, scanning everything, taking careful steps. Nearby, something stirred, crunching leaves and tearing branches. His bio-suit sounded the alarm, beeping. Its location and high threat level were now confirmed. It snapped tree limbs as it charged! The barbear was many times bigger than the cat. *How could I have lost my spear?* thought Michael, knowing an important duty of his was taking care of his weapon. He prepared using his dagger. Piercing the monster's thick black coat of fur looked impossible—so he aimed for its head to take out an eye. Its muscles rippled as the ground beneath it shook. Michael missed! His dagger bounced off to the side. *Running may have been a better choice*, he concluded, fleeing back up his tree. A heavy paw missed his foot, lopping out a chunk of bark. The giant bear was not letting up—the tree or its prey was coming down.

Michael could not wait it out any longer as his tree creaked and groaned. The bear's face was vulnerable; its mouth was all he had to avoid. He jumped! Landing behind the bear's massive head, his dagger dug in deep, the force from his fall making it possible. He tried stabbing its eyes but was flung off. Landing, Michael rolled over, startled to see another bear's face blanketing him with its steamy breath. The white bear bellowed furiously before attacking. But a tiny spot on its back suddenly caught fire, sending him back. Its companion had the same happen to it, as a tiny spot smoldered, until fully igniting. *Where the heck did that come from?* Michael questioned, relieved to see both bears gallop back into the trees.

Two red discs retracted back into its nose; its laser did the trick. Archimedes hovered overhead, tilted vertical, and then descend between the trees. Michael was incredulous as he spotted his guardian from above. Archimedes' six spidery legs grasped branches and tree trunks, keeping his fuselage stabilized the whole way down; his razor-edged wing-frame removed any obstacles. Touching down with only two limbs, he kept the other four wrapped around a tree. He opened his hatch.

"I've been searching for you, Michael," Archimedes' voice gave Michael goose bumps. "Do you wish to leave?" his guardian added. Michael's answer was simple, rising to his feet and walking toward the open hatch. Using one of Archimedes' legs as a ladder, he had no trouble making the climb. Once secured, they crawled back up through the trees. Before liftoff, Archimedes sat still, perched like a spider on a web.

"I take it I'm the only one you've found?" asked Michael, wondering what course of action they should take.

"I came across three others. They were all killed before I could get to them," the sublime aircraft responded.

"Was Peter among them?" queried Michael, worriedly.

"Yes," replied Archimedes. Michael sat back.

"We must go find the others," decided Michael, but Archimedes did not budge.

"Your bio-suit is reading high stress levels. Your body needs fuel" was Archimedes' reply. Taking off, Michael said no more as Archimedes got them out of there.

24

"He will come again, but this time, his kingdom on earth will be in heaven," an old man dogmatically proclaimed to a small crowd. Wolf overheard the English as he drew near. He'd been walking through the vast, vibrant village for hours, hearing different earthly languages he did not understand—until now. He was ignored by adults but eagerly followed by children.

Who are these people? Wolf pondered, surprised by their diversity. Jaxifer and Bracken said little else before he left, only telling him to go explore. Presently, Wolf was doing just that, wandering aimlessly. *This place is incredible.* He stood near a tree and listened, fascinated with the man speaking.

"This millennium has been both an opportunity and a gift—at the beginning a fresh start, so to speak. Yet spoiled as humankind is, and continues to be, we continue to squander it. We won't have a third chance, those of us who stray from the triune God. Do you not see why He has spared his two most precious creations—man and Earth?" the man stopped to take a breath and then continued, "spread the Word, a voice told me in a dream. Have others help spread the Word as well." A man wearing only a loin cloth around his waist suddenly stood up.

"Why do you keep insisting on telling us this? What are we to do about it? You preach this day and night, constantly talking about the end and spreading the Word. How are we supposed to leave? The jungle will swallow us whole. The Milagro Tree can't produce enough repellent for all of us to leave," the man finished and sat back down.

"In nature, beauty cannot exist without the ugly. I have seen what lies beyond this jungle. Those beyond our nations cannot be helped. So, we must keep reminding those closest to us," the old man answered, returning to his wicker chair and laying his staff across his lap. Wolf was taken by his words, scanning over the man's sleeveless robe. Wanting to know more, Wolf walked out into the open.

"Don't give up on those who live beyond these trees. You are being kept here for a reason—I think. ... Perhaps—" Wolf paused, directing his next phrase more to himself, saying, "I've come to this great city for a reason. I've never heard your words before. My knowledge of the past thousand years has mostly been limited to war. You, young man." Wolf pointed toward the half-naked man who spoke moments ago. "What is your name?"

"My name is Paul—and yours?" Paul said curiously. Wolf appeared larger than life with his shimmering bio-suit and its awkward glow; his battered book in one hand also stood out.

"Commander Wolf," replied Wolf. All eyes were on the commander as he approached the old man. "How long have you been living here?" Wolf inquired next, looking over dozens of faces; villagers beyond went about their business.

"Generations—centuries," the old man replied, looking surprised and startled by Wolf. *Where does this man fit into all this?* the old man wondered, thinking of past dreams to find possible answers.

"Do not be afraid, beneath this armor is flesh, just like yours," Wolf eased some tense stares. *I guess word of my arrival hasn't spread this far.*

"Where did you come from? How on earth did you arrive?" the old man finally asked, coming out of his ponderous stare. *He is not from our village—but one of God's creatures—just like us*, concluded the wise man.

"What is your name, sir?" asked Wolf before relaying his unbelievable tale.

"Daniel," the old man replied, shifting his staff into his right hand.

"Please, stay seated, and I will tell you all about my people and others like me—others far from here. I will tell you how I miraculously arrived in one piece—by a storm—if you can believe it." Wolf began telling his story, revealing all, even some wandering to and fro in the background wandered in. *May as well start with these people*, Wolf determined.

25

"These are my nicest," the lady informed Dray.

"What do you think?" asked Dray, turning to Jamie and John.

"I like it," said John.

"Not too bad, I guess," answered Jamie. Dray's black pants had zipper pockets, and his new black vest did not look much different than the one he wore upon entering. His original white-sleeved shirt fit snug underneath. Dray appeared satisfied.

"Now, let's get something for you," Dray said happily to Jamie, but Jamie smiled back and said, "I think I'll bring my mother back later. This way, it will be a surprise." John and Dray looked content. Dray handed over twenty coins before exiting. Bruce sauntered toward the back of the shop, and with a needle protruding from one lower limb he raised a pant leg. He looked toward Dray with amber eyes. Dray was glad to have him back.

"What? You don't want to keep them?" asked Jamie.

"I have so many pairs. I think I'll be fine," replied Dray, grasping Jamie's hand as they turned the corner outside.

There was commotion on the street. Bruce moved in front as Dray let go of Jamie's hand.

"Bill Hagen is dead!" yelled one Endeavor.

"Someone murdered Bill Hagen!" shouted another.

"That can't be right. We just met with him," Dray said to Jamie and John. The crowd approaching was not the ordinary citizenry—Commander Tarpin was at the head of the group. They encircled Dray and Jamie. Tarpin, Dray knew, thought he was responsible. It was human nature to fear what you cannot control. *I know you've been watching me—there must be an explanation*, Dray assured himself.

Ordinary citizens stood watch. Though murder was rare, one had never gained this much attention. Tarpin's company became silent.

"Dray! Where were you an hour ago?" asked Tarpin. His words were nothing short of accusatory. Tarpin had never trusted Dray and was not going to trust him now.

"All four of us were meeting with Bill Hagen. He was fine after we left," answered Dray, confirming with Jamie and John. John looked a little scared, having been surrounded once before. But his worrying ceased as suddenly as it had begun—the madness one would have to have to take on Bruce—and Dray's other side.

Jamie took Dray by the arm, offering some comfort.

"Cults are tricky—they have stealthy power..." Tarpin shocked those around him. He, too, felt the gravity of his own words.

"This is crazy! What on earth are you talking about?" John got in Tarpin's face.

"Dray is not what he appears to be. I will no longer keep this a secret. I won't be the only one losing sleep at night. We're going to take care of this right now before it gets out of hand. We'll put it to a vote—the entire city will have their say," Tarpin paused.

"What happened? What is it?" a voice from behind asked out loud. It was Dr. Roberts pushing his way through the crowd.

"Ah, good, Dr. Roberts. *You* can confirm Dray's a Cult," Tarpin posed to the doctor. Gasps and whispers circulated throughout the city. Dr. Roberts was speechless. This was exactly what he had hoped to avoid.

"Why are you doing this?" was Dr. Roberts' first question.

"We have suspicion to believe that Dray killed Bill Hagen," replied Tarpin.

"That's ridiculous. … But I'm glad you came out into the open with this rather than make a really bad decision behind closed doors," was Dr. Roberts' response. He hadn't prepared a speech but knew it was time to give one—a good one—if possible. His words were is only instruments now. He was not certain of Dray's condition but would defend him. Dray had nothing new to offer in his defense. He was relieved to see Dr. Roberts.

The cat's out of the bag, Dray acknowledge.

"It is true, Dray does have a certain anomaly that I can't explain," announced Dr. Roberts, adding, "I'm working on finding its origin, and I have Dray's full cooperation. I haven't had enough time, however, to diagnose its full capacity—that is to say, the extent to which the Cult in him will react. Listen carefully to my next words," Dr. Roberts raised his voice, saying, "It's vital that we work with Dray and continue to study his phenomenon," he ended. Dr. Roberts studied their reactions. *Was it enough to convince them not to turn on Dray?*

"Well said, Dr. Roberts, but that doesn't deny the fact that he could still be a potential risk to our people. He should be locked up or released," offered Tarpin.

"Released?" said Dr. Roberts.

"Yes—let go, banished. I first thought this would be dangerous, him joining others like himself, but I suspect the Cults won't want anything to do with him. He did kill many of them, even their leader. The other beasts will have different desires. If we're lucky, he'll continue hunting our enemies." Tarpin turned toward Dray, adding, "Tonight, Endeavors and Survivors will cast a vote. They'll decide on locking him up, releasing him into the wild, or leaving him be. He'll have tighter security if it's the latter of these three. Unless someone confesses to Bill Hagen's murder, the vote will go ahead as planned." Tarpin nodded to one of his men. Dr. Roberts had nothing to say. Tarpin's vote seemed fare, better than locking Dray up and throwing away the key. Dray decided to speak.

"How was Bill Hagen killed? Since I didn't do it—I would like to know?" Dray asked.

"He bled to death through every pore. No natural death could have occurred in such a way," answered the commander. Dray looked at Jamie with indescribable sadness, and then looked toward the crowd.

"I will honor the outcome of the vote. I understand how my condition may cause concern—but locking me up is not the solution. If your fear prevails, for your sake and mine, I'll be better off in the wild. I'm not a bad person." Dray turned away, preparing to leave.

"Wait one moment, Dray," said Tarpin. Dray halted with Jamie. "We must confine you until the vote," Tarpin informed. A soldier took out handcuffs.

"I can assure you that won't be necessary," Dray replied. Dr. Roberts stepped between the handcuffs and Bruce.

"And I can assure everyone that confining him until the vote won't be necessary. He just stated that he would comply," insisted Dr. Roberts.

"Hey! What's going on?" asked Jason, rushing through the crowd, with Grace not far behind him.

"They're about to handcuff me. They think I killed Bill Hagen," replied Dray, happy to see his friend. *Handcuffing me was not part of the deal*, Dray angrily concluded, adrenaline creeping up his spine. He had come to terms with having to leave the city one day—and leave Jamie. Never returning was hard to process. Banished forever—for something he did not do.

"There's no way you're putting him in handcuffs," Jason looked furious, stepping up to the soldier with handcuffs. But he was held back by Grace. Dray's eyes turned fiery-orange and bloodshot, and his round pupils morphed into something feline-like; all took heed, cautiously stepping back. Dr. Roberts liked what he saw; not his eyes, but the fear they could command. Bruce warningly moved into position, altering his stealth coating. Tarpin had a sudden change of heart.

26

Michael and Archimedes tumbled through the sky. It was a slow rotation and an odd way to fly, as Archimedes bent his wings, triggering thrust in opposite directions—it practically made Michael sick. But it was necessary.

"Helps avoid detection. I encountered many threats while pursuing you," Archimedes informed.

"I feel like I'm in space," Michael shakily replied, hitting his chest, revealing his pale face. Archimedes leveled back out.

"Threat detection avoided," Archimedes reported.

"Thank goodness," said Michael, recovering.

"ETA five minutes. Target detected," Archimedes warned. A clock popped up in front of Michael, counting down.

"What?" said Michael, confused. "What target? Where?" he asked. But his question was soon answered. His screen zoomed in miles ahead, zeroing in on a woman.

"You might have to deploy, Michael. I can bend and fold, but not that much," cautioned Archimedes. The target fled into a narrow ravine; cavernous holes the size of men compassed the entire stretch. The real target was the one in pursuit of the other.

"Wait a second—" doubted Michael, the clock counting down.

"I was given this, and the occasion is timely," Archimedes interrupted. A weapon slid out directly beside Michael. "I was going to present it to you upon our return," revealed Archimedes.

"Are you kidding me? A sword?" was Michael's reaction. Michael inspected the weapon. It had a deep purplish hue. Archimedes explained its origin.

"The storm carried me into the upper regions of the earth's atmosphere. I crossed paths with a black bird. It had a wingspan longer than mine. In its talons was a scroll and a sword. We locked together like two seabirds dueling near a cliff. No natural predator could have existed there. The thin frigid air was immobilizing. A voice told me not to fight. It told me to present these items to the first living soul I encountered. You, Michael," Archimedes finished with a minute to spare on the clock. Michael hit his chest with a determined fist, taking hold of the sword. A sensation like no other coursed throughout his body.

"You have an Icarus wing should you need it," additionally informed Archimedes. The silky wing had been present the entire time. It had fashioned itself to Michael's bio-suit without him noticing it.

"Where will you be?" asked Michael, angling his double-edged blade toward the hatch.

"I will accompany you down as far as I can," comforted Archimedes.

The countdown was up. Archimedes touched down with hardly a sound. He proceeded over the edge of a cliff, vertically, like a black widow spider. Michael had never used an Icarus wing. He was happy to have it should he fall into a bottomless pit.

Upon crawling to the bottom, Archimedes halted and opened his hatch.

"Archimedes. Can you hear me?" whispered Michael.

"Affirmative," replied Archimedes, nose facing the ground.

"It's dark in there," Michael said before his vision kicked on. With sword in hand, he walked into an opening no taller than himself.

With outstretched hands helping steer her way, she did the best she could to soften collisions, running as fast as humanly possible in the dark. A dead end soon obstructed her path. She tried desperately seeking an opening, a way through, feeling high and low with quivering hands. It was too late, though, as she heard the clopping of rocks approaching from behind. The chase was over. She hunkered down, wrapping her arms around a boulder. Stomping its hooves, making its presence known, the four-legged she-monster approached. The monster had the fangs of a lion and face of a woman, and its glossy mane was like that of a horse's. It had a man's torso with hairy arms like a gorilla. Its lower body looked like a goat's but with a long serpent's tail. Its tail swung wildly, chipping loose rock from the cave walls. The chimera discharged steamy, hot breath. Terrified, her prey cried for help, but all she got was a meaty hand grabbing her by the neck. The she-beast held her like an infant before strangling her.

Michael hastened his pace after hearing the scream. The struggle had ceased by the time he arrived. But before passing out, the dying woman saw a flash of light. Michael came down with an ax-like blow, severing the chimera in half; its entrails spilling all over the place. Its death roar was chilling, turning its devilish head toward its attacker. Its eyes locked squarely on Michael.

"*Tetelestia!*" cried the monster, keeling over.

Michael's attention turned toward his dripping sword. The blood-soaked blade suddenly grew hot, incinerating the fluid covering it. He turned toward the woman. She felt her neck and tried standing up. But fainted. Michael rushed to her aid. He slumped her over his shoulder and made his way out.

27

"We are the Almas," answered Daniel. "We're descendants of great nations," he added, guiding Wolf through a maze of people.

"That's incredible! I didn't think there was any unity left after the Great Divide," said Wolf enthusiastically.

"Our ancestors were fortunate souls. They took refuge in the jungle. A mystery man appeared and showed them the Milagro Tree. He told them how it offered protection—and then poof—he was gone," responded Daniel, adding, "May I ask where you got that?"

"A man named Jaxifer gave it to me."

"You're fortunate. Not many books exist. Much of our ancestors' history was lost, destroyed during their journey," revealed Daniel, stopping in front of a hut. "This is the only available space at the moment," he said as he opened the door. Wolf saw a table, two chairs, another door in the back, and a bed.

"That's a bathroom in the back. I apologize. I know it's not much. I'll send someone to fetch you some clothes if you'd like," Daniel pointed toward Wolf's bio-suit.

"Yes, I would greatly appreciate it, and no—it's perfect." Wolf looked around. "Do you by any chance have a strong container, preferably made out of metal?"

"I'll see what I can find." Daniel turned, giving orders to a young man outside.

"Please, don't be offended by my next question," said Wolf.

"No, go ahead, ask anything," said Daniel, still fascinated by Wolf and his people, the Endeavors.

"I've noticed a certain lack of technology around this place, minus the canisters you use to spray back the jungle" was the question on Wolf's mind.

"Our ancestors came here with little, just the clothes on their backs. They lived simple lives, passing down the only knowledge necessary to survive. As you can see, it's worked out okay. We live in harmony. We have very little crime but do have laws. Ostracism is the greatest deterrent. Would you want to go out there without Milagro?"

"Absolutely not," agreed Wolf.

"In any event, technology's most basic need is power. We lack the power supply, a source, to produce much of anything in mass. Don't get me wrong, we can smelt plenty of minerals from the ground in our fires, and understand ancient technology, but we have no need. At night, we use candles and torches," Daniel admitted. Wolf thought about their primitive fires giving them comfort at night. "Our most important source of life-saving energy comes from the Milagro Tree," Daniel added.

"Could this help?" asked Wolf, reaching behind his back.

"What a strange-looking object," uttered Daniel, studying Wolf's cylindrical tube.

"Stand back and cover your eyes," cautioned Wolf, hitting his chest with his fist. He activated his spear ray, its white orbs lighting up the room. Daniel covered his eyes. Wolf deactivated his ray, saying, "The harder I squeeze, the stronger the light."

"The things you asked for, sir," announced a man at the door. He placed a large metal container near the door, and on top he placed some clothes. Wolf walked over, tossed the clothes on his bed, and then slid the container away from the door. He opened it and stepped inside. Reaching for his plug, inserting it, his bio-suit glowed. The scene captivated Daniel, shielding his eyes once again. Seconds later, Wolf stepped out, groaning. At the same time there was thunder outside. Almas took shelter before the rainfall.

"Jeez! I haven't done that in a while. Without a biotank, we're trained to do it this way. I'm supposed to practice— but boy that really stung," admitted Wolf, turning toward a startled Daniel. Wolf 's black suit matched the black of Daniel's robe, but hugged Wolf like no other material Daniel had ever seen. Wolf 's face looked sun-burnt.

"My God, what a sight." Daniel caressed his forehead.

"If you don't mind, I'd like to try on those clothes now." Wolf pointed toward his bed.

"Yes, of course. Come out when you're ready. I'll begin preparations for a special dinner tonight—in celebration of your arrival," said Daniel before turning to leave.

Wolf gently placed his spear ray inside the container. It sunk into what was once his bio-suit.

"I'd like to see someone try and steal that without knowing how," Wolf said to himself, looking down at his dead armor. He knew he'd never be able to wear it again without a biotank. But for now, he was safe, and his spear ray was secure.

28

Hours passed while Dray sat in his room waiting with Bruce.

"I've quarantined myself after all, Bruce," said Dray, looking down at his scout. Bruce didn't reply, but Dray knew he was listening. A knock rapped on his door. "Come in!" shouted Dray, louder than necessary. In walked everyone: Dr. Roberts, Jamie, Madge, Al, Jason, Grace, Eric, and John. Next to Dray, Bruce sat like a bronze statue, dutifully turning toward those entering.

"I took the liberty of making sure it's an honest vote tonight. The results should be coming in within the hour," informed Dr. Roberts.

"How are the votes being taken?" asked Dray, but from the tone of his voice, it appeared he did not really care.

"Everyone of voting age was given a black, white, and red marble, and additional instructions on what the colors stood for. Various locations around the city have drop boxes where they can drop them; they're scanned and counted automatically. It seems reliable," finished Dr. Roberts.

"Dray, when Eric and I discovered what was happening, we immediately went to talk with Tarpin. He's not budging," reported John.

"If you have to leave, Dray, where will you go?" asked Al, stepping closer to Dray.

"I'm going to retrace my steps from Compound 40. Bruce and I will find the Pectore and hopefully get some answers. I agree with Jason—they must know more. I'll also try and track down Commander Wolf and the rest of his team," revealed Dray. His objectives were clear and made sense to all. In fact, it was a mission that Jason wanted to undertake.

Jason came forward, begging, "Let me go with you. The Endeavors will equip me with a bio-suit and spear ray. You won't have to worry about me," he pled. Dray stood up.

"I know, Jason, I know, but I think you'll be more useful here. I know you'd be a great help. But I'll be moving fast," Dray said. Bruce cocked his head to the side. The intercom next to the door beeped.

"Final count—red. Dray must exit the city. All personnel accompany him to the main portal," the announcement spread throughout the city.

"So how did you guys vote?" Dray comically asked, giving Jamie a hug.

"I'm sorry it had to be like this," Jamie smiled, her eyes welling up with tears. Eric stepped forward.

"I asked Tarpin what provisions you'd be given, if any at all. A bio-suit and spear ray were denied. So, here, I thought this might come in handy," offered Eric, handing over a sheathed sword. It was the katana Dray had given him on their journey.

"This may just come in handy, Eric, thank you. Thank all of you for being here—" A knock sounded on the door. Tarpin and others stood outside.

"Shall we go?" Dray said to Bruce and the others.

The walk to the portal was long but gave them additional time to talk, particularly with Jamie, afraid of losing Dray for good this time. The atmosphere was languid. Most felt like they had betrayed Dray, especially the ones whom he had saved. They apologized, and Dray forgave them.

Dray and Bruce halted at the portal.

"You can trust me! Your location will follow me to the grave," proclaimed Dray, shaking everyone's hand. Giving Jamie a final kiss good-bye, hugging, he whispered, "Be careful. Whatever killed Bill Hagen is still here." He and Bruce stepped toward the wall, vanishing.

29

Dray and Bruce appeared under an archway. The frigid wind beyond howled and pulled inward, coaxing them out. On the outside he appeared calm, but he was livid. He would have loved taking command, but unbeknown to him the portal was locked. Whatever kindled his fury could only help him survive. Without a bio-suit, any rage was welcome. The maelstrom of weather matched his temper. Dray swung out his sword and violently struck a boulder. He shattered the blade and tossed it aside. Bruce stood idle, unable to process the attack.

"Let's go, Bruce, lead the way," loudly announced Dray, ready to finally make his way down. A familiar membrane grew over his eyes, shielding them from the wind.

"Bruce!" roared Dray. Bruce was snatched up like a toy! Startled, Dray staggered backward. Devouring Bruce whole, it revealed its true form as it split from the mountainside. Its scales were gray and tan, matching every nook and cranny of rock. Dray dove for cover but was too late. The predator's raven-black eyes caught him. But the monster halted—then shrieked. It had to be Bruce. *It must be*, Dray determined, waiting in angst for his scout to rejoin him.

Bruce began heating up, crammed inside the creature's viscous throat. With cyclical claws, spear-tipped nose, and a jolt of thrust, he jettisoned through muscle and bone. Bursting out through a wall of meat and tissue, he landed on brittle ground. The scout tauntingly looked up with iridescent eyes. The beast mistook him for prey. The colossal creature slumped to the ground, obstructing their path. Bruce was not deterred, using his flesh-tearing claws to climb. He halted once reaching the top. Looking down, his intrepid eyes gave his master the all clear.

Dray's heart raced, and his flesh crawled. His fingernails grew black. His skin hardened into scales, changing color, matching the rock beneath his feet. Dray poked his left hand with his right hand, surprised by their leathery toughness. Black strands of hair fell on his sleeve; he pulled out a fistful. The Cult in him had come out. Bruce matched his phantom-like nature, blending into the environment. Dray lapped his tongue across his lips. He homed in on Bruce. New senses detected what his eyes could not; he felt more vibrations beneath his feet. Dray cursed the heavens with a gravellier voice. He had become what he trained his whole life to defeat. He tore off his shirt and vest and ran.

30

"It's Drake!" declared hoarsely an alarmed Cult. Cults shuffled about the control room, flipping switches and checking monitors.

"How far?" barked Commander Spiels.

"Twenty minutes!"

"Take out his aircraft!" roared Spiels. Cults snorted and huffed, sending out orders. Spiels' entire army was on alert. Vehicles of all shapes and sizes rolled, jumped, or launched into the late afternoon sky. Spiels disrobed, smothering on a lotion that removed his makeup; beneath its pale hue were hardened scales. *He should have brought an entire army to retrieve my flesh,* growled Spiels. His chameleon guise now absorbed the bland colors of the control room.

Drake ejected, gambling with his life it appeared. *Nothing risked, nothing gained,* Drake grumbled in midair. His cloak flapped incessantly until he removed it. His scales were black as night, and his golden fierce eyes never blinked. Reaching terminal velocity, he spotted a wave of targets below. With both fists pointing downward, he targeted one, emitting a melting current its way. His unsuspecting target lost control and ejected into a black form—Drake and his fist. In their rapid descent, he harvested the warrior's flesh, hastily draping himself with it. But nothing happened as they quickly lost altitude. Drake's adrenaline surged. Soon enough the flesh took hold, sticking tightly to his own. His fall came to a halt. His wings appeared more eaglelike than the last. Sullenly pleased, Drake watched the ongoing pursuit in the distance. His aircraft continued without him.

"He's come for you!" snarled a warrior Cult, pointing a spiny finger toward Spiels. The others in the room stopped what they were doing; their commander was being challenged. Spiels swiftly moved across the room, taking the warrior by the neck.

"You wish to defy me," blandly stated Spiels. "He slaughtered my centurion guard. What makes you think he won't do the same with you? He's come for all—"

"No! He's come for you. You killed his soldiers. Now he wants your head—not ours," another Cult coolly interjected. Others circled them like hyenas. Spiels' eerily smiled, exerting more pressure on the warrior's neck. Attempting to pry himself free, the warrior pulled on Spiels' arm. The others looked on, imagining the same vice grip around their necks. Spiels finally snapped his neck. He knelt beside his kill, cutting and tearing with scalpel claws. He, too, prized the flesh of other Cults. He stood back up, holding the dripping flesh out like a trophy. With another crazed smile, he walked over to the wall and hung it. With torturous stares, the others suppressed their rage, falling back in line.

Drake reached Spiels' outer compound wall. He landed softly, and to his surprise spotted Spiels and two guards. Drake charged, and within fifty yards jumped, his massive wings shortening the distance. All three kept watch, but not above. Drake smashed both guards with his wings! He picked up Spiels. Spiels' thrashed wildly, cursing the predator behind him. They rose high before Drake let go. He could not have planned it any better. Spiels' flesh was left intact, unspoiled from not having to shoot it. The two guards lay unconscious until Drake broke both their necks. Unquestionably painful, Drake had to remove his wings before boarding a snug cockpit. He jumped high and came down hard on the edge of an aircraft wing, severing both of his wings. They fell to the ground and shriveled up. Guessing what they had once been was impossible. Drake's agony was surreal, bending over on his hands and knees. The gaping wound on his back stung until closing. Staggering toward Spiels, he picked him up and boarded the aircraft.

31

"Just as you don't need different words to write different books, you don't need new genes to make new species. You just change the order and pattern of their use," Dr. Roberts told Jeffrey, peering back into his microscope. "Humans have twenty-three pairs of chromosomes in each cell. Cats have nineteen. If you were to rearrange or invert just a few cat chromosomes, you could conceivably convert its gene order into the human pattern. To replicate this with a dog or mouse can require a hundred chromosome rearrangements."

"So how does this explain the Cult?" queried Jeffrey.

"Well, that's what I'm trying to figure out. It all has to do with uncontrolled cell division and a specific gene. The Cult can trigger this gene. It's responsible for the differentiation of organs and tissues in many species. How Dray can do this I can't explain. It makes no sense. The Morphic Formula I designed was meant to trigger this gene once, temporarily. Why he even has Cult in him in the first place is still the million-dollar question. Compound 40 couldn't have been infiltrated. Dray was, and is, the only known case of this anomaly."

"Can it be airborne?" pondered Jeffrey

"I don't think so…it can't work like that," replied Dr. Roberts hesitantly.

"What if we all have it in us, some more than others," responded Jeffrey.

"Go on?" Dr. Roberts looked intrigued.

"What if we're all born with it? It just takes more time for some to change. Scientists have always tried to explain the origin of evil, put a face on it, so to speak. Maybe we've overlooked this possibility."

"I've always believed that the Cult is the embodiment of evil. Are you trying to say that we're all going to eventually turn into Cults? Dr. Roberts asked dismally.

"No, I'm trying to say that if evil exists in all of us, could this not make us more susceptible to the Cult, airborne or not?"

"Interesting theory, but I think there's a scientific explanation for all this," Dr. Roberts convincingly stated. Dr. Roberts obviously knew more than he was letting on. Jeffrey was trying to get at the origin of the Cult, and while Dr. Roberts knew exactly where it had originated, Dray's Cult origin was his quandary. Dr. Roberts turned in his chair, considering Jeffrey's words. "So simple, too simple. Airborne, impossible," concluded Dr. Roberts, yet could not escape the fact that Dray had it. Had Dray's mother or father shown any signs they would have been discovered right away.

"Hi, Dr. Roberts," Jamie greeted as she entered the lab. Dr. Roberts swung around in his chair.

"Jamie! So good to see you. How are you holding up?"

"I'm doing okay. How 'bout you?" Jamie nodded at Jeffrey.

"As good as one can be. Jeffrey and I are going over some samples," Dr. Roberts went back to his microscope. Jeffrey took a seat nearby.

"I wanted to discuss something with you, alone if I could,"

Jamie said, glancing toward Jeffrey. "Sorry, no offense, Jeffrey," she added with a look that would drive some men lustily mad.

"Yes, sure thing, can you excuse us for minute, Jeffrey," uttered Dr. Roberts, still peering into his microscope. Jeffrey left without hesitation. Jamie paced back and forth behind Dr. Roberts.

"I don't know where to begin. You're going to think I'm crazy when I tell you this," Jamie kept pacing.

"At this point, nothing would surprise me," replied Dr. Roberts. "Please, tell me something crazy." He swiveled around in his chair.

"Not long ago, I had an interesting encounter with Dray. The word *interesting* can hardly describe what that encounter entailed. You ready for the crazy part?"

"Shoot," reacted Dr. Roberts.

"Dray wasn't physically there. … I mean, he was there, but wasn't," Jamie ceased pacing back and forth. Dr. Roberts was intrigued with Jeffrey but now looked astonished with Jamie.

"Jamie, please, a little more detail," inquired Dr. Roberts, crossing his arms around his chest.

"I couldn't see him, but I could hear him, feel him, even smell him," Jamie went back in time, reliving her magical encounter with delight—her and Dray's first kiss.

"Where were you? When did this happen?" asked Dr. Roberts, his face unmoving. Jamie came back down from the clouds, amazed that a memory that could stir up such bliss.

"We were on the Great Mantle, right before Dray and the Endeavors left on their mission. I was taken aside by Dray. He was invisible, Dr. Roberts, a ghost, can you believe that?" Jamie explained, shaking her head and smiling. Dr. Roberts was sure to think she was crazy now. "I wish Dray had told you before he left. You'd probably think he was out of his mind, too."

"I don't know what to say, Jamie. Could you have been hallucinating, imagining all this, perhaps?" was Dr. Roberts' only suggestion.

"At the time I thought I was dreaming. He told me that he was in his bio-suit, but it just wasn't possible to touch him like I did. He wanted to keep it secret. I wasn't hallucinating. It was real. I couldn't explain it then, and I can't explain it now," Jamie revealed, keeping eye contact with Dr. Roberts.

"I want to believe you, Jamie, if what you say is true. People have had out-of-body experiences since the beginning of time." Dr. Roberts looked away and up toward the ceiling. "Who would have thought, Cults, evil incarnate, somehow able to control it, use it to their advantage—"

"No! Dray isn't evil! He's not a Cult!" cried Jamie, unable to believe it.

"Jamie, why did Dray come see you that day?" Dr. Roberts asked suspiciously.

"He wanted to say good-bye. You and Tarpin didn't allow him to—that's why he came to me," she answered.

"Anything else?"

"We kissed," said Jamie sulkily.

"Not exactly evil, but..." Dr. Roberts shook his head satisfactorily.

"I just thought you should know. Maybe it can help you find out more" were Jamie's final words. She wiped a tear from her cheek before turning to leave. Dr. Roberts was steeped in thought as Jeffrey rounded the corner.

"Jeffrey, oh, Jeffrey, you may have been on to something," relayed Dr. Roberts.

32

"The human spirit is our sixth sense. It's what makes us conscious of God," said Daniel, seeing Wolf tear off a chunk of meat.

"Do you have this sixth sense," chewed Wolf, "because I sure don't." He swallowed and burped. Almas sitting across from Wolf quieted, reproachfully staring his way.

"I mean, God doesn't speak to me like he does to you," added Wolf. Almas nodded understandingly. Their table was outside and lengthy and sat at least a hundred people. Lanterns lit up the surrounding houses, and kids played.

"I said it's what makes us conscious of God, Commander. Humans gave up the ability to communicate directly with God a long time ago. At one time, the soul and full spirit both had homes in the physical body of man and experienced harmony in their innerworkings. Can you imagine what that must have been like?" Daniel imagined for himself.

"Yeah, that must've been something," Wolf said as he continued relishing his food. "Daniel, remember when I said my coming here may have had a purpose? What I meant was—I think I can help the Almas."

"Help us how?" asked Daniel.

"You have many warriors, and with the protection of the trees, you have the freedom to move about," Wolf spoke loudly so all could hear. "With the power from my spear ray, we can build, rise out of the jungle, and fight." With a warrior's spirit, Wolf wanted to fight the enemy and not hide in the jungle. For all he knew, his Endeavors were still out there, fighting. An Alma sitting across from Wolf spoke up.

"It would take quite an event to rally all nations to leave and go fight. But—I agree—it wouldn't hurt to be better prepared. Relying solely on our environment for protection is foolish," said the Alma, returning to his food. Wolf knew they were not going to fight unless they had to defend themselves.

"Good! At the very least we should start building weapons for defense. It's only a matter of time before the Cults figure out a way to repel the jungle," reasoned Wolf, but doubtful anyone could ever get through those trees. "I think everyone can acknowledge this. Help me spread the news. I want the greatest thinkers at my side. Tomorrow, we begin to build—for defense," declared Wolf spiritedly.

One Alma listening nearby raised his cup, agreeing, "For defense!" he shouted. The cheer spread down the length of the table, everyone saluting. Wolf was happy, too, smiling a hardy smile; he got what he wanted. He, with the help of the Almas, could now build weapons unlike any they had ever seen.

On the other side of town, Bracken stood next to a bonfire with Jaxifer and other warriors at his side. The sound of crackling wood was predominant. An attractive woman stepped out from the shadows, carrying a bowl of Milagro. Bracken stood tall and was prepared to be rubbed down. Jaxifer cleared his throat, beginning to chant; a ritual was being carried out. The scantily clad woman moved with grace and patience, careful not to miss any spots. Satisfaction quivered up her spine, giving her goose bumps as she smothered Bracken's biceps. Moving on to his palpitating chest, she felt her own heart skip a beat. He glistened all over, standing in the firelight. The slow chant sped up as Bracken was handed a spear. Stroking the back of her long black hair, the Milagro woman said, *"Buena suerte."*

Bracken jogged off into the night. He had done this many times, and so did many other warriors. It was a test of manhood. He listened to his environment, smelling and feeling to find his way in the dark. With the chant's protection, Bracken hoped to avoid night-vision predators. Howler monkeys went wild in the treetops. He wondered why the jungle never shut them up. If he could only reach one—the hunt would be over.

Bracken made an arc, veering off the beaten path and into the dense undergrowth. After approximately a mile, he heard something nearby. It moved, thudding—an animal perhaps, but a strange one. He halted, flexing his muscles and adjusting his grip. The thudding turned into rumbling, louder and heavier than before. Bracken squinted, peering into the dark. His nose and ears could not tell him what was coming his way. It was not one but many, Bracken now ascertained. They sounded like locusts; the thudding and rumbling were the trees beating the jungle floor. Bracken swung his spear! They swarmed him. He flailed and bellowed. The howler monkeys went crazy. The evil horde had never entered the jungle. Bracken's remains were gone, not a single piece of him was left.

Jaxifer was distraught. The others ceased chanting. Bracken's cry was heard by all. He was one of their best; he always returned with a kill. His death was an ill omen. Villagers wanted answers. One suggested a night-vision predator took him. Jaxifer, terror-stricken, suspected much worse.

33

She sat limp in Michael's arms, sleeping in peace. Her head lay right beneath his chin. For quite some time, Michael wanted to unmask, but he did not want to wake her. Deciding it was time, he carefully propped her up. Stirring awake soundlessly, and after blinking a few times, the whites in her eyes grew wide—she was about to scream. But an invisible, gentle hand suppressed her lips. Slowly turning, she peered into human eyes, and froze.

"It's okay, you're safe now" were Michael's comforting words. The sound of his voice was like a gift from God. He, himself, had to be a supernatural being, for his celestial body was invisible. She was floating in a tiny bubble, it seemed, warm and comfortable. Cockpit lights brightened, articulating more of the face that accompanied his eyes. It was dark outside, nothing for any human to see.

"Who—are—you?" she whispered, trembling.

"I'm Michael," he answered.

"I'm alive?" she asked petrified.

"Sure, you are—see..." Michael softly pinched her cheek. She pulled away, raising her hand to her face. Calmly averting her gaze, she glanced down, seeing her tattered tunic in shambles. Leaning forward, she managed to better

149

cover herself. With her bare back facing Michael, she hesitantly asked, "Where are you taking me?"

"We're going to the city of Endeavors," he answered.

"How's all this possible?" her voice changed in pitch and tone, less frail.

"How's all what possible?" retorted Michael.

"This, where we are? What are you? I can't see the rest of you," she uttered, turning to her side. Her legs now sat across his lap, and the closeness of her stare seared into him, temporarily stunning him. Unbeknown to Michael, his gaze was having the same affect.

"I'm a Survivor, living with the Endeavors. I'm as human as you are," assured Michael. His eyes unlocked from hers, momentarily glancing down. Focusing back up, he continued, "This is a bio-suit, and underneath it is me—the rest of my body." Michael touched another part of his chest, revealing more to his true form. "Each suit is unique to the individual wearing it," he added as made his suit glimmer. With the help of the scan she looked him over searchingly, sitting on what she discovered to be his lap. "What is your name?" he then asked. It took her a moment to respond, navigating through her befuddled mind.

"Veronica," she answered abruptly.

"Where were you heading?"

"I was heading nowhere," Veronica said defensively, but soon warming up to Michael. "I've been raised to run, educated to think, and outwit the monsters that hunt me," she said rapidly, as if programmed. Michael did not know exactly how to respond; he was startled but impressed all at once. "This must be a dream," cried Veronica. "There are others out there like me, men and women. Some give up right away, others find cliffs and jump." Michael could not imagine a worse fate. And he could not help noticing the strength in her voice.

Alluding to death so courageously, he thought admiringly. "That's all over now. You don't have to run anymore. The monsters I fight are a little bit more sophisticated—"

"What is this contraption?" she asked, shifting her eyes off Michael, toward the rest of the cockpit.

"This is Archimedes. Say hi, Archimedes,"

"Hi," responded Archimedes. Veronica's heart jolted, perspiration beading everywhere.

"It's okay, it's just an aircraft. You've never seen one?"

"I've seen strange things in the sky, but I never heard one talk." Veronica leaned closer toward Michael, still frightened.

"What's our ETA, Archimedes?"

"Thirty minutes," the scary voice replied.

"Any threats avoided so far?"

"Many."

"This aircraft saved our lives. We should be thankful," acknowledged Michael, taking out the scroll. Turbulence jostled Veronica, and unknowingly she took hold of the joystick between Michael's legs, grasping anything for stability.

"What is this?" she asked. Michael was distracted, looking over the contents of the scroll. He glanced below his parchment.

"Wow! It helps steer Archimedes," he replied, making sure Archimedes was still on autopilot.

"What's that?" she asked, reaching for the floating paper separating them.

"I'm trying to find out," Michael answered. The scroll, however, was illegible. He could not make out a single word.

"I'm going to miss my blood relatives," said Veronica sadly. Michael stopped pretending to be making any progress.

"You have family?" asked Michael.

"Yes, we were separated before the chase. I'd like to see them again," the strength in her voice faded, upsetting Michael as he rolled up the scroll.

"Archimedes, did you see anyone else down there?"

"No, Commander, she was the only one," answered Archimedes. Veronica sat back to her original position, her head beneath Michael's chin. She felt defeated.

"You'll make new friends, perhaps even start a new family." Michael tried convincing, but all he got in return were tears. He had never seen a woman cry before. He joined his arms around her waist. She took heed to his new positioning, readjusting herself. In the lap of her protector, Veronica continued to mourn. The two became at ease and, simultaneously closing their eyes, both fell asleep.

34

Incorporeal as it seemed, a solid form followed behind his nocturnal eyes. Dray crouched low in the dark, waiting, as Bruce cantered ahead and snuffed out the menace. Creeping up from behind, Dray whiffed the animal predator-like but did not take a bite; its demise came swift like the rest. He and Bruce were on a killing spree it appeared, killing for fun, and not for food. They ran for hours, covering considerable ground. Using Bruce for transportation was considered, but the less attention the better. Soon after twilight, the temperature dropped tremendously, and Dray could no longer run, trudging along as best as he could. Finally coming to a halt, breathing heavily, he called Bruce.

"I can't run," grumbled Dray. Bruce came to a halt, oscillating his head. Dray assessed his condition, looking over his limbs. His hardened flesh was an inch thicker, making his pants tighter. And his spiny toenails had torn holes through his shoes. He wondered how the Cults handled the cold, collapsing in the dirt, panting. With Bruce standing guard, he involuntarily gazed up, wishing he could draw warmth from the stars.

"I'm cold, Bruce, so cold," said Dray exhaustedly. Bruce looked downward, scanning his master. Stepping closer, he lowered down against him, heating. His exuberant warmth brought Dray back to life. Dray wrapped his arms around Bruce, making as much contact as possible. The scout's amber eyes never ceased scanning the terrain.

"I guess Cults need more warmth than Humans," determined Dray, fortunate to have Bruce at his side. Now heated, he separated from his scout. "I guess we'll have to do that every so often," he concluded, shouting, "Move out!" Bruce trotted back into the night, his master energetically following behind. Compound 40 was not far ahead. Bruce clawed his way up a hill. Dray did the same, digging in his hands and feet. Vibrations tickled his fingers, alerting him to what emerged from the shadows below. Dray clung to a ledge as they gathered in force. Drones! He had only one option—outrun them.

"Bruce!" roared Dray. Bruce turned, focusing downward. "Let's fly!" Bruce took form, flexing and bending. Dray crawled on, took hold, and flew.

The first drone landed, but only found scorched earth. It jumped skyward! It missed Bruce and Dray with one razor-sharp limb. It plummeted back down but shot straight back up on its springy limbs. A sky drone appeared, emitting its crushing sound waves. But Dray and Bruce were miles away. Something new had just popped up on the Cults' radar.

Dray and Bruce cleared the valley, steering left and right, pitching and rolling, escaping the odious drones. *The sooner we arrive, the sooner I can choose.* A wicked grin popped up on Dray's face. Craters and metal littered the terrain, revealing telltale signs of war. Bruce came in fast, shutting down, extending his limbs. Dray jumped off and felt the ground. *Nothing,* he found. The two descended into a familiar dark tunnel; Bruce had no need to plow his way through this time.

Dray and Bruce arrived at *Ancient Weapons and Memorabilia.* Since he no longer had a bio-suit, a simple harness or belt would suffice. Equipping himself with enough ammo was essential, but he had to choose fast—he did not know how much time he had. Dray removed his torn shoes and pants. *If I can't find another pair, I'll make do in my underwear,* he concluded, comforted by his new armor-like flesh. Rummaging through Al' boxes, he found a pair of camouflaged shorts, large, with hefty pockets. Next, he walked alongside display cases. He found survival knifes, 9 mm pistols and rifles of all shapes and sizes. Though a rifle packed more of a punch, it was too cumbersome. Randomly, he picked up a 9 mm Glock, filling as many cartridges as he could. Toward the back of the shop were more scattered boxes, their contents spread all over the place. Lying peacefully on the floor was a Smith & Wesson Magnum 500. Its rubber pistol-grip fit snug in his hand. Caressing its 10.5-inch long barrel, Dray opened its five-shot cylinder. *Empty.* He pillaged through box after box, searching for its high grain rounds. He was becoming frantic, looking inside the last box. He found five rounds. *Only five?*

"I'm ready, Bruce," announced Dray. Bruce stood watch at the entrance scanning Dray's new equipment. "This stuff could help," coolly uttered Dray. Before leaving, something caught his eye. It was partially covered by rubble. *There's no way that belonged to Al. It must have come from a warbot,* thought Dray, uncovering a modified Dillon Aero mini-gun. Dray propped it up, discovering that it did indeed come from a warbot. Since he could not take it with him, he pointed and squeezed. Smiling a malevolent smile, he hosed the place down with its 7.62 mm rounds. He knocked in doors and shattered windows not already broken. The biting flash from its six rotating barrels came to a stop. Dray detected the damage in the dark. What did he care? The place was already a mess. Bruce simply watched, discovering his darker side. *What am I doing?* a part of Dray wondered, imagining live targets, both monster and human.

35

"People were given superhuman power to advance his work on the earth. Inventions have come from the spirit world, and fantastic creations have occurred just as foretold by the ancient text," said Daniel, standing behind Wolf and working Almas.

"Well, I can assure you, Daniel, this machine will be fantastic," Wolf turned from Daniel, ordering, "Place those support beams over there! Move that pulley toward the very end! Good, now, someone, please, get me some water." Wolf wiped sweat from his brow. They'd been working all morning in the tropical heat. Even under the shade, the humidity took its toll.

"What exactly is this behemoth going to do?" asked Daniel.

"Ah, thank you," said Wolf, taking a big gulp of water. "It's going to help us beat back the jungle. I figure, in addition to using Milagro, it wouldn't also hurt to have some brute force. I don't know how far we need to go or how much Milagro we'll need. Since no one here has ever left, I'm not taking any chances," answered Wolf.

"I'm usually not the pessimist, but there are some pretty big trees out there," Daniel was highly doubtful, but Wolf ignored him, barking out another order.

"Has the blacksmith finished smelting those shapes I drew out for those parts?" Wolf asked an Alma nearby.

"No, I don't believe so," answered the Alma

"Could you go find out?" said Wolf. "Thank you." Almas moved about like worker ants. They came from all parts of the city and put their skills to use, taking orders from Commander Wolf. Most looked content as the massive structure began taking shape. It was a towering heap of wood, rope, and metal, and nowhere near being complete.

"How does your spear ray fit into all of this?" queried Daniel.

"You'll see. It's going to move this entire thing," replied Wolf, smirking.

"Wolf, one of the elders has requested you," announced an Alma coming down a path.

"Who?" wondered Wolf.

"Jaxifer," the Alma responded. "He says you've met."

"Yes, how could I forget, Jaxifer. I'll be right over. I want to see this cross section in place by the time I get back," was Wolf 's final order before leaving. He headed up the same path taken by the Alma. He took his time, needing a brake. *Jaxifer—what could this old man want?* Wolf pondered, passing children at play. Along the way, Almas went about their daily lives in peace. Wolf pictured the same one day for all humankind living in peace, not just here.

The houses sitting in the treetops were unique and constructed well. Milagro dripped down their sides; some had automated timers releasing it at the appropriate time. *I'll use the same mechanism on my vehicle*, Wolf determined. People greeted Wolf kindly, some greeting him in their native language. When he began hearing more, "*Buenos días, señor*," he knew he was close. Wolf detected a branch move his way. He stopped at the next Milagro barrel. Jaxifer and several others walked up.

"Wolf, good seeing you," greeted Jaxifer. Wolf turned from the barrel, smothering his limbs with Milagro.

"Jaxifer, good to see you. What's going on?"

"Bracken is dead, he die last night. We honor him. We have a warrior ceremony. All warriors attend. You come too?" asked Jaxifer.

"Of course, just let me know when and where," replied Wolf.

"Today—now," said Jaxifer sadly.

"What happened? How did he die?" Wolf had to ask, knowing Bracken was a tough warrior, and healthy.

"He die in the jungle. But jungle not eat him. Something else."

"A predator?" queried Wolf.

"Yes, a predator. We track him and find his spear, nothing else. No bones, even." Jaxifer turned toward the others as if to confirm. Jaxifer extended his arm toward Wolf, and Wolf accepted; they walked arm in arm.

Women, men, and children were gathered in a wide-open circle between houses. In the center was a firepit with a spear sticking up. *Must be Bracken's*, surmised Wolf. Jaxifer and Wolf entered the circle.

"Bracken *fue un soldado! Recordemos eso!*" proclaimed Jaxifer. Shouts rose up from the crowd.

He was a soldier, let's remember that, translated Wolf. And that was it. Wolf noticed a boy and girl standing closer than the rest. *Must be his kids*. Bracken was not a brother, father, or son—he was a soldier. Wolf admired that. The boy tossed a lit torch into the firepit with the spear. It went up in flames. There, in the center of all these Almas, was Bracken's burning spear. Had Bracken's remains been found he may have accompanied his spear. Jaxifer took Wolf by the arm again and walked him from the circle.

"That's it?" questioned Wolf.

"*Sí*," answered Jaxifer, adding, "Our song no protect him like does normally."

"How so?"

"Protects from night-vision predator. But Bracken strong warrior, he kill many night-vision predator," Jaxifer looked just as confused as Wolf. All Wolf could glean was that Bracken's death was unusual.

"Whatever killed Bracken is still out there," assured Wolf. "We are building weapons and a device that can protect your people. This confirms it—time is of the essence. We need more help—more blacksmiths—we must build faster," Wolf explained to Jaxifer, confident in all those helping so far.

"I send more help," responded Jaxifer. Jaxifer had long sensed something unnatural out in the jungle. But raising alarm and spreading panic was counterproductive.

"I have to go, Jaxifer. I'm sorry for your loss. Come see what we're building some time," finished Wolf, giving Jaxifer a handshake. Jaxifer nodded.

"Thank you" was all Jaxifer said in return.

Somewhere, out over the jungle, a voluminous sphere hovered close to the treetops; its coiled neck and head extending as low as possible. The trees below swung wildly at the poison it dropped—but they were too small and too many. The sky drone continued deploying ant fragments.

36

Drake gutted Spiels, eviscerating him with natural pleasure. Entrails and organs were delicacies; once devoured Spiels' power lived on. Nothing went to waste—the flesh was the main prize. The stench was awful, but it did not bother him. Flesh played an important role in Cult society. Its strength was not predetermined from birth, but rather from the length one went to condition it. The secret behind their tough skin is not widely known; and only a few know what it can do—Spiels being one of them. Drake could feel it now firsthand, what is father had taught him long ago—the joining of superior flesh. He controlled it now, when and where he wanted it to expand.

Coarse Bay was a coastal base occupied by a handful of Cults—until the Great Dome arrived. Floating a mile off shore, it sat big and luminous. Cults on land felt its presence. Drake's coincidental arrival was not planned. Landing, the crew knew in advance it was him. Two Cults greeted him.

"We received your message, sir," said one Cult, lowering his head submissively.

"Send word to Spiels' men. Their commander is dead. They will obey me now," finished Drake. The two warriors took note of their commander's crawling flesh. Had they known the anomaly's origin, their reactions may have been one of terror and not dismay. A third Cult came running up from behind holding a black and red cloak. Covering his eye-catching flesh, Drake walked toward the dome's grand entrance. One Cult carried out his order while the other two followed him inside. Many stood beside the walkway just as they had before his departure. Drake's quick defeat of Spiels surprised them. He was truly the black angel of death.

"Our enemy grows stronger by the day!" roared Drake, sounding madder than ever. Growls and hisses spread throughout the crowd. "Leach! Begin mobilizing!" ordered Drake, turning away from savage stares. Leach nodded to his warriors nearby.

"Where will we send them?" asked Leach, walking behind Drake's fluttering cloak.

"North, where my father lost his mind. Our enemy has a stronghold in that region. I was close."

"Did you find what you were looking for, Master?"

"My only concern is finding those responsible for taking our prison. I want all troops deployed at once." Drake entered his room, but before closing the door made a final request. "Fetch me Echo."

Echo knocked, then entered once receiving permission.

"Have a seat, my sweet Echo," said Drake. Echo sat, crossing one leg over the other. She seemed at ease, for this moment had been played out a million times in her head.

She took a deep breath, beginning to say, "I am delighted—"

"Don't speak, just listen," interrupted Drake. "I want you to go north and accompany our troops. My mission for you is simple. Stay out of their way and observe. You will report back to me on their progress. Inform me of any disloyalty."

"May I speak?" asked Echo dryly. Drake nodded. "Why me? You wish to send me away? Not stay at your side?"

"What in heaven made you think I wanted you at my side? We are at war. Show me your loyalty and strength."

"How will this impact our warriors' morale?"

"Ah, yes. You're already proving your capacity to think. I should think that it will affect morale greatly. They will have no choice but to accept you. In what manner and form is up to them."

"It will be dangerous," replied Echo, realizing what her supreme commander was asking her to do.

"Yes, it will, and if you return, perhaps I will let you stand at my side. Now go."

"Yes, Master," obeyed Echo, standing up to leave.

"Echo." Echo turned feverishly. "If you find yourself in an inescapable situation, don't be afraid to use your best asset," he advised, glancing over her flesh.

"Yes," said Echo. She was terrified. What he asked her to do was unprecedented—a female Cult accompanying troops into battle. Having to potentially face the enemy was one thing; it was handling her own kind that worried her.

The room slowly darkened. Drake sat in total darkness.

Only the strongest will stand by my side.

37

"Who did it?" asked John, sitting next to Eric and Al inside the *Sky Bar*. Beneath their feet was glass, the entire floor. Looking down, anywhere in the bar, one could see the commotion of city life below.

"Whoever murdered him is still here. Tarpin is still convinced it was Dray. But until he starts thinking otherwise, they'll never search for the real killer," John angrily stated.

"Why don't we try?" suggested Al.

"I have a feeling this murderer will strike again," said John, "and when he does, everyone will know it couldn't have been Dray. If there isn't another murder—then great," John tipped his glass, making a small gesture of a toast. Eric took a gulp, then cleared his throat to speak.

"What if Dray was framed? Tarpin strikes me as a man who would do just about anything to keep order. Dray was a threat to his order. Best way to get rid of someone, if you ask me, is to make him out to be a criminal," Eric surmised, taking another swig. A round, flat robot scurried under his feet, cleaning the glass floor. With arms pressed against the bar, Eric looked downward, distracted by the robot. "Hey, check her out," said Eric, pointing.

"Which one?" John uttered, seeing many people walking far below.

"Well, men, I have a date," Al interjected.

"You have a *what*?" asked John, looking back up.

"I was invited to go hunting—by a woman—so I'll see you guys later," Al chugged the rest of his drink, slid his glass across the bar, and then turned to leave. Collecting Al's glass, the bartender glanced over at John and Eric disapprovingly.

"I hope you guys can cover that," said the bartender. John joined Eric people-watching. The crowd at the bar grew. John and Eric hardly noticed.

"You boys don't stick out at all," quipped a woman. John and Eric slowly lifted their heads. She had perceptive hazel eyes, red hair, and wore a red T-shirt with an illustration of a heart roasting over a fire.

"What do you think, Candice?" her companion said smilingly. Her friend wore tight jeans and a plain white T-shirt. Her sandy blonde hair and blue eyes gained John's attention.

"Not my type, Sarah, you know that," replied Candice. John glanced at Eric to think of something to say.

"Not your type?" said Eric, chuckling.

"What exactly is your type?" asked John.

"They wouldn't be talking to us if we weren't their type, John," Eric mumbled.

"What's so funny?" said Candice, ignoring John and focusing on Eric. Eric took a drink. John had not removed his gaze from Sarah.

"I once read a book on body language. You'd be surprised what movements can say about someone," answered Eric, finishing his drink and setting his glass down. Sarah turned from John, joining her friend studying Eric. Although Sarah had never met Eric, something familiar about him drew her attention. He looked sad. Candice, Sarah would never admit it, had a similar sadness.

"What does *my* body language tell you?" asked Candice.

Confidently, Eric replied, "It tells me you're gorgeous."

At the far end of the bar sat a quiet, lonely soul, drinking away. It was Jason. In walked Grace, gloomily approaching the man she wanted to spend the rest of her life with. She took off her coat before taking a seat.

"Are you okay?" asked Grace.

"Do I not look okay?" replied Jason, sounding surprisingly sober. He had been there for quite some time.

"You said you were going to meet me at *Olfactory Perfume*."

"You smell nice," said Jason, downing the rest of his drink. Their meeting had completely slipped his mind. He did feel bad about it, but it really did not show. She did indeed smell nice. The clove extracts, jasmine, and rosemary, all synthesized down into a perfume, offered Jason's senses an escape. The fragrance took his mind off Dray.

"They tell me you quit teaching. Is that true?"

"For the time being. I'm not quite fit to teach," answered Jason, inching closer toward her.

"He'll be okay, you know. You can't beat yourself up about this," Grace uttered softly, leaning in and giving him a kiss. Jason pulled away.

"It's not just Dray. What about Michael and Peter? They're all gone. And here I am, kissing you," he said guiltily. Jason's three best friends were either dead or fighting for their lives. It was understandable, Grace realized, how miserable this made him feel. She wished she could cheer him up.

"What are you going to do?" she somberly asked. "I mean, what *can* you do?" she added.

"What *can* I do? I can't do a damn thing," he answered, almost relieved by her question. There really was not anything he could do.

"So, you like my new perfume?" Grace cleverly switched topics.

"Yes."

"That's why I wanted you to come with me. This place is like stepping into another world. It's like the gardens but even more potent," she cheerfully stated, taking him by the hand.

"You're all I have left," Jason admitted.

"Don't go crazy on me. Look around you. What are all these people? What about your fellow Survivors? Surely you care for them?"

"You want the truth, Grace. No. I don't. How's that?" Jason wobbled his head.

"You've had too much to drink," replied Grace, "and you don't look so good."

"A couple more rounds! Down here! Have a drink with me, love," Jason slammed his glass on the bar.

"I don't think so. Maybe a couple rounds of water," Grace huffed, letting go of his hand. "You're falling apart, Jason. I'm trying to help you get through this. I'll see you later."

"Ah, come on. What's wrong!" pleaded Jason, but she was already out the door. Two drinks appeared in front of him. Jason stared at them for a minute, saying, "More for me."

"They seem to be getting along," acknowledged Sarah. She sat next to John, peeking over his shoulder. John was leaning on the bar, his hand pressed against his cheek.

"I got to admit it, Sarah, I've enjoyed your company," John could not help saying. She did find John to be intriguing. He had given her a firsthand account of his perilous journey to her city. He also mentioned Dray. She felt bad, admitting her voting for him to leave. This did not lessen John's interest in her.

"I've enjoyed our talk, too, John," replied Sarah, casually sipping her drink. "What's it like starting over? It must be fun starting a new chapter in your life."

"It has its ups and downs, I guess. Though I can't really say how it's been overall. I've only just begun this new chapter. Tell me more about yourself," queried John, his hand still glued to his cheek.

"My life is boring—not interesting at all when compared to yours," stated Sarah, disheartened.

"I find that impossible to believe," responded John, not knowing how else to respond.

"Well, I've obviously lived here my entire life. For work, I design clothing. I supply a few stores, not many. It keeps me busy. It's my passion. Interesting stuff, right?"

"Go on," encouraged John, looking as though he had just struck gold.

"For fun, I like hanging out with Candice and meeting new people. I enjoy walking in the Hanging Gardens. My life is very complicated, you see," she joked.

"No, it's perfect—"

"John, my boy, how's it going?" interrupted Eric, patting John on the back. "I told you we'd find a couple of lovely gals." Sarah smiled, embarrassed. Candice giggled, one of many that had been coming from her and Eric's side.

38

Loping along, Bruce detected movement ahead. The passage from which they had come was not far, but Bruce halted mid-stride, homing in on his quarry like an English pointer. Dray told him to check it out. As designed, Bruce plowed forward, mowing over fallen shards of Skyscape and through a concrete barrier, bravely jumping into the unknown beyond. Yelling and screaming erupted! Dray ran toward the shouts. With eyes blazing, Bruce spotted ten humans in the dark. He had two pinned to the ground. The others ran.

"Bruce," called Dray devilishly. Dray jumped down and landed next to his scout. Bruce lowered his head and, with eyes glowing, two faces lit up in the dark. Horror-stricken, his quarry did not move. "Who are you? What are doing here?" interrogated Dray.

"We—are—Survivors," trembled one.

"We heard noise," told the other, groaning.

"Bruce, get off them," commanded Dray. Frightened, lying on the ground, the two boys contemplated running. They collected their nerves.

"Call the others," said Dray. The two hesitated, thinking it was a trick. "I'm not going to hurt you. I'm a Survivor like you. I'm an Elite," revealed Dray. Bruce moved closer, his eyes still glowing. Dray saw instant relief spread across their faces.

"Corporals!" shouted one corporal.

"It's okay! You can come out!" shouted the other. Dray could not believe it—they were corporals. Fifty feet away, faint light from their lanterns drew near. Before coming any closer, Dray ordered them to stop. Their lanterns halted and swayed.

"You guys corporals?" asked Dray.

"We were in corporal training," said one.

"We were left behind. They didn't find us," said another.

"How many of you are there?" pondered Dray, surprised he did not detect them earlier.

"Seventy-seven," answered one corporal. A little boy approached Dray in the dark.

"Can you take me to my mom?" quavered the boy. The light from Bruce's eyes faded but remained bright enough for the boy to detect Dray.

"How old are you?" asked Dray, ignoring his seemingly impossible request.

"Nine," he trembled.

"We range from seven to seventeen," an older corporal informed. It did not surprise Dray, recalling how young he was when he was sent to training.

"Did anyone else survive? Our families?" asked a different corporal.

"Yes," Dray replied.

"Where are they?"

"They're safe, but far away from here."

"Can you take us to them?" There was a long pause. Dray found the question difficult to answer. The odds of his survival were still an unknown, but theirs?

"It would be suicide," Dray finally answered, adding, "It's too dangerous." Dray still wondered how he could help.

"Why can't we come any closer? Why don't you want us to see you?" the question came from someone in the group.

"Don't be afraid. You can come closer now," Dray permitted, kneeling next to Bruce, eyes now level with his scout's. The lanterns moved in, gradually shedding more light on Dray's grotesque body. They gasped, stepping backward. Though none had ever seen a Cult up close, many had had nightmares of one—their nightmare had just come to life.

"Hand me that," requested Dray, extending his gargoyle-like hand. The boy warily came forward and handed over his lantern. Dray peered into it, and once adjusting his eyes, saw his reflection for the first time. "This can't be permanent," he said out loud.

"What's wrong? What happened to you?" asked a startled corporal. Once again, Dray took his time answering.

"I can't say—I don't know," answered Dray truthfully, setting the lantern down. "Something has happened to me. I won't hurt any of you, I promise. I want to help you. I used to be one of you." Dray was scared, not for himself but for them.

"We've been living like rats down here, too afraid to go above," said the biggest corporal among them. Dray formed a plan.

"I want all of you to split up into groups. Find someone close to your age. Hurry," ordered Dray. The corporals shuffled about, grouping as best as they could in the dim light. "Form lines," instructed Dray. As they moved into formation, Dray counted exactly seventy-seven. "I want seven rows," calculated Dray. They lined up perfectly into seven rows of eleven. "Okay, good," he said, walking in front of each row. He could approximate height-wise oldest to youngest. "I'm placing you into squads. Each group of eleven will consist of different ranks, ranking according to age. I want each of you in this line to pair up with one of the youngest in that line." The entire line of eleven split up, each pairing up with the youngest corporal in the other line. Dray moved to the next group and had them do the same. "As best as you can, I want the rest of you to divide up. I want as many different ages as possible in each group. Keep your squads at eleven." The corporals shuffled once more; varying heights now stood in each squad. "The oldest corporal in your line, step forward," ordered Dray. Seven corporals stepped forward. "You're squad leaders now.

They're your responsibility. Stick together and you'll be fine. Now, everyone, follow me."

Corporal morale was on the rise, but there was still tension. Dray did not blame them. They finally halted at *Ancient Weapons and Memorabilia.*

"Squad leaders! Step forward! You'll find an assortment of weapons, clothing, and ammo in there. I'm leaving it up to you to supply your men."

"Sir," one of the squad leaders approached Dray. "We have not been trained on any of these."

"Trust me, you'll learn quick."

The corporals descended on Al's shop, one digging so deep he found fragmentation grenades, missed earlier by Dray. As ordered, the seven corporals made several trips in and out, carrying handfuls of hardware. Dray grew more comfortable by the minute, seeing the corporals arming up. The youngest ones were handed survival knifes; by the looks on their faces, they could have been handed swords. Torn pants and shirts were switched out. Vests with pockets were distributed to those big enough to wear them. Some donned Kevlar vests unknowingly. Dray walked among each squad. One held a Heckler and Koch MP5, another had an AK-47. There was an array of battle rifles, submachine guns, and shot guns. A myriad of pistols glinted. A couple of belt-fed weapons were also heaved out, along with crates of ammunition, and boxes of spare magazines. BARs and M-16s were among the array. An optimized sniper rifle also caught Dray's attention. One must have scavenged all the way in the back, what used to be Al's backroom, as he lugged out a rocket propelled grenade. *That must have been hidden,* Dray thought disappointingly, wishing he had found it earlier. He wondered if it even worked. Dray took a knee next to one young corporal inspecting his survival knife.

"If anything dangerous comes near you, thrust that as hard as you can. Is that clear?" instructed Dray, patting the corporal on the back. The whites in the boy's eyes expanded. "Okay, listen up!" called Dray. "You all want to reunite with your families, which is understandable, but in order to do so, you'll have to survive long enough for help to arrive. I can't say when that will be, but I can say that there are soldiers out there who will come for you. They just don't know you're here. The noise you heard earlier was me firing a gun, but I did so recklessly and could've been heard by the enemy. I was obviously heard by you. But you all do need to test your weapons—but not here. We must go deeper underground."

"We could go to the Running Grounds," suggested one corporal. "It's where we've been hiding."

"The Cults didn't find the grounds?" asked Dray, surprised.

"No. Their drones didn't find it," revealed the same corporal.

"The light drones still work? There's still an ecosystem down there?" Dray could not believe their luck. *That's how they've survived all this time.*

"Yes."

"Take what you can carry. Move out!" Dray helped one corporal with his gear, even using Bruce to help carry boxes of ammo. With the right harness, Bruce could carry quite a payload.

"How many of those were there?" asked Dray, pointing toward the corporal with the rocket propelled grenade.

"This was the only one."

"Don't test-fire it then. Save it for when you might need it. Just make sure you point it in the right direction."

Dray and Bruce brought up the rear. On the way, Dray thought of anything else that could help. Their guns might protect them from predators, but not from drones. Only gun barrels with high-muzzle velocities stood a chance. Dray thought of warbots and their artillery. He then had an idea—it was a long shot—but one that offered hope.

Their path slanted downward and crumbled beneath their feet; the corporals navigated through tight passages and around cave-ins made by bombs. Along the way, they passed many blocked passages sealed before the invasion. Dray was amazed that they had found their way up. Upon entering the final stretch, a lengthy, unstable tunnel, Dray recognized a familiar archway. *If only Jason were here,* he imagined, recalling the many occasions he had to run through it.

The grounds were dark, but wildlife could be heard. Plants and trees saturated the air, and the ambient temperature was warm. Dray felt at home. Near the entrance, the corporals gathered in their squads, checking their weapons. Once locked and loaded, Dray had everyone stand shoulder to shoulder in firing positions.

"Always keep your barrel facing downrange. If your safeties aren't already switched off, switch them now," Dray instructed. Some corporals took some time while others appeared to be naturals. They all took aim. "Fire on my mark. ... Three. Two. One. Fire!" The grounds absorbed the cacophony of gunfire and hail of lead riddling the trees. Lanterns did little in showing them what they hit. The scent of gun smoke hung in the air. Dray added to the symphony of ear-splitting fire when he took out his own two sidearms. His Magnum was one of a kind, turning a few heads after he pulled the trigger. He only fired one round. His 9 mm was nothing special, barely audible amidst the high-powered rifles. Successfully testing their guns, the disciplined corporals ceased firing, mindful to conserve ammo. Over by the archway, crouched low in the dark, unequipped youngsters covered their ears.

The ground's lighting came back on. Inspecting their weapons, looking downrange, the corporals thought that they would see more damage.

"Good," announced Dray, gaining everyone's attention. Dray's chameleon-like flesh absorbed the green and brown beneath his feet, blending well with the environment. His shorts and eyes were all that stood out. "For now, this is your home. Keep hidden. Don't fire your weapons unless you must," he ordered, adding, "Bruce, locate the armory." Bruce popped open his nose and was about to display a holographic blueprint of Compound 40. "No. Just show me the way."

The armory was near where Elites and warbots deployed. Bruce steered them there, clearing any obstructions along the way.

Bruce and Dray finally arrived. The giant armory door was sealed, and Dray did not have a key. Bruce trotted toward the other end of the corridor. Raising his right limb, protracting a claw, he rotated it like a drill bit. In no time at all, he bore a hole, and several others below and above it; the explosive thrust from his rear sent him smashing through the rest.

"Good work, Bruce," complemented Dray, stepping through the passage. On the other side, Dray found the armory control panel. He flipped a switch, and to his astonishment, the lights came on. Many robots were present, primarily those responsible for installing and transporting equipment. In one corner, staring Dray in the face, sat a rapid-fire, double-barreled 25 mm Bofors cannon. It was specially modified to fit a warbot, but the warbot was nowhere to be found. Wasting little time, Dray prepared the weapon to be transported. Once activated, an unmanned four-wheeled vehicle went to work.

"All right, Bruce, make your entrance a little wider."

39

The corporals huddled back into their groups. Squad leaders met with each other, deciding each squad would hold different positions throughout the grounds. They moved out when there was light. Although feeling safer, armed, the corporals were still on edge, wondering what else was drawn to Dray's noise. It was dark and, like many dark hours inside the massive biosphere, it became more alive.

"Do you think he ditched us?" murmured one corporal to another, positioning his rifle like a sentry.

"So, what if he did? He did all he could," replied the other, hugging his rifle appreciatively. The earth beneath their feet trembled, caused by something not already in the grounds. Lanterns were tactically dispersed between each squad, challenging those to get by unseen. On high alert, they listened to what sounded like bulldozers, but what moved the earth was anything but a bulldozer. Creatures performed like bulldozers, seeping and cutting through, pushing aside rock and dirt. Breaching the grounds, they snaked around with incredible speed!

"Everyone!" shouted team leaders. "Get ready!" The tumultuous encroachment moved in from all corners, but to their advantage, the corporals had cleverly positioned themselves at the right angles.

"Fire!" screamed the first corporal to see one coming tearing through the underbrush, knocking over lanterns! Ear-splitting rounds peeled away at the beast, sending it up in a halo of red mist.

"Hold your fire!" yelled a squad leader, trying to ascertain what they had hit. In the opposite direction, in an open clearing, the corporals heard more movement. Picking up his lantern, he hurled it toward the sound shedding more light on what came their way. It zigzagged through the grass, consuming everything in its path.

"Fire!"

Dray felt vibrations, placing his hand on the tunnel wall—he read the staccato tremors as gunfire. Detecting his master's sudden rush, Bruce readied himself for lift off. Dray jumped on and, once taking hold, the ordnance between his legs ignited. They spun through the tunnel like a bullet rifling down the barrel of a gun. The infamous archway lay directly ahead. Like one massive cannonball, they burst out into the open! Behind, a cell-cloud of energy accumulated in a vacuum, and once released from the tunnel, the pent-up pressure boomed! And as if prompted by the shockwave, the light drones lit up. Stationed near the entrance, startled corporals glanced up. Their austere faces brightened once discovering the sound's source to be Bruce. Hovering under a light drone, Bruce's transparency seemed to magnify the light's intensity. Before verdantly transitioning, Dray locked eyes with one corporal. Transfixed and scared, the corporal resumed firing. Dray and Bruce mapped out the erupting battlefield below.

"Protect the corporals!" ordered Dray as Bruce dropped to the surface. Jumping off, Dray hit the ground on all fours. He kept his head low, crawling through the tall grass as bullets buzzed by overhead.

Back in the tunnel, rolling at a sluggish pace, the unmanned lift continued its linear path.

Dray moved comfortably and instinctively, removing his sidearms and parting the grass; a hideous sight lay directly in front. Bullet holes festered boils, spewing forth tiny volcanoes. Speckled throughout, the creature swaggered awkwardly, gargling, and coming closer. At the end of its neck was a head full of teeth. Dray pulled the trigger on his Magnum, causing a hole the size of a grapefruit to blow out its back! Its innards, similarly, looked like grapefruit. Convulsing, it flopped to the ground.

Unleashing his rifle's final round, a nerve-racked corporal pulled out his Glock, soon discovering how less effective it was. Fifty yards to his left, amidst the mayhem and mind-numbing blasts, one corporal was separated from his squad. His weapons were spent, and his spirit waned. Dangling from his vest was a fragmentation grenade. Removing the pin and about to toss it, the corporal attempted to make an escape—but was too late. His legs and arms separated from his torso, chewed, then swallowed. Inside the monster, floating, was his dismembered hand, still clenched tight to his bomb. Two seconds later, it and its carrier went up in flames! Shrapnel tore out through the creature like butter. Pockmarked with steel, the other garish monsters nearby spilled to the ground; burnt earth and charred tissue hung in the air.

Hiding in the dense brush, like lion cubs, three youngsters stood firm. One brave little corporal stepped out of hiding, wanting to get in on the fight. Quivering uncontrollably and looking up at the enemy, his tremulous hand let loose his knife. Though the beast had no eyes, it appeared to be staring down at him. Frozen stiff, the corporal could not move. As if cast by a spell, a green flash shot upward! It impacted and discharged out the creature's back! Warm, sappy fluid showered down on all. The boy's guardian angel had four legs instead of two and had a heck of a thrust acting as its wings. Never stopping and doing what he did best, Bruce moved on to the next. Mesmerized, the little corporal hastily picked up his knife and decided best to rejoin the others in hiding.

Bruce lunged forward and decapitated one; a torrent of steamy goo dispersed from its neck. Wave after wave they came, but Bruce was just as unrelenting, devastating everyone he encountered. The massive, wormlike creatures were taken by surprise, never having confronted a scout. Zipping around with outstretched claws, it did not take much for Bruce to slash open large vital organs. A few pings and dings from gunfire washed over him, not slowing him one bit.

Many corporals were down to their pistols. One group was holed up in a circle, the tinniest among them taking cover in the center. Dray appeared at the feet of one corporal, startling him half to death! Staying low to the ground, crawling, Dray managed to get by undetected and unharmed. Among the hail of different rounds, Dray unloaded his last two. The entire place was still crawling, and inch by inch the grounds' vegetation shriveled away. Facing down the rapidly advancing enemy, the only weapons Dray now had left were his claws and teeth. Soldiering on, he stood tall alongside fighting corporals.

"Sir!" shouted a corporal. "Get down!" A gaseous vapor trail passed by over Dray's head; it looked as good as it sounded, sailing magnificently into an oncoming wall of teeth, having an abrupt, halting effect on the assault.

Al's RPG worked after all, praised Dray, making a mental note to thank the old geezer later. *If I get to see him again.*

On the other side of the grounds, crashing forth on a scale never heard before, was the sound of a colossal upheaval. Dray ran for the tree line and scanned the terrain. It was the mother of all earth dwellers!

"The entrance!" shouted Dray to the nearest corporals. They fled like mice back into the maze of tunnels. Running in the opposite direction, Dray went to retrieve the rest of the scattered corporals.

With a heavy thud, Bruce landed in front of the queen. His stealthy cloak was gone, painted over by colored chunks of biomatter. As if taking an X-ray, he sought out the predator's most vulnerable spot. Launching forward, he ascended in an arc, rocketing toward one side of the giant like a heat-seeking missile. As he came in for the strike, the queen caught him by surprise. Using its own, sheer weight, the creature flexed and smashed him back with its neck, crushing him up against a wall. Bruce was stunned for the moment, but not out of the fight.

Shifting his attention away from the corporals, Dray saw Bruce get swatted back like a fly; he wondered how long until his scout would make the ultimate sacrifice.

Charging after Bruce, Dray stopped dead in his tracks. At the Running Grounds' entrance, pulling up idly was the unmanned vehicle. He ran for it, dodging and weaving past wickedly close attacks! Most every corporal was out of ammo, many preparing to wield knives.

Dashing toward the four-wheeled vehicle, Dray jumped on, positioning himself behind fixed, twin-mounted barrels. Since its modification, the cannon, pneumatically fed from below, allowed for continuous fire. Its two triggers were also modified; two holes were present, large enough for two fists to fit inside, likely where a warbot placed its two firing pins. Trial by error was Dray's only option. Acquiring his target—

which was too big to miss—he clenched his fists and punched forward up to his elbows! His fists hit two plates, like gas pedals, internally prompting the real firing pins below. From the ground up, hell rained! In the space of thirty seconds, everything at his twelve o' clock expired. He made Swiss cheese out of the gargantuan queen, outmatching the Richter scale upon her arrival, and unlike with Bruce, she could not swat his projectiles out of the air. Beneath his feet, under the vehicle's main frame, were housed the rapidly moving rounds; the belt fed clips sent tingles up his leg. After hitting each breech, spent shells fell off to the side, clinking together like wind chimes.

The corporals covered their ears, crouching low in fetal positions, thinking the end was near. Dray felt like he had died and gone to heaven. Killing was what he was born to do. The destructive power at the end of his fingertips was thrilling to his senses. Joy seemed to emanate out from every pore; his adrenaline asked for more. The deafening thunder made him slam his fists forward harder. Still standing atop the vehicle, he searched for more. Bruce vanquished the remaining slugs, or at least whatever else still twitched. Once given the all clear, corporals began creeping out into the open, trudging over the mush that was once the enemy. Letting go and jumping off, Dray was happy to see that many of the corporals had survived.

"There're still plenty more rounds," Dray pointed toward his two smoking 25 mm cannons. "You'll need them against drones."

40

Lionized, Dray was inundated with corporals praising him. And as if he were a living, breathing person, Bruce, too, received looks of thanks.

One young corporal walked up and said, "You saved me, Bruce," extending his hand, touching Bruce on the nose. Unmoved, Bruce just sat there, ignoring stares and everything else being said.

The grounds were unrecognizable. Much had been obliterated, either cut down or knocked over. Holed up in their deep burrows, many mole hogs had survived; one emerged and scampered across a clearing, drawing immediate attention from Bruce. Also emerging was a group of corporals exiting the grounds' entrance.

"Okay," said Dray, "is everybody still in one piece?" The corporals checked themselves, some finding minor cuts and scrapes. Thinking he had gone unscathed, one corporal pointed toward Dray's leg; it was difficult to miss, centered squarely on his right upper thigh. Pulling up his shorts, Dray noticed the gaping hole slowly closing in on itself. Twisting his leg and checking the back side of his thigh, he found the exit wound. Scanning his other seemingly unaffected limbs, he suspected some had been hit but had already healed. The corporals watched, seeing up close and firsthand a magnificent feat of Mother Nature, as one of Dray's fingers grew back. As for Dray, he raised his hand, thinking the painlessness was on account of his adrenaline, yet unbeknown to him, it was his flesh's molecular makeup. There was little blood flow. His circulatory system slowed tremendously, blood vessels sealed until coagulation was successful—no need for a tourniquet. It was a bloodcurdling moment, literally, as his cold, viscous blood began impacting his movement. Dray appeared sluggish as he drew closer to Bruce. Hugging his scout, he said, "Heat." Bruce's amber eyes radiated, and his outer frame heated. Dray's vitals were okay, and he was still very conscious, staring back into seventy pairs of eyes. Still wrapped around his scout, the Elite spoke, "Retrieve more ammunition. There's not much left. It should only take one trip. If any of these things return," Dray looked toward the bloody ground, "use the tunnels for protection."

"What should we do with this?" asked one corporal, placing a hand on the cannon.

"Construct a pillbox, somewhere. Or use the tunnel as a bottleneck," Dray suggested, unraveling himself from Bruce. "I have to leave you now and go find help." The corporals were hopeful that he and Bruce would return. A few wished that they would stay, particularly Bruce.

Dray and Bruce quietly made their way back up. Reaching the last tunnel, stepping out into the causeway, they detected movement. Crawling on hands and knees, peering around a corner, Dray spotted drones. They walked about the wreckage like worker ants. Among them were smaller drones, crawling into tighter spaces like those used by the corporals. Dray turned to Bruce. He knew that they and the corporals were trapped. He remained hidden in the shadows, out of view from the Endeavors who would eventually be watching his message.

"Commander Tarpin, these corporals need your help. Bruce can take you to them. Jason, you should have seen them in action. John, Compound 40 still has power—the light drones still work. Al, your shop came in handy. ... Jamie, remember me as I used to be," Dray ended his message. One thing he could not hide was his scratchy voice. "Return to the Endeavors, Bruce. Show them what we've seen," commanded Dray, adding, "Wait until I'm gone, then move out." Bruce statuesquely stayed put as his master came out of hiding.

Thirty drones suddenly stopped prowling about, turning their praying mantis heads toward Dray. Springing over Dray's head, they surrounded him. Zooming in on his face, they analyzed his every Cult-like feature. Dray analyzed them as well. One drone moved in. Dray braced himself for an attack, but it did not come. Instead, swerving to the side and lowering its back, the drone presented itself like his scout would do for an inspection. It looked like a gesture for him to climb on. Surprised, Dray was not entirely sure what its intentions were—perhaps take him somewhere else to be interrogated and executed. Either way, he knew he had to steer their attention away from the rest. He climbed on. Sitting on top of its back, taking hold of its neck, Dray wondered how many of them he had killed.

The drones scampered out of Compound 40, having successfully obtained what they were looking for. Between each leap, high enough for a deadly fall, Dray clung on to the drone for dear life.

In the fog of night, two starry eyes watched his master disappear out of sight. Once again, Elite and scout were separated.

41

"Vulcan," said Drake, "you found it?"

"Yes, Master," the space droid replied. Vulcan had mollifying gray skin and widely set black eyes. His white robe was equally soothing. He was self-aware and acquiring more intelligence with each passing day. Mimicking Drake's destructive pursuit of humankind came naturally.

"Their defenses?" queried Drake.

"Strong, but not impregnable."

"Hmm," reflected Drake, "we'll send an air strike in advance. How did you get in?"

"One used candlelight. The thickest of walls cannot keep me from it. I molted his skin, took his form, and went undercover."

"Did you find anything else of importance?" Drake asked obliquely.

"I sensed I wasn't alone," Vulcan responded with dizzying eyes, suddenly turning azure blue.

"How so?"

"I felt the presence of another like myself. I had difficulty zeroing in on it. It was not there in its entirety."

"They have a space droid?" Drake replied in disbelief.

"No. They do not know it is there."

"Accompany our troops then. Find out what it is," concluded Drake. Vulcan nodded, heading gracefully for the door. Drake returned to his plans of world dominion. *I've found their stronghold*, he relished. It was hard to see in the dimming light, but for the first time a genuine smile spread across his face. Distracting him briefly, however, was the thought of an unidentified space droid. *I thought all were accounted for*, pondered Drake. At the very outset security precautions were taken to ensure that all could be controlled indefinitely by their masters. Many years have passed since their inception. *There's never been a double-cross*, Drake thought assuredly. *The only others must be light-years away.* After the Great Divide, the last six were never launched. Spread across the globe, the Cults had kept them for themselves.

42

Wolf 's nights were peaceful and pleasant, alone in his bed reading Jaxifer's book. Tonight, however, he was not alone.

"What is it?" she asked, brushing her auburn hair from her sleepy eyes. Wolf lay awake, looking up at the beams supporting his roof. He had become obsessed with beams and supports.

"I can't sleep. Tomorrow we finish."

"Isn't that a good thing?" she asked, puzzled. She was awake now.

"I want you to come with me," restively stated Wolf.

"Come with you where?" she uttered, leaning up on one elbow. Her winsome words were her greatest appeal. They hooked Wolf the moment they met.

"When I first arrived, all I could think about was how to leave. Now, tomorrow, for the first time I'll be able to, but I don't want to." Wolf turned all the way over, facing the container holding his spear ray.

"Stay here, then—stay with me," she offered. The zeal in her voice, combined with a firm arm, rolled him back over. Cupping his cheeks in her hands, she continued, "We can get married. You'll be happy."

"You sure are something," garbled Wolf, his cheeks still clamped to his mouth.

"We're safe here. Why can't you see that?" Her hands fell from his cheeks.

"I know. I know. You should stay—where it is safe. I don't know what I was thinking, asking you to come with me," Wolf said, getting out of bed. "It is dangerous out there," he added. An airy breeze permeated the mesh curtain draping his window.

"Come back to bed, Commander. We can talk more in the morning."

=

The benign sun woke Wolf early the next morning. Outside, the variegated foliage was as sinuous as the Alma still asleep in his bed.

"Heck of a party," Wolf mumbled to himself, stepping out the door. To his immediate right, an Alma laid sprawled out with a cup still in his hand. Raising his arms and yawning, two arms wrapped around Wolf's torso.

"We should build like that more often," she said, turning her gaze toward Wolf's megalithic creation, "that way we'll have reason to celebrate more often." Wolf turned, still wrapped in her arms.

"Come with me. I want to show you something." Wolf took her by the hand and walked back inside. He opened the container holding his spear ray. The transparent glob that used to be his bio-suit made it impossible for one to reach in and take it out. "You want to see how I take it out?" asked Wolf, retrieving a box of matches. Striking one match and holding it over the container, a purple hue covered his cylindrical spear within; it began rising to the top.

"What a beautiful color," she uttered, transfixed by the fleeting light. Soon after rising to the top, the light vanished.

"Here we go," informed Wolf. "We're going to finally test it."

"Can't wait," she responded. He kissed her on the cheek.

Boy am I going to miss you, Wolf thought, procuring his spear ray. "Come on, let's go," encouraged Wolf. Excited, they briskly made their way to the Caterpillar. Almas were still fast asleep.

It was a monster of a machine, comparable to a turned over battleship. Standing on twenty centipede-like legs, ten on each side, it gave the appearance of a massive creepy-crawler. Each leg took a village to construct. Four buzz saws, the size of tiny houses, were placed on all four corners, front and back; they were raised five feet horizontally off the ground, just high enough for the behemoth to clear tree trunks. Pincer-like claws accompanied the round saws, situated directly above to divert falling limbs from its path.

"It's amazing what some men and woman can do," stated Wolf, marveling at their creation.

"Well, Commander, where exactly does that fit in to all this?" asked the Alma, her eyes fixed on his spear ray.

"Follow me," replied Wolf, reaching for the ladder up to the hatch. Inside, the interior was spacious, enough capacity to seat a hundred people. Standing, it could hold twice as many. Along the sides, circumventing the entire structure, were cigar-shaped windows, spaced every six feet. Toward the front, which looked identical to the back, was a compartment only big enough for Wolf. "This is where this goes," Wolf showed, fitting his spear ray snuggly into a metal box four inches thick and twenty inches long. "It pretty much works like a battery," he added. Upon insertion and flipping a red switch, the Caterpillar giant woke from its slumber. Creaks and groans sounded. Wolf's Alma companion grabbed him by the shoulder, worried that they may have made a mistake. The vehicle was replete with components allowing it to tick. Stepping out of the engine compartment, sealing the hatch, Wolf headed for the controls. Close behind, the Alma tried not to make any sudden movements. She was one of the many who had helped work on the project; yet seeing it grow and take form was one thing, hearing it charge up and come to life was entirely different.

The control panel was simplistic, nothing more than ten buttons, three switches, one trigger, and a joystick. Had Wolf had more time he could have added more to the experimental machine.

"Wow!" she stumbled backward, falling into a seat. The Caterpillar jolted forward once Wolf moved the stick.

Turning 360 degrees, the noisy limbs stirred the entire Alma population from their sleep. Its buzz saws spun on cue, and big cylindrical canisters ejected Milagro down each limb; it sounded like a living, breathing beast.

Rolling out of bed, Daniel hobbled over to his tree house's window; in the distance, he saw what had awakened him—the awe of it pulled back the wrinkles on his face. Like moths drawn to light, Almas throughout the city went toward the commotion. Wolf had gained quite a crowd of spectators. Taking his hands off the controls, he halted all testing, seeing too many people getting too close. He walked up and down the aisle checking for cracks. Above his head, tops of seats faced down at him. The control panel on the other side was much different than the last; this one was inverted above the window. Tilting his neck and turning his head, Wolf pushed the button he was looking for. Outside, atop the other end of the Caterpillar, a propeller spun. Exiting the hatch and climbing down, Wolf joined the crowd.

"I still don't see why that was necessary," said one Alma, looking toward the prop.

"If I make it to open water, I can assure you, it'll be necessary. If I could test it I would, but I can only flip this beauty once. The last thing I want to do is maroon all our hard work."

"Commander, I see your spear ray has worked," said Daniel, parting his way through the crowd, his staff leading the way.

"It's only using a fraction of the power it can muster," Wolf replied, turning his attention to the Alma stepping down from the hatch. "I have to hand it to you," Wolf announced to all, "you all exceeded my expectations. Congratulations."

"So, what now?" asked Daniel.

"Well, a few more trial runs, I suppose. The gear boxes didn't explode. The frame held up under the stress. I'm confident it'll take its occupants far."

"I'd like to go inside," said Daniel.

"I bet you would. I'm sure all of you would. Please, allow me," said Wolf, ushering Daniel toward the ladder and helping him up. A long line gathered behind, waiting for their turn to climb aboard. Once entering, Wolf retracted the prop and retrieved his spear ray. Making his way back down, Wolf went to retrieve the finishing touch.

"This is something else," admitted Daniel, turning toward the Alma next to him. Some took seats, others stared out the windows. Many had already experienced being on the inside, having brought in building material. Before today, it only appeared to be a big house—now it was something that could move.

Wolf returned carrying a familiar metal container. Almas waiting to go inside stepped out of his way.

"I'm going to need everyone to move all the way over there—and you might want to cover your eyes," warned Wolf. He climbed up, hoisting the heavy container on his shoulder. At the top, he placed it precariously sidewise, approximately in the middle, making sure it did not slide off. On the way back down, in front of the hatch, he leaned in, cautioning, "Stay inside. This will only take a second." He closed the hatch. Daniel and the rest did not know what to make of it. They looked out the windows, noticing Almas standing many feet away. Wolf stopped and turned, bending his knees to the side, taking aim. He activated his spear ray and hurled it! Seeing the bright light streaking toward them, those inside the Caterpillar dove for cover. His spear hit the container dead-on! In the eyes of some, it was perhaps not the safest act, but Wolf's confidence superseded any doubt. He knew getting any closer could do him harm; those inside were shielded. The inertia of light thickened, covering the entire surface area below. Wolf's bio-suit imploded, melting away its containment and spilling forth its Olithium. A clear coat of supercharged energy dispersed, covering the entire Caterpillar evenly; the protective field now encompassed the entire vehicle. Not a scintilla of damage was left behind. Wolf's spear ray rocketed sky-high, undamaged. Still activated and falling back down to earth, it landed ten feet from an Alma; the Alma winced when it pierced the ground and deactivated.

"How's that for a christening," said Wolf, patting the Alma on his back and unplugging his spear ray from the ground.

43

Almas came and went in droves, young and old, all morning, to see what their family members had contributed to. Many were proud, yet one questioned the practical need for the vehicle Wolf called the Caterpillar. It also bothered some that he was the only one who held the power to operate it. Wolf explained it was for safety reasons, never keeping his spear ray out of reach.

Wolf returned to his hut and sitting on his bed he thought out his next move. *The time has come,* he thought, *to put together an elite squad.* It would be challenging to convince them, he knew, but the city was a big place, and there were many brave, able bodies. *What am I thinking?* Wolf paused. The idea of leaving now suddenly seemed ludicrous. He had grown too attached and comfortable working with the Almas. Several minutes passed before his pallid face filled with color. *That settles it then—until it's absolutely necessary, I'm not going anywhere,* Wolf determined. "I'm staying right here—" He turned his head, commotion distracting him. Beyond his thin walls the unrest grew louder. There was a knock at his door.

"Wolf! Commander! Come quick!" shouted an eager soul outside. Wolf jumped to his feet and opened the door.

"What is it?" Wolf questioned the out-of-breath Alma.

"Something has happened on the far side of the city. The east side—a plague," said the Alma with an ashen face. Wolf was suspicious of it being a plague. To his knowledge, no outsiders other than himself have entered the city. Had he brought something biological they would have seen its impact a while ago.

"More detail?" queried Wolf.

"It moves! It's chasing us," replied the Alma. Wolf confirmed it was not a plague. Almas began racing toward him; the entire city was moving west. Panic was in the air!

"Has anyone tried using Milagro?" said Wolf as men and women hurried past.

"It hasn't worked. They're using fire now. Wolf—they're burning the city."

=

Inside her house, many feet above the ground, she laid out an outfit. After the Caterpillar unveiling, she had returned home to change. She wanted to look her best for Wolf— before continuing their conversation from the night before. Her skimpy dress was fashionable for an Alma. The thin-laced fabric hardly covered her flesh, and the parts it did cover were practically see-through. Putting her hair up in a bun, she abruptly paused; shouting outside caught her attention. Poking her head out her window, blinding smoke immediately sent her back. She ran toward the door! The staircase was blocked! They ate away at the steps, ruing all chances for an escape. If the ant fragments did not get to her first, the raging fire spilling upward would. She fell backward onto her bed and sat upright. Her angelic face calmed as she passively closed her eyes, crossed her hands, and dreamed of being somewhere else. They were voracious little killers.

=

"Paul! Listen to me!" Wolf caught Paul by the shoulder. "Get as many provisions together as you can and head for the Caterpillar." Wolf ran in the opposite direction, dodging Almas as he went. He went to look for his Alma—his soul mate.

They ran past the Caterpillar in droves and continued west. No one thought to take refuge in the giant vehicle. Paul tried convincing many to come with him, but no one believed it was safe; and who could blame them with the fire coming their way—the entire structure would make a hellish oven.

"Mom! Dad! Help me with supplies!" shouted Paul, spotting his family among the wave of people.

"Paul! Get down from there! What are you doing?" his mom shouted.

"Just listen to me," replied Paul. "Go get food and water. Dad, get Milagro," demanded Paul, going to retrieve the same items, collecting close friends along the way.

"Are you sure?" a startled Alma asked, helping Paul carry a barrel.

"Yes, Wolf is coming," reiterated Paul, sweating profusely.

"Paul, what's going on?" asked Daniel, bringing up the rear.

"No time to talk. Grab as much as you can and come." Daniel spotted a sack of grain by a house and scurried toward it; with one arm leaning on his staff, he carried the sack under his other.

Wolf halted! He watched those unable to outrun them be eaten alive. Almas with flame throwers torched everything in their wake. Wolf had never seen ant fragments up close. From the way the ground moved, he could tell they were tiny and numerous. *The fire's working*, he noticed, as one flame-throwing Alma reached him.

"There's nothing left back there!" said the Alma, spraying the path he had just taken; it went up in a blaze! Wolf looked to his left and right, seeing a wall of fire steadily approach. He knew if she were still alive, she would have made it to him by now. Ant fragments caught in the fire made popping sounds as more began dropping down ahead of the fire. The Alma standing before Wolf sprayed his flames upward, but not quick enough as the enemy fell past his flames landing on his face and neck. There was nothing Wolf could do to help—the Alma was dead before he hit the ground. Finishing him up, the ant frags now came for Wolf. Wolf suddenly found himself trapped. He swung out his spear attempting something he had never done—on account of its draining impact. He had no choice now. Centering his grip on one end of his spear, he squeezed as hard as he could, transferring all energy to its other end. It was not working! They closed in! His hands turned red from the strain; his truculent battle cry drowned out the roaring fire. The ray's heat and light were immense, elongating toward the direction he pointed. Finally, one transitory beam exploded outward! Its intensity scorched his hands, forcing him to release his hold. The fleeting beam paved an instant, clear path. The ant frags disappeared! With blistering hands, Wolf picked up his spear and ran. It pained his hands, but he had to hold on.

Sky drones flew over the tenebrous jungle, their flimsy, coiled necks scanning downward. They dispensed their deadly cloud like crop dusters. When smoke rose up through the trees, accompanied by muffled screams, their eyes glared. Releasing its final load, the last balloon-shaped drone hovered off toward distant rain clouds.

"Children! Follow me!" huffed Wolf to a group of weary children. Tired and crying, they had fallen behind; their parents had left them. *Cowards,* thought Wolf, picking up the smallest. He barked another command, demanding they move their tiny legs faster. Not far behind, ahead of the stentorian fire, more merciless ant fragments approached. Wolf hurried. The stolid Caterpillar came into view.

"There it is!" shouted Wolf, trying to pick up the pace.

"Commander!" called Paul, seeing Wolf leading a group of children toward him. Paul ran out to help.

"Stay there! I'll hand them to you!" ordered Wolf. Paul rushed back up the ladder. One by one, Wolf heaved, even tossed the children up to Paul. Inside, the Caterpillar was not at full capacity.

"Is this all?" asked Wolf, making his way toward the engine compartment; the spear ray's housing cell had somehow deformed. Wolf frantically jammed it in, but nothing happened, the vehicle did not budge.

"What's wrong?" asked an Alma. Ignoring him, Wolf ran toward the front. Outside the window, ant fragments arrived but were at a standstill. The Caterpillar was the mother of all ants, it appeared, and something about it hindered the ants seek and destroy mission. Built by humans but not human, the Caterpillar was an imposing figure. Unbeknown to the Almas, Wolf's exterior clear coat acted as a shield; its energy field scrambled the ant frags nanocircuits. Wolf dashed back toward the fuel cell and, after tinkering with the metal housing, slammed in his spear. The Caterpillar came online! It adjusted to their additional weight, bending and swaying, Almas staggered left and right.

"They're not following us!" exalted Paul. Wolf was too distracted, steering the Caterpillar in the opposite direction, away from the incoming firestorm. Hemmed in by trees, he switched on his buzz saws. The jungle awoke to what sounded like a construction site. Extending outward, above the saws, pincers moved massive trunks away from the Caterpillar's main body. High up, from the vantage point of a cloud, a black line was being drawn through the jungle. Wolf's path of destruction took down trees as tall as buildings. Outrunning the fire, they traveled west for quite some time. With their Milagro canisters set on timers, spraying every hour, Wolf and the Almas went unmolested. Wolf finally came to a halt.

"Is everyone okay?" Wolf asked. Almas filled the seats, wanly staring back. Many were recovering from smoke inhalation. Wolf, too, felt a little light-headed. He went to take a seat, giving his sore legs a break.

"You don't look so good?" said Daniel, coming over to check on Wolf. Daniel inspected Wolf's hands; how he had managed to handle the controls shocked Daniel. "Here," decided Daniel, tearing off a sliver of fabric from his cloak. Wolf appeared too exhausted to respond, accepting the cloth, bandaging his turgid hands. He dampened the liquid rupturing his bubbly skin; touching them now hurt even more than the controls.

Toward the center of the Almas' city, the Milagro Tree went up in flames, its sacrosanct life-blood going up with it. Fleeing the city every which way, panicked Almas forgot to take more Milagro. The oily balm saturating their skin would eventually wear thin. When the time came, escaping ant frags and fire would be the last things on their mind.

44

"Oh, girl, I really do miss him," said Jamie, caressing Tulip's back. Tulip's eyes were large and vividly brown. Her tongue lapped out, catching Jamie on the cheek.

"Good night, Jamie," said Madge, shutting her bedroom door.

"Night," replied Jamie. Tulip jumped up next to her. "Tulip, down," Jamie persisted, but Tulip did not obey, hunkering down on top of her covers. Jamie knew at some point she would harmlessly kick her to the floor as she tossed and turned at night. At the bottom of the bed, the four-legged brute stood up and circled. After finding the right spot she plopped back down; her head now laying snuggly between Jamie's legs. After yanking up the covers and closing her eyes, sleep came quick tonight.

=

Hundreds of miles from Compound 40, Dray had a hard time keeping his eyes open, being lulled to sleep by the fluid motion of his drone. In the long hours since first setting out, the innermost recesses of his mind was where he found comfort. A slow drizzle alerted him, sharpening his senses. Traveling over desolate land, far from city lights and without moonlight, it was overwhelmingly dark. Rising and falling in long, spaced intervals, Dray's heart beat uncontrollably; though he had grown used to the movement over level terrain, knowing when to hold tight and when he could loosen his grip was still challenging. The terrain quickly became uneven, and each descent felt like falling into a bottomless, black pit; it was difficult knowing when his drone would hit bottom. Landing inside a deep ravine, his face slammed against his drone's back! Blood trickled down his nose. He was knocked out, but incredibly his flesh still clung to the drone.

Standing over Jamie's bed, Dray took comfort in watching her sleep. She was strikingly beautiful. Her lips were full, and her breathing was steady. Tulip was there, too, near the bottom of the bed, breathing through her nose, snorting and sighing. *She must be dreaming*, concluded Dray, looking at both warm bodies so entranced in their sleep. *I must be dreaming*, he thought further. It all looked so real. The lights were off, but he could still detect stark contrasts with the moon and starlight pervading her curtained window. Kneeling next to her bed, with his monstrous hand, he touched her softly on the forehead. She stirred, saying his name out loud. Astounded, Dray jumped back! Tulip's head popped up; the direction of her eyes unmistakable.

"Shhh," calmed Dray, sensing a slight growl preceding a bark. Tulip bounced up, glaring white teeth. Dray did not know what to do. *She doesn't recognize me*, he concluded. *And neither will Jamie.*

"Tulip, what's wrong?" said Jamie, perturbed from awakening so suddenly. Dray stood in the corner, hiding in the shadow. Being bitten by a canine was something every human feared; it was the same for every specie—even Dray. Tulip jumped down from the bed and came toward him. He did not want Jamie to see him—if she even could. Tulip's teeth were too close. Dray responded savagely, but quietly with a slow hiss and glaring rapacious teeth. Tulip stood down, slinking back toward the bed, sitting beside Jamie.

"You frightened, girl? You have a bad dream?" Jamie whispered. Caressing Tulip under the ear, Jamie went back to bed. Tulip no longer stared directly into the shadow's eyes; there lie a monster more formidable than her.

Dray's mind wandered from her loveliness to his ugliness, thinking he could never see her again. All he wanted to do was leave, but he could not; his libidinous thoughts kept him rooted in place until his wraith precipitously withdrew. The dark shadow in the corner no longer breathed. Dray's surly eyes were his last features to leave. Tulip was lying on the floor and, as if nothing had ever happened, she lowered her head and went back to sleep.

45

"Al, I'm going over your tests here, and I can't find anything. You seem extraordinary well for your age," Dr. Roberts reported.

"My X-rays?" replied Al, surprised.

"Nothing. Whatever you had is gone. Since I wasn't the one treating you, I have no explanation."

"I guess, then, I'll just go back to work now," said Al, standing up and buttoning his shirt. Al shook Dr. Roberts' hand before leaving. Exiting the lab, Al's quizzical look turned into a grin. He had long dreaded this day but, in the end, the news was better than expected. He received a clean bill of health, plus, he was told his health was extraordinary for his age.

"How's it going, Jeffrey?" said Dr. Roberts, setting down Al's test results.

"The samples I took from the deceased, Bill Hagan, are inexplicable," replied Jeffrey, adding, "It's as if he shed his skin. I can't find any trace evidence of what could have done this."

"Do you have any theories?" queried Dr. Roberts, sitting in his chair.

"My guess is, perhaps, some kind of spontaneous combustion, impacting only his epidermis."

"That's quite a theory. Have you considered a biological agent?"

"No. By the looks of the autopsy photos, heat was present. If I had to equate this to anything else—it's as if he was dunked in a pot of boiling water, cooked, and then peeled like a potato. The only problem with this, however, is that his organs were unharmed."

"Have you given any thought to our last conversation?"

"Dr. Roberts—I have. And I can't imagine it. I just don't believe man is in the process of evolving from a one-celled organism to some kind of superhuman creature. If you ask me, I think man is in the process of devolution—a degeneration. Why else would we be on the brink of annihilation? We're being replaced."

"I'm shocked to hear you say that, Jeffrey," responded Dr. Roberts. "If I were to tell you, hypothetically, let's say, that humankind had something to do with the origin of the Cult. Would you still hold the same belief?"

"How so? What do you mean?"

"What I mean, is, what if the Cult was that superhuman creature?"

"A Cult isn't human," Jeffrey said in disgust.

"You're right. A Cult can't be human," Dr. Roberts looked away. It was eating him up inside—the knowledge he had to bear. He wanted to tell Jeffrey the truth but could not bring himself to it. What good would it do? It would only cause finger pointing, bitter resentment between Survivors and Endeavors, who had finally mended relations after Dray's departure. The Endeavors did not see the Cults the way Dr. Roberts did; to them, the Cults were an unfortunate act of Mother Nature. They did not look human or act human, therefore, they could not be human. To Dr. Roberts, though, they were human—and indeed superhuman creatures.

"Man wanted a finely tuned killing machine, and he got one," explained Dr. Roberts.

"What're you saying?" Jeffrey asked.

"My formula. If there's one thing history teaches us, it's that we don't learn from history. Stop all research on the latest formula," ordered Dr. Roberts.

"Wait, why?" replied Jeffrey, uncertain of the command.

"Jeffrey, listen very carefully. I need your help. I need to round up the first Survivors who arrived with me. I don't want Tarpin to know, though."

"I don't get it. I thought the formula was safe?"

"It very well could be. That's why I don't want to make a big spectacle over this."

"You said the formula was the best way to fight the Cults?" posed Jeffrey. Meanwhile, Dr. Roberts wrote down a list of names.

"It has helped, this is true, but I fear it may be a gateway to something else. Something we don't want. Bring these

217

people to me," Dr. Roberts handed the list of names to Jeffrey.

"What shall I tell them?"

"Just tell them I want to see them. That's all," replied Dr. Roberts. "Jeffrey," he added, "this fight must be won with *our* minds and bodies. Not something we create in a lab."

46

A harried Tarpin sat at his desk thumbing through a manual. Pounding thuds at his door startled him.

"What!" Tarpin shouted, agitated.

"Sir! Archimedes has returned!" announced the Endeavor knocking. Tarpin jumped to his feet and ran to the door.

"Where is he?" Tarpin asked.

"There," the Endeavor pointed toward the Great Mantle.

Archimedes came down from the Stargaze like a falling feather, swaying side to side until landing on the massive helipad balcony with hardly a sound. Endeavors gathered earnestly, watching their beloved aircraft flex its spidery limbs. Archimedes' translucent frame altered back and forth in visibility, stopping on a chrome hue so all could see. Michael and Veronica appeared beneath him.

"You made it!" said Tarpin, approaching. Veronica was startled by everything and everyone, feeling naked in front of so many eyes.

"Yes," replied Michael.

"And the others?" questioned Tarpin.

"They fought bravely" was all Michael could say. A female pushed hurriedly from the crowd, having breached the distracted security by the elevator. She halted in front of Michael. She did not say a word; news of her loved one had finally come.

"How did Archimedes perform?" asked a curious Endeavor.

"He did great," said Michael, gazing back at Archimedes. Turning back to Tarpin and the Endeavors, he additionally informed, "Everyone, this is Veronica. She needs medical attention, food, and clothes." A female Endeavor wasted no time taking Veronica by the hand. Veronica turned toward Michael, who in turn gave her an assuring head nod; hesitantly, she went with the Endeavor.

"Michael!" greeted Jason, slapping Michael on his transparent, slippery shoulder. Michael's limbs slowly began to materialize.

"I've got something to show you," replied Michael, walking back toward Archimedes.

"Where's Peter?" asked Jason, still content. Michael shook his head, indicating clearly what he did not want to say. Jason's jubilant mood instantly turned.

"Look at this," said Michael, distracting Jason, pulling out his glistening sword. It sparkled vibrantly for all to see, as if it had a mind of its own, emitting a bio-luminescent glow. Michael handed it over to Jason as he reached back in for the scroll. Jason's face lit up in the sword's light. "Just don't ask me where it came from," remarked Michael.

"Come, Michael, I want to hear all about your mission. But first, go armor down," said Tarpin, adding, "Oh, and Archimedes, report below for an inspection." Archimedes closed his hatch, retracted four of his six limbs, and stood perched over the Great Mantle's railing. Hopping off like a giant bird, he circled the great expanse beyond; a torrent of wind grazed Endeavor faces. Floating upward, in much the same way he had come down, his departure looked just as wondrous.

Michael turned toward Jason with an outstretched hand.

"Here, see if you can make any sense of this," Michael exchanged his scroll for the sword. "Commander Tarpin, if you don't mind, I'd like to take another way down." Michael stood over the railing. He jumped off! Endeavors and Survivors gasped astonishingly. After falling thirty feet, he sprung back up. His Icarus wing was invisible to all, and remained so, gliding him through the air. Tarpin did not seem to mind; though he would have advised against it.

Holding out his magical double-edged blade, as if wanting all to see, Michael swiftly made his way down. The lack of wind cut his flight-time short, but enough to give him a thrilling ride. Michael aimed for the netting hole circling the gardens. Touching down before a shocked crowd, his Icarus wing dislodged with ease. With sword in hand, he made his way toward the elevator.

On their way down, watching Michael the whole way, Tarpin and Jason stood in silence, shaking their heads smilingly.

47

Jaxifer stopped to take a breath. The rest of his followers did the same. Pockets of Almas were spread out in all directions, wide-eyed and frantic. Only a few had canisters of Milagro and used it sparingly. Jaxifer found one Alma with a canister.

"*¿Está lleno?*" Jaxifer asked morbidly.

"*No,*" replied the Alma emphatically, eyes agape. Jaxifer knew they did not have much time. With sweaty forearms, they wiped grime from their foreheads. Instinctively looking up at the trees, they moved on. A millionth of a second later, far behind, an Alma was snatched up.

"¡Julio!" was a woman's cry. Her booming voice caught the attention of all. Jaxifer signaled for Milagro, but the victim was too high up, out of reach. Their beastly toil was unfathomable—the manslayer was everywhere. Their death march had begun.

=

Commander Wolf rose to his feet. The task before him was daunting. Venerable Daniel stood by his side.

"You've left all that you've known behind," announced Wolf. "Some of you may have left more than just a home, perhaps a friend. I know it's hard, but I need everyone to focus on the task at hand. We have a limited supply of food and water. We must make it last. Our objective is to make it out of this jungle. I can't say how far we'll make it before this thing breaks down," Wolf pointed up, "but I can assure you, we'll have enough power so long as it does hold." Wolf turned toward Daniel.

"Are there any questions for the commander?" asked Daniel, unsure of what else to add. One Alma raised his hand.

"Yes," said Daniel.

"Shouldn't we go back and look for survivors?"

"Your city is gone. We barely have enough here to sustain ourselves. Say a prayer for them," offered Wolf. Wolf saw another hand go up. Her creamy skin made him think of his stinging hands.

"I'd like to know what Daniel thinks?" Daniel looked at Wolf, surprised.

"I agree—a prayer is all. They're in God's hands now," answered Daniel. Wolf cleared his throat.

"Good, then, if there's nothing else, we'll get on our way. Paul, let me show you how to drive this thing." Paul stood up and walked toward the front. "If my hands were better, I'd do it myself, but as you can see," he raised his hands, instructing, "forward, left, right, you got it. This controls the saws. Everything else is on timers. Now go," finished Wolf. Paul nudged the joystick forward and woke the sleeping giant. Wolf bent his knees, carefully making his way back to his seat.

"Where am I heading?" asked Paul, keeping his eyes ahead.

"West. Follow the compass," replied Wolf.

"Why west?" asked Daniel.

"It's the quickest way to the coast," said Wolf. Daniel was genuinely puzzled. "Let's just say I have a gut feeling," added Wolf, looking out his window. Creatures big and small scurried about, fleeing the Alma monster and the trees it devoured. "They seem immune to the jungle. Why is that?" Wolf wondered, still keeping watch out his window.

"Man, and anything man-made is what it seeks. I guess it sees us as its only threat," Daniel paused, listening to the sound of the grinding buzz-saws.

Wolf leaned back and shut his eyes, saying, "Well, my friend, if it saw us as a threat before, I'd hate to think what it sees us as now."

=

A thorny branch snagged an Alma. Her scream was heard for miles. Maroon blood trickled down her leg as she tried desperately to yank it off. Thorns pierced her hands; she was not going anywhere. Before despair overcame hope, a machete came slicing down beside her leg. A warrior strapped with many knives came to her aid. Slipping his blade between the vine and her skin, he slowly removed it and its thorns. Surgically removing the last thorn, he helped her up.

"Let's go," the warrior said in English. Tears of pain streaked down her cheeks. A half a mile away, others faced similar organic barbed wire. Bleeding and limping were good signs, for staying put was death. They meandered on, tired and hungry.

Rain flooded over Jaxifer, funneling down through massive, gutter-like branches. Halting beneath one such branch, with water spilling off to the side, he stuck out his tongue and drank. The others did the same. Though comforting and replenishing, it did little to boost morale. Jaxifer had never traveled this far and was as lost as everyone else. The rain washed away the last traces of oily repellent sticking to their skin. Things could not have been worse. Peering drowsily out into the open, Jaxifer made peace with his predicament. He sat down. One young warrior tried lifting him back up but was pushed aside. Every muscle in Jaxifer's back, neck, and shoulders told him to stay put. He needed rest.

"*No puedo. Ayuda a ellos. Adelante,*" said Jaxifer. The warrior hesitated, but coming to his senses, he stepped out into the cascading rain, calling for the others to follow him.

Brushing back his long wiry hair, Jaxifer leaned back. The tree behind him, as if welcoming him home, engulfed him. Rushing water muffled his groans—his mouth was gagged, and his limbs were immobilized.

=

The Caterpillar moved with impunity. Paul could not help feeling untouchable—all powerful—as he moved aside everything in his path. In their wake was a magnificent clear trail. The rain did little to slow them down. Paul, except for a few Almas, was the only one still awake. It was getting darker, and there was a shortage of lights onboard. The console before Paul was the only area aglow. Adapting to the ups and downs of their vehicle's noisy limbs, the Almas found comfortable postures and slept. The kids felt safe, tuckered out, curled up on the floor. An Alma approached Paul from behind.

"Will we make it out in time?" asked the Alma.

"Make it out in time?" replied Paul, momentarily averting his gaze.

"Before we run out of Milagro," clarified the Alma.

"I hope so—at the pace we're moving." The front window was dark, not much beyond was visible.

"How can you see where you're going?" was the Alma's next question.

"I can't. See that compass," pointed Paul. "As long as I keep heading west, that's all I need to navigate."

"This is going to be quite an adventure," the Alma said with some excitement. Paul had not considered their escape and subsequent journey as an adventure, but soon found himself agreeing with the young man.

"Yes, an adventure. Wolf hasn't said it, but I think our ultimate destination is where he came from. I have a feeling we'll be heading north once we hit the ocean."

"And you'd be right about that," said Wolf, appearing from behind. The young Alma went back to his seat.

"You should have built a seat here," uttered Paul, standing at the controls.

"How are you holding up?" asked Wolf, carefully clutching a handlebar, grimacing.

"Okay," replied Paul, seeing that Wolf was in no condition to take over.

"At first light, we'll stop and take a break. I'll have to find you a replacement. We'll need to start taking shifts."

"Sounds good, and maybe we can work on that seat," suggested Paul.

"We should have spare parts on board. Had we had more time, this thing could have been fully loaded." Wolf imagined what else he could have installed. Thinking of additional material and equipment, a whole minute had passed before Paul regained Wolf's attention.

"What is your home like—the city of Endeavors?" asked Paul. He and Wolf rocked up and down as if onboard a ship at sea.

"I think you'd like it, Paul. The people are nice. And you feel safe inside. It's hidden, too," answered Wolf, removing his bandaged hand from the handlebar. "Boy, I hope these guys heal quick," Wolf said, raising his hands in the dim light. "I'll be useless until they do."

"I'm sure you'll be able to still give orders," replied Paul with a grin.

"Yeah, right," replied Wolf, catching Paul's sarcasm. "My order for you is to keep this thing moving till dawn. If you need to stop, stop, but we must keep moving."

"Yes, sir," replied Paul.

=

The rainfall had given way to a still morning air. Many Almas had given up, overtaken by exhaustion, then the trees. Suspended high and low along game trails were the cocoons of young and old, wrapped tightly from head to foot. A lucky few had received quick deaths, but the majority were left to suffer. Mother Nature can be cruel. For those far behind, still on the move, catching up to the eerie sight was riveting. One Alma was about to attempt a rescue, poised to spray the little Milagro he had left toward one in need. Her eyes moved left to right. The rest of her face and body were smothered.

"No! We need that!" said an obstructing Alma.

"She's still alive," replied the frightened man, unsure of what else to do. Some of the vines holding her carried thorns, an all-natural Iron Maiden.

"You going to try and save them all," pointed the opposing Alma. Both turned to see the long line of cocoons ahead. Irrepressible anguish gave way, for he knew it would be in vain.

She'd most likely bleed to death anyway, thought the Alma, turning one last time toward her. Her eyes were suddenly moist.

"Come on! Let's go!" shouted a warrior. Zeroing in straight ahead, they hustled down the trail; beside them, squirming and yelping accompanied moans and groans. With a flicker of hurt in all their faces, those trapped knew that there would be no rescue. Toward the end of the trail, many eyes were empty and unseeing. One deceased Alma looked frozen in time, with his dark blue eyes and wavy hair.

Charging ahead, into the green monster, the last four Almas hacked away, fighting for their lives. An empty canister discharging its last vapory mist was distressing; an attempt to use the empty tank as a shield was equally distressing. Realizing the futility of it all, he tossed the tank and ran wildly, separating himself from the rest. He did not make it far, as a plant doused him with a grayish mist of its own, stunning him and choking him to death. The battle for the other three ensued. One showed great skill with his lackluster blade, ducking and dodging, but one plant got the better of him firing prickly needles. Roaring in pain, the warrior fought on desperately; his willpower overcame the paralysis creeping up his leg. His arms flailed, one hand grabbing, the other slicing; but soon enough his arms, too, went into shock. Convulsing on the jungle floor, white foam boiled out from his mouth. Turning stiff as a board, the Alma's valiant struggle abruptly came to an end.

Alone, the second to last warrior skillfully used his knives. Smaller than a machete and lighter, he was having success with his twelve-inch blades; he was conserving energy and avoiding being tangled up. In a fit of rage, he hurled a knife—like trying to avert an attacking dog. Bursting out from a wall of green webs, the Alma fell into a massive pit—a living plant with a crater for a mouth. The bowl plant's sole purpose in life was to wait for its meal to stumble across it. The Alma did not disappoint. The carnivorous plant awoke hungrily, and closing like the hood on a car, it was about to have its next meal. Spikes on the rim of its mouth formed bars, like that on a cage. Its prey was simply left to rot; human was rarely on the menu. Using his knife, the Alma dug his way up a slippery slope, tearing and releasing more slimy fluid keeping him down. Strenuously reaching the elliptical mouth, he confronted green bars. He sliced through one, making space for an escape. But before squeezing through, he was noosed. Suspended, being carried back down, his neck luckily did not snap. With knife still in hand, one swipe above his head released him. He fell! Looking back up, with the little light that entered, he saw many more nooses dangling down, preparing to snag him. Crying out in frustration, he dropped to his knees, stabbing like a blood-crazed murderer. He was determined to burrow through. Sensing its prey's grit, the giant plant sprang into action. The Alma never saw it coming; the organic rope caught him unaware, first ensnaring his arms, then legs. His dripping knife hung limp in his hand, useless. Unable to wiggle free, tugging at each limb, he lowered his head, defeated.

The last Alma still standing made it to a river. Unarmed and out of breath, he jumped into the water. The current swept him away. On either side of the riverbank, menacing movement reached out for him. But the greatest obstacle lay ahead. The roaring crash grew louder, its white foggy mist coming into view. The towering waterfall, alive and always moving, rivaled all that encompassed it.

48

Over and over, Dray rehearsed his cover story—who he was and where he came from. *Perhaps they already know who I am,* thought Dray presently, his drone sailing through the early morning sky, shimmering. Landing on rocky ground, his drone sprung up fluidly, absorbing pressure and balancing over varying inclines; energy from each landing fueled its movement. The praying mantis crawled only when necessary. Surrounded by drones and, seeing many more sky drones ahead, he determined jumping off and making a run for it would be pointless. A part of him desired to know where he was being taken anyhow, no matter what the danger.

Squinting his eyes, Dray saw it in the distance. The massive troop buildup was too big to miss. Jingling metal and gleaming microbands sparkled silver against the shadowy forest backdrop. Bright green and reddish-orange banners also shined bright under the sun. Cults and machines flooded the area, beyond and inside the prison walls. Dray recognized the prison; his victory was still gloriously fresh in his mind. His triumph was of little comfort now. The swaths of microbands were intimidating. With every bounce, high up, he took in a better view.

Formations snaked away from the prison, led by Cult vehicles. Dray guessed it was preparation for a war. *But where?* he pondered.

Dray's drone changed course, avoiding the outer perimeter housing tents. From afar, his nostrils picked up the rotting corpses they transported. The odor was distinctly Cult. Having come across the stench once before, Dray had zero clue why they carried it with them.

The drones accompanying Dray split rank, teaming up with an array of Cult warbots lining up. They formed an immense wall around their masters. Aircraft flew by overhead, low and fast, startling Dray with their closeness. Hugging his drone's neck, facing sideways, Dray glanced back. To his right, at a hundred yards, the convoy was still in progress. *There's so many of them*, he counted, as he and his drone kept leaping south. Attentive Cults noticed the sole drone heading in the opposite direction. Dray sighed when they did not give chase. But his drone suddenly took bigger leaps. His heart, already racing, now raced even faster.

Like a marauding pack of wolves, they picked up Dray's scent. They looked like horses, minus long eel-like tails on their backsides; and they had black wings. Their round, black eyes homed in on Dray. Jumping and flapping, one creature flew skyward, near enough for him to see its gnashing teeth. They ran with the help of their wings, like water striders skipping across the water, their tails acting as rudders. Speeding up before takeoff, one by one they took to the sky. Gaining altitude, they came for Dray. Holding tight, there was nothing he could do. One came down like a screaming falcon, its two hammer hooves leading the charge. Dray's drone bucked like a wild bull, spinning sharp limbs, tearing the guts from their attacker's underbelly. Falling back down to earth, its shrill whine ended with a splattering smack. At their twelve o'clock, a flying horse attacked head-on, but was met with two scythe-tipped limbs. His drone pierced and sliced but lost its momentum as a result. Falling backward, it turned upside down, Dray with it. Before landing on its back, the drone reversed its four springy limbs. With his back mere inches from the ground, Dray held on with all his might. Bouncing back up, the drone righted its position. Circling high overhead, beaten, his attackers fluttered back toward the convoy. Dray's hands were glued; every part of him making contact had suctioned itself to the drone. His core temperature had fallen, and his limbs were fatigued. He resumed breathing as calmly as one could. The carnival ride had to come to an end soon—if not, a smelly corpse would be the only thing arriving.

Dray's drone managed to put the barren plain well behind. They came upon a hilly countryside with plush, tall grass. Each time they landed, Dray wanted to let go; lying flat on the ground never seemed so tempting. He was utterly exhausted and saw no end in sight. He maintained control— mind over body—and soldiered on. In the distance, below the endless sky, stood a great, dark form, measuring a great length.

A city, Dray marveled, approaching rapidly. His mind went blank—he had forgotten everything—his whole cover story. His mind, too, had finally succumbed to exhaustion. Yet he did not care; he'd soon dismount and be done with it. The wall grew bigger and wider. To his left and right lay dirt paths, zigzagging every which way, but with another leap the paths turned into paved roads. His drone ceased jumping, now crawling. Relaxing his grip, Dray wondered what on earth to expect. His inner visionary eye suspected great strife and humiliation. Cults and warbots manned the city gate.

"Here it goes," Dray said tiredly, approaching the gate. They looked at him with curiosity, sizing him up. The drone halted at the closed gate, but it soon opened. Dray was incredulous. Avoiding eye contact, he and his drone entered. Inside, Cults and machines tramped about in all directions.

The adult males wore long bland robes, mostly black or gray, whereas the young dressed in pants and coats. Uncovered limbs were covered with a pasty white substance resembling human flesh. The females were not at all what Dray was expecting; in fact, up until now he had never given them much thought. Unlike their males, they were stunning to the eye, exotic in every way imaginable. Sporting necklaces, wristbands, and earrings, in addition to long flowing hair—they looked human. Something under the surface, however, told Dray otherwise. Their flesh reflected whatever mood they were in, able to dissuade as a repellent or tempt as a lure. This became evident when he saw one being scolded by a male. Her silky, copper-toned skin transitioned right before his eyes. It turned lumpy bluish, unappealing, and contagious-looking. The Cult male turned away, uninterested. One thing they all had in common was their unhappiness.

Dray's drone came to a halt. Taking it as a sign, he slid off. His feet hit the ground, absorbing information just as his nose, ears, and eyes did. Blending in, his thick skin turned gloomy gray. His shorts remained their usual brown tan camouflage. Gazing back at his drone, he uttered, "Now what?" But the drone cocked its head to the side and took off. He never felt so alone, even amidst what appeared to be his own kind. *Had the drone mistaken me for a lost Cult?* Dray wondered, wandering off. He was determined to find clothes, food, and shelter, and someplace to rest. Nearby, off the main road, he saw an empty alley. Only a few eyes darted over him as he made his way there. In the alley, he found two warm air vents and sat down. Rest was all he craved for now. Dray satisfactorily closed his eyes. He would need sharp wits the next time he opened them.

49

Hunger and voices woke Dray early the next morning.

"Quietly," said one course voice.

"Get him around the ankles," directed another cruel voice. They had already managed to tie one leg.

"What's going on?" Dray demanded to know, his voice low and threatening.

"You're coming with us," replied one.

"He looks healthy. They'll give us ten pieces for him," one said contently. Descending on Dray, they grabbed his limbs, hoisted him up, and carried him out. The burly Cults were dressed in tattered tunics and wore leather belts.

"Heaters work every time," said one Cult, holding Dray by the wrist. Dray guessed he was referring to the two vents.

"Look at these ridiculous shorts?" said another, scratching Dray's left thigh.

"Where're you taking me?" asked Dray, growing concerned. Outside the alley, a cage on four wheels awaited.

"In you go!" shouted the Cult in charge, slamming the gate behind Dray. "To the games, along with every other slouch we pick up."

"He's probably a deserter," Dray overheard the last Cult say before boarding the front cab. The wheels beneath creaked, grinding to life on worn-out axles.

All morning they drove around the city inspecting alleys and dark places. Heating vents were the popular spots, but all came up empty, except for the last.

"Move over!" growled the trapper, shoving a young bound Cult inside the cage. Dray, sitting cross-legged, with his hands bound, moved over. The prisoner sitting across from him doggedly moaned. He was barefoot, and his pants and shirt were filthy. Staring down, as their cage rolled on, he did not say a word.

"What's your name?" asked Dray. The Cult's head lifted, making eye contact with Dray.

"Mo."

"Do you know where they're taking us, Mo?" Dray queried.

"The games," Mo squeamishly replied.

"What are the games?" asked Dray, guessing something unpleasant.

"Have you lost your mind?" stated Mo, concluding he was caged with a loon.

"I'm not from around here," responded Dray.

"Yeah, right, keep your crazy talk to yourself." Mo lowered his head between his legs, mumbling, "I'm going to die with this guy." His voice was frail, not as coarse as an older Cult's.

"That makes two of us then," said Dray, turning toward a passerby.

"What?" asked the demoralized Mo, head still facing down.

"You don't call that crazy talk? We're not going to die together. You'll die alone. Trust me," notified Dray, smirking.

"How old are you?" asked Dray. Mo felt small and weak. If his cellmate was indeed a loon, he had better not anger him.

"Thirteen," answered Mo.

"Why were you captured?" questioned Dray, leaning forward.

"They take anyone. Trappers pluck us off the street." Mo glanced toward passing civilians. "Often, they only go for those out of view, away from the rest. Loners—like me."

"The games? What are they?"

"Entertainment for nobles. They're going to feed us to wild beasts," Mo dully revealed.

Dray leaned back, saying, "Just my luck. … If you knew dark places were risky, why were you there?"

"I needed warmth," replied Mo, playing along with the loon.

"Warmth?" responded Dray, remembering his own need for it.

"I had nowhere else to go. Even the warmest nights can't satisfy the need." Dray could not believe the treasure trove of information sitting across from him. Best of all, the treasure trove did not have an inkling of suspicion. In Mo's eyes, he really was sitting across from a loon.

"How do warriors in battle stay warm? How do they regulate their body temperature?" asked Dray.

Mo pensively replied, "Microbands."

The cage slowed until coming to a halt. Dray looked to his left. There was a massive gate, and beyond it stood gigantic, black marble towers.

Uncertain if he and Mo would be separated, he quickly asked, "The warriors? Where are they going?"

"What warriors?" replied Mo.

"The troop buildup not far from the city," added Dray impatiently. Mo's silence was deafening.

"Out! Let's go!" ordered a savage voice. Obeying their captors, Dray and Mo got out. Dray stood a foot taller than Mo.

"Good luck, Mo," said Dray, taken away by a brisk arm. They inspected Mo.

A throaty voice explained, "This one's too young and scrawny. Get him out of here!" A passage opened, and out came a rolling cart of red meat.

I'm being traded for bloody gobbets? Dray pondered, passing through the gate, whiffing mouth-watering chunks of beef. Distracted by the savory slabs, Dray had not noticed the walls closing in; the gate behind him sealed with an ominous clank and ding. Ahead, more checkpoints came into view. Vituperative, red-cloaked Cults were counting prisoners, jeering and jostling them around like bullies on a playground. Lower ranking thugs, garbed in black and white cloaks, marked the chests of the condemned. Dray's captors continued shoving him forward.

"Here you go!" one captor panted, pushing Dray toward an enormous Cult towering over the rest. Slapping foul goo on Dray's upper right pectoral, he looked down on him questioningly.

"Are you too good to obey the law?" asked the giant Cult, his voice heavily baritone.

"What law?" replied Dray, more curious than afraid.

"The way you come dressed. It's going to cost you," he ordered, poking Dray in his shoulder. Like the others in front, Dray's bound hands were now tied to a long leash.

"To the Pit Plank!" roared the giant.

50

Sprinting long, cheetah-like strides, Bruce flew up the mountainside and reached the city of Endeavors as fast as mechanically possible. Dirt and pebble kicked up as he came to a halt. Eager and alert, he walked toward the invisible entrance, his limbs sparkling like chrome. Once crossing the line, he was instantly screened; access was granted. He trotted at a hastened pace. Startled bodies made way, surprised to see Dray's scout. Headlong, Bruce leapt over the railing, igniting and launching skyward. Endeavors rushed toward railings on every level. Sitting with his advisors, discussing the latest, Tarpin heard the missile fast approaching. Rising to their feet, they waited. The inflamed warbot burst over the railing!

"We saw you coming, Bruce," said Tarpin, standing still as the rest. Bruce appeared as though he were searching for someone. Stepping up to the conference table, he ejected a mini cylinder. Rolling to a stop, the nearest Endeavor snatched it up. "Play it," said Tarpin. The Endeavor opened an audio and video chamber built into the table. Taking all by surprise, Bruce dove back over the railing. Landing on the level directly below, he went to go find Jamie. Retracing his steps, as he had done many times before, he found Jamie inside her room. Extending one forelimb, he beat twice on her door.

"Bruce!" shouted Jamie happily, looking left and right. "Where's Dray?" Her question was answered solely by the strength of Bruce's gaze. Tulip went wild with happiness, swaying side to side, licking her chops. Bruce stepped inside, molested by Tulip the whole way. "Tulip!" shouted Jamie, grabbing her by the collar. Like a mother lioness, Bruce ignored Tulip's raucous, cublike behavior. Jamie eyed Bruce with suspicion, thinking of only one reason why a scout would return without his Elite. Jamie let go of Tulip, falling exasperatedly back on her couch. Tulip ran toward Bruce. Shutting his jaws with a snap, Bruce instantly halted her approach. Bruce opened his nose and played his last recording with Dray. Tulip whined with suppressed eagerness. Jamie heard an unfamiliar voice, discernable only upon hearing it address the people closest to her. *It's Dray*, thought Jamie, happy just to know he was alive. But something was different. He sounded distant and foreign—changed. His words sounded from the heart, genuine, but underneath the sadness was something else. The tense silence lasted only a minute before there was a knock at the ajar door. It was Al.

"I got off early. I just thought I'd stop by and see my favorite gal—Bruce!" Bruce's outer frame shone with the sheen of silk. "What's he doing here?" asked Al, his cheery words lightening Jamie's mood.

"Dray sent him. He just delivered a message," replied Jamie.

"About what?"

"Dray found corporals hiding in Compound 40. Their situation is dire. The Running Grounds are still intact. They're surviving."

"That's incredible. Have the others been notified?" Al and Jamie gave Bruce a glance. Bruce nodded, comprehending their every word, also expert in human body language.

"Then, we should go see what they plan to do," determined Al.

=

Jason sat on his bed fixating on the scroll. Unraveled, the parchment stretched four feet long and made absolutely no sense. The random markings were difficult to see, except for a few odd symbols that stood out. It could have been a language, but none that any earthly human, past or present, had ever spoken—at least to the best of Jason's knowledge.

"God, this is hopeless," uttered Jason, gently placing the scroll beside him. By his dresser, a sound and movement caught his eye. A tube of ointment fell to the floor and rolled his way. Jason's eyebrows lifted, and so did every hair on the back of his neck.

Across the hall from Jason, Michael was sprawled out on his bed—rest and relaxation had finally come. By his night table, his sword leaned idly up against the wall; its aura strengthening. Its hilt suddenly jolted and raised, beginning to twirl on its blade. The mad swirl whistled furiously until lift off! Michael rolled over on his side, thinking he was fast asleep and dreaming. With the speed of an express train, the sword plowed through his door, bursting out into the hall and then bursting into Jason's room! Already mesmerized, Jason fell back and tripped. His miracle ointment combined with the sword and scroll, transforming and growing, illuminating even greater once the sword entered; the white light in the room grew even more blinding. Michael arrived rapidly on the scene, and like Jason shielded his eyes. Their flesh grew hot, and their exposed hair was about to singe. They both inwardly pleaded for it to end. Near and far, Endeavors heard the loud bang and felt it beneath their feet. Then, as spontaneously as it had come, it was gone. The white light, along with its intense brightness and heat, vanished. Jason and Michael uncovered their eyes. Their jaws dropped. Between them stood someone all too familiar, appearing exactly as he had not long ago; his gray eyes eloquent and not an ounce of superfluous flesh. His white garb played tricks on the mind.

"Jason, Michael, my friends—so good to see you," said Simone, stately and dignified.

"Simone!" responded Jason, on the floor, leaning back on his elbows. Michael stood in the doorway.

"I don't understand," said Michael, confused and excited.

"You kept my ointment, Jason," explained Simone, turning toward Michael. "And Michael, I've been with you ever since healing your wound." Simone turned back to Jason, extending his hand and helping him to his feet.

"The scroll? The sword?" Michael wondered out loud.

"A matter of convenience. I can be in many places at once," answered Simone.

"You've been watching us ever since?" queried Jason, more of a statement than a question. "Why haven't you revealed yourself sooner?" he added.

"It wasn't time. Come, I must address your leadership. I've gathered intelligence."

=

"Is anyone else enjoying this?" admitted an Endeavor sitting at the Great Mantle's conference table. Bruce's video revealed scenes of a killing spree, all the way up to his arrival at Compound 40. The last soundbite made their stomachs turn. Hiding from view, Dray's report revealed he had become what they had feared most, and unless helped arrived, Survivor corporals were as good as dead.

"There's no way. He could be using them as bait," said one Endeavor.

"Yeah, and why would he care?" remarked another. Tarpin felt relieved, having banished Dray, but was hesitant to say it out loud. He knew others must have felt the same.

"Did anyone else feel that?" asked a Survivor, acknowledging vibrations underfoot. "Earthquake?"

"Too abrupt," replied Tarpin.

"So"—the Survivor leaned forward on his elbows—"it came from within?"

"It must have. Check the sensors," ordered Tarpin. "Locate its origin."

"Sir, it's showing corridor 57, three levels down," the Endeavor's monitor indicated.

"Let's go!" Tarpin jumped to his feet. Out of the elevator came Dr. Roberts, Eric, and John.

"What's going on?" asked Dr. Roberts, everyone hustling his way, Tarpin at the front.

"What *was* that?" posed Eric, having felt the same disturbance.

"That's what we intend to find out," responded Tarpin, hurrying past Dr. Roberts. Those that could not fit in the elevator headed for the slide. By the slide's hatch was a keypad. Endeavors and Survivors, including Dr. Roberts, Eric, and John, went down.

Taking the staircase from above, Jamie and Al entered the corridor, Bruce bringing up the rear. Endeavors from adjacent rooms were already on the scene, inspecting two blown-out doors. Down the hallway, the elevator came to a halt; and on the opposite end the slide hatch sprung open. Jason and Michael's hallway soon flooded with people. Out of one room, amid hanging dust and smoke, appeared Simone. Standing on either side were Michael and Jason.

"What's happened here?" demanded Tarpin, leading the charge.

"Commander, this is Simone," announced Jason, eyeing everyone reassuringly.

"My apologies for the damage. It was the only way," said Simone calmingly. Whispers at both ends of the hall hushed. Dr. Roberts knew what he was seeing but it still gave him goose bumps. "I've come to help," continued Simone. "One of my kind has infiltrated your city and has since reported back to his Cult masters. They are amassing their forces as we speak. I bought you some time, intercepting communications. Their leader, Drake, grows more powerful by the day."

"The infiltrator?" questioned Tarpin.

"Is a long story, Commander, and one that I will gladly tell. But first, your city must be warned. War is coming."

51

The Caterpillar came to a stop. Rays of sunlight splashed through the windows. Sleepy Almas rubbed their eyes and yawned.

"This looks good," said Wolf, scanning the terrain, then turning from the window. "Okay everyone! We're taking a break. Anyone who needs to relieve themselves, now's the time. Stay close."

"How much farther do you think?" asked Paul, meeting Wolf at the hatch.

"Well, we might have to deviate from our course. Our elevation has risen. We're either approaching steep hills or a mountain range. In either case, we'll have to find a way around or through. It could take more time."

"I'm going to get working on that seat then," replied Paul. "How's your hand?"

"It's doing better," answered Wolf, tightening his bandages before opening the hatch. "That aloe really helped. ... All clear," the commander announced as he glanced down below. Birds chirped and fluttered between trees, and nearby, a play of colors looked peaceful—lilies, azaleas, and roses were a welcoming sight. Stepping off the last rung, Wolf inspected rivets and swivels connecting the

Caterpillar's turbo charged limbs. Women and children were next in line. Spurts of Milagro mist hazily made its way down, covering all those caught in its path, and any malicious shrubbery growing on the surface. Directly behind the Caterpillar, their path revealed just how thorough their vehicle was. A twenty-foot-wide trail displayed stumps of all girths, standing knee high, as far back as they could see. Mighty trees were splayed out, like parted grass in a meadow.

"How's everything holding up?" queried Daniel, looking over what he could himself.

"Seems fine," remarked Wolf, testing and tugging on an extending rod. "Let's not take too long, people," Wolf said to a group of lingering Almas. On the other end of the Caterpillar, a man and woman conversed.

"Not in my wildest dreams could I have imagined this," the man gloomily said.

Heavy with doubt, the woman replied, "I believe in Commander Wolf. He'll get us out of this." The two turned and faced the others. The feeling of being watched was ever present. In their heart of hearts, they knew that their grizzly surroundings reluctantly waited, hell bent on savoring their meat and bones. One could almost hear the anticipative creaking and groaning.

"I wish I could have said good-bye," said the man, pausing. "I could have gone back. Mom and Dad would have had a chance." A cool breeze passed between them.

"They're watching over you right now. They're with you. Stay focused. Live for them," she encouraged. Placing her arm over his shoulder, she added, "Come on, let's go back in."

Wolf carried out his last inspection in the front, right next to the buzz saws. Thirty feet to his back, Daniel verbosely spoke with others, diverting his attention. A rotary kicked on beneath a blade, moving the entire plate laterally several inches.

"Huh," braced Wolf, stumbling backward, managing to keep his hands and torso intact. Almas heard the commotion.

"You all right?" asked Daniel, reaching Wolf.

"Yeah. I think it was a power surge," replied Wolf, blotting sweat from his brow.

"Wolf!" called Paul from the hatch above.

"I'm okay!" the shaken commander replied.

"Ah—good," Paul reacted nonplussed, "but that's not why I'm calling you. Come check and see what I've got."

"I'll be right there!" shouted Wolf, facing Daniel. "See to it that everyone begins coming back in." Daniel turned and clapped his hands.

"Round up the children," said Daniel, clapping. "Let's get going."

52

The Pit Plank's cells were spacious. Dray stood tirelessly quiet in his. Prisoners in adjacent cells were riled up. They were drawn to the scented gobs of carnage, what they saw through the slits in their bars—what awaited them. The Cult waste was abominable, sickening Dray as much as the merciless beast eating away at will. It loosened its teeth from the flesh of one prisoner's arm, then prowled up and down the pit. Dray's gate held it at bay. Its face and body were marked by the teeth of many, and its throat, constantly thrumming, drove the noble Cults above crazy.

Above each cell, circling the pit's perimeter, warrior Cults walked out on planks chumming the prisoners with raw meat. Clueless to when their gates would be opened, prisoners were in a constant state of fear. Above Dray, a warrior tossed down a heavenly morsel, but as intended it snagged on his cell, dripping. Starving, Dray jumped for it but missed. Pains of hunger altered his state of mind. He thought he was different from the rest, unwilling to be used as entertainment. But he had finally reached a tipping point; they had successfully worked him up into a frenzy. Drunk with rage, he turned from the bait. Through his cell bars, he spied the gory beast and now saw its monstrous form as food.

Its muscles showed tight rolls underneath its skin, a ton of grit and virility. The Cult eater had two long horns on its head, both capped with metal spikes. It moved on four lithe legs. Its long, whip-like tail, clad with jagged razors, lashed out at its prey. The first prisoners to enter expired quickly. None had combat experience, evidenced by their careless frontal attacks. One prisoner, presently, dodged a horn, ducking to his side, but got his head smashed in by a tail. Stinking corpses began piling up. No tactic, absent of a blunt weapon, stood a chance.

The beast's searching eyes darted side to side, scanning for movement. The next gate sprung open, prompting another aggressive soul to run out. Dray turned. He needed a weapon, and he needed it fast. The prisoner was plowed over, his dangling dead weight now sticking to the eater's horns. He and the beast blindly slammed into a gate. The collision shook the room, loosening a chain over Dray's cell. The gate, just rammed, now had a mangled body smudged between its bars. Dray went for the dangling chain, freeing it down. Balling it around his fist, he came up with a plan.

Skirting the dead, mouth laughing, the creature seemed overjoyed. The diabolical image was imprinted in Dray's mind. With chain in hand, fueled by hate, Dray hungrily waited behind his gate. With each passing second, his time drew near. It opened! Like the others, he ran out so as not to be pinned inside.

"Urgh!" grunted Dray, deflecting the horn with his chain-linked fist; he next dodged its tail sweeping in from behind. Casting the chain in the hopes of netting its horns, he missed! The chain tumbled down its back, one link catching hold on a bony protrusion. Latching on, Dray somersaulted and landed on its backside. Riding the bucking beast, trying to steady his posture, he attempted lassoing its head. Enraged, the beast tore off around the pit. The spectators above rose from their seats. Again, Dray twirled the chain and threw, and this time catching a horn! They circled the pit as fast as a race horse. Directly ahead, a gate stood ajar. Tossing the free end of his chain, it wrapped between the bars with a loud clank. He jumped, tucked in his legs, and rolled. The beast's snapping neck cracked with the magnitude of a thunderbolt. Dashing toward its throat, the victor took no chances; his animal instincts took hold. Dray was incapable of drawing back. The taste of blood never tasted so sweet, and having gone days without food, the taste of fresh meat was intoxicating. Gnawing flesh and digging in with his hands, the beast conqueror continued feasting; the warm fluid dribbling down his body was a delight.

"Potentate!" cried a noble up above. His tears preceded fury as if he had just lost a son. A firestorm of abusive language and murderous stares hailed down. Without a care, Dray tore off another chunk. Like caged dogs, the fretful prisoners nearby barked up a storm.

"Luck!" shouted one noble.

"Scoundrel!" yelled another. "Send for Watcher!"

"Watcher! Watcher!" angry nobles chanted.

Dray's blood-stained feet matched his blood crusted shorts. His whole body began turning red; to those above, he was a little red devil.

"Bring him to me!" demanded Dray, huffing fervently and tearing off more flesh. The mysterious force that drove him made him wonder if he would ever change back. Intent, he focused on his next target until nothing else existed. With his name still being chanted, Watcher entered ceremoniously, lowered down by crane. Standing nine feet tall, outweighing Dray by hundreds of pounds, it did not take long for Dray to size him up. His hands were the length and width of cookie sheets, and his arm span was twice that of Dray's. He smiled malevolently. Dray smiled back, happy to see a pulsing femoral artery completely exposed.

"Kill him!" a noble shouted from above. Lumbering forward, the super Cult's scales transitioned silvery, until blending in with the mucky pit. Crouching low, bearing sharp teeth, Dray dove for his inner thigh! Watcher counterattacked, grabbing him by the waist and taking his arm. Dray roared as his limb gravitated toward Watcher's drooling mouth. Watcher tore his limb clean from his elbow, hurling the rest of Dray across the pit. Not much blood came from the severed arm, and surprisingly, Dray felt little pain. His adrenaline kept him alert and his body tingled. Bone and tissue grew in place of his arm. Dray could not believe his eyes, keeping one eye on Watcher. Dray felt his new arm with his other. Picking bone from his teeth, taunting the other prisoners, Watcher turned back to his opponent. Nobles squinted, wanting a closer view of the rapidly growing arm; the only thing left to grow now was a hand. Keeping his distance, Dray sprinted around the arena. With longer strides, Watcher closed in fast behind. Exulted, Dray raised his new hand. Potentate's long horns starkly stood out ahead. Dray dove for them. Thrusting his shoulders into Potentate's carcass, he angled one horn upward. It shot through Watcher's kneecap. Gently pulling it out, the giant roared. The nobles and prisoners were enthralled. With his mouth wide open, the little red devil went for Watcher's inner thigh. The gash he opened must have hit an artery, blood spurted out everywhere. The giant swung around, knocking Dray back. In a fit of rage, he took Potentate by the horns and heaved him. Catching Dray off guard, he crushed him.

The nobles fell back in their seats, relieved. The prisoners panicked, knowing that they were next. Watcher's triumph did not last long. He awkwardly scratched his throat as blood rippled out from his neck; he choked, dropping to his knees.

Dray had become a knife-wielding spirit, tearing at Watcher's neck like a crazed badger. It was a horrible death, having his neck eaten away by an unseen entity. Watcher fell on his back, making it easier for his unseen foe. Dray chewed tendons and vessels keeping his head attached. Finishing, Dray rushed to his trapped body beneath Potentate. With all his might, he pried him off. He awoke in devil-like form. As for Watcher, for all those watching, he succumbed to a flesh-eating bacterium. Though rarely attacking with such rapidity, its spread was normally kept under control. Dray leaned against Potentate. The prisoners chanted words he did not understand; he surmised they were for him.

"Open the pit!" shouted a noble. The muck beneath Dray's feet trembled. The gate to his cell slammed shut, and an invisible wall kept him from holding the cell bars.

"Wait!" shouted one noble. He was a high-ranking Cult, face lined and craggy. Dray dug in, peering into the pit that was about to consume him. The muck slowly gave way. Potentate and Watcher tumbled in. "Stop!" the noble roared again. The opening pit came to a halt, leveling back out. "This one's going to war."

53

They were at an impasse, all sitting around the Great Mantle's conference table. Bruce stood off to the side looking tame and bland. Al, frail and hallow-cheeked, shifted in his seat.

"We should send them something, at the very least," said Al. Tarpin turned toward Bruce, responding, "Why not send back Bruce? I'm surprised he hasn't already returned to Dray."

"Dray must have ordered him to stay here for some reason," answered Eric.

"Sending Bruce won't be necessary," spoke Simone. "The corporals, soon, will be in good company. Plus, Bruce, has a new reason to stay. I suspect he already knows." Simone gave Jamie an undecipherable look. She swooned at his otherworldly beauty. His soft words made one woman's knees buckle.

"Very well then, shall we begin? We don't have much time," Tarpin closed the meeting. Endeavors and Survivors moved out, tasked with having to prepare defenses and call for troops.

"Simone, may I have a word?" asked Dr. Roberts. "How can we win this? They decimated our compound in one day, took out all our warbots and Elites, and took the remaining population prisoner. I don't expect much difference to take place here."

"They will come in greater numbers this time also," added Simone, not helping ease Dr. Roberts' fears.

"Yeah, even worse," Dr. Roberts uttered, appearing distracted. Simone could tell that the doctor had something else on his mind.

"You should have more faith. Just because you were defeated once doesn't mean you should assume it will happen again. What is it, my friend?"

"I can't figure out what's happened to Dray, and worst yet if the same will happen to me and a few others. I don't know what else to do—or if I should warn them."

"Give it some time. Mystery is at the heart of life," comforted Simone. The late afternoon sun collided with the Great Mantle, making Simone glow an aura as if he were a source of light. Dr. Roberts stood up.

"I take it you can't help me out then?" queried the doctor.

"There is much that is outside the bounds of human experience."

"Simone," interrupted Tarpin. "You said one of your own took out one of their satellites—correct?"

"Yes, and many more, by now," replied Simone blithely.

"Okay," Tarpin turned toward the Endeavor next to him. "They're going to hit this mountain with everything they've got. Send word for civilians to begin evacuating."

"You want to abandon the city?" countered the Endeavor.

"No, you and I will be staying along with our very best," Tarpin starkly stated.

=

"Bruce hasn't left my side once," noticed Jamie, walking beside Al.

"Maybe Dray told him to keep an eye on you. Make sure you don't go chasing after any of these Endeavor soldiers," Al joked.

"Very funny, Al," replied Jamie, slapping Al on the arm.

"Jamie!" called Madge, Tulip steering her forward. "Thank God I found you."

"What is it?"

"They want us to evacuate, go deeper underground."

"The entire city?" asked Al.

"Yes. I told them I wasn't going anywhere without you." Tulip incessantly barked at Bruce. Bruce discharged a frigid vapor her way, calming her down. Turning her attention away from Bruce, Jamie came to a decision.

"There's nothing else we can do. Al, Mother, let's go."

=

"Well, Eric, I guess we can say good-bye to Candice and Sarah," said John.

"Ahaha!" chuckled Eric. "Just our luck," he said as he checked his watch.

"Is it time?"

"To the armory. I'll lead the way."

=

Veronica wore an Egyptian-style gown with shoulder straps—she looked almost indecent.

"Michael," she called. Michael turned toward an amazingly beautiful woman; cuts had been cleaned and dirt had been washed from her face and hair.

"Yes," responded Michael.

"I wanted to give you something before I evacuated with the others."

"Of course, what is it?" Michael wondered. She took Michael by the hand and took him toward a bench. Endeavors busily moved past them. She sat on his lap and undid her hair, letting it spill over him. She kissed him with warm lips.

"I wanted to thank you properly," she kept kissing. Michael became blissfully drowsy. Everything around him had suddenly become silent.

"It's quiet," said Michael, turning toward the last Endeavors boarding the elevator.

"Silence makes the spirit grow," replied Veronica, unfolding her arms around his shoulders. "You're my angel," she said, passionately adoring him. They were worlds apart in where they both came from, but both felt the same feverish love.

"Veronica."

"Yes." She kissed.

"We must go. I'll walk you to the elevator."

=

Jason firmly held Grace's hand.

"I guess the fight's coming to us," said Jason.

"Are you afraid, my dear?" Grace joked.

"Afraid? My love, this isn't the first time I've stared death in the face. But yes, I am a little afraid."

"We'll both go together. I'll be at your side." Long lines of Endeavors circumnavigated the city, all leading toward escalators and elevators.

"You sure about that? I wouldn't want your pretty face getting disfigured," said Jason. Grace punched him in the stomach.

"Don't make me hurt you. Especially if I need you to watch my back."

"What's that?" pondered Jason. A large cylindrical tube, dwarfing everything around it, lowered down.

"It's called a Vortex. There are many. They carry troops from one side of the city to the other. Handy if one side needs rapid reinforcements." Jason leaned over, kissing Grace on her delicate ear.

54

Thin brows arched over small, bright eyes, and her muscles were well defined, amplifying her commanding, attractive profile. Echo stared into the vast and solitary desert, ignoring the athletic male Cult standing directly behind her. He had a broad, high forehead, and strong chin under a long, slightly hooked nose. Echo turned, her eyes distant and demanding.

"You really don't get it, do you?" said Echo unbendingly.

"I haven't seen a female in years. And the first one I see is a goddess," responded the warrior Cult. The troops behind him kept silent. A giant centurion held three, dark haired lions on a leash, all pointing toward Echo; each let loose a fearful roar. Their blazing manes made them look like victorious warriors.

"I was sent by Drake himself. I'm to personally report back to him. Don't step any closer," insisted Echo.

"He'd never send a piece of treasure like you out into the wild," replied the unbelieving Cult. He stepped closer. Echo stepped backward, reaching behind her back for a dagger.

"I won't warn you again," hissed Echo. He came in with outstretched hands. Echo outmaneuvered, plunging her dagger into his torso.

"Er!" he groaned, pulling out the dagger from his side. "Your turn!" the warrior shouted with the dagger raised. Echo's eyes flashed, hinting at what lay in wait, but it was all too brief as a loud thud erupted from the sky. All turned, including Echo. An aerial transport ejected crates and barrels. Two warriors appeared holding the arms of a chained prisoner.

"This one's going to the front. Don't give him anything," ordered one warrior. Dray glanced up, catching Echo's gaze. Warriors began encircling, taking an interest in the condemned newcomer.

"Take caution," warned the warrior. "He killed Potentate." The silence of death shot through each warrior; even Cults from afar, miles away, halted, feeling a sudden tingle. Echo also grew excited; not from hearing the name of Potentate—she did not know who he was—but from witnessing everyone's response.

He must have been a great warrior, Echo thought, seeing the crestfallen face of one male. Teeth flashing, even the lions felt the same excitement and bewilderment.

"This puny lug? I don't believe it," said one brute.

"Believe whatever you want. I'm putting you in charge of him. If he tries to escape, fry him. He is not to come near microbands. Is that clear. We clear?"

"Yes, sir!" the warrior replied.

"Move out!"

The timely distraction allowed Echo to leave unnoticed, as she hastily made her way behind abandoned tents. She decided to follow from a distance, aware that she was leaving the safety that their numbers provided. Dray was the only one to notice her elegant silhouette infusing with the morning mist.

"Put this on!" roared Dray's new guard. He handed Dray a brightly colored jacket; its orange and pink hues could be seen for miles. "Farther! Go!" ordered the warrior, pushing Dray out toward the very front. As Dray grudgingly slipped in his arms, others disrobed cloaks and other visible items. They wore Speedo-like underwear underneath. Like their microbands, in unison, the chameleon-like fabric blended in with their flesh.

"Mine's the toughest," giggled one hideous Cult, hitting his leathery jockstrap. Their forms seemed to take on different shapes, Dray noticed. He guessed that their infamous gaits might have shown differently to a human— or not shown at all. He now mostly felt their presence. One warrior whistled, and others responded with their own melodic tune. Dray saw his environment through a new prism of sound and touch. They communicated like whales in the blackest depths of the sea. Dray tugged at his highly visible sleeve, determining he was dead meat. It would not be long until prowling eyes spotted him, but he was not alone—the centurions and their beasts had not changed one bit. They flanked the invisible army; and though they were not garbed in bright colors, they too were undeniably a target.

Many yards out in front, Dray thought about making a run for it. But glancing over his shoulder, he decided not to, for a line of radiating microbands stood poised; and a fleet of bloated sky drones flew overhead.

55

"Be that as it may, I still have to go out there and look," said Wolf, responding to many objections, principally Daniel's, whom had just advised that whatever snagged the Caterpillar could be alive. Paul slammed the joystick forward and, again, the vehicle jolted back and forth, stuck. "Okay, that's enough. Anymore and you'll do damage," Wolf ordered, a little perturbed.

"Your hands—how are they?" asked a dispassionate little girl.

"They're fine," replied Wolf, looking down at her round face and plump cheeks. Kneeling, Wolf quietly stated, "We can't sit here forever—" An impetuous rumble sounded beneath their feet.

"What was that?" questioned a young boy, trembling and sweating. Wolf looked out the window and like the others was unable to detect any movement.

"The first design flaw. We can't see underneath us," uttered Wolf, turning back to Daniel and Paul. "We know it's not the jungle—we still have Milagro." Wolf gazed over heads of varying heights.

"Your spear ray," suggested Paul.

"Too risky, I could lose it. And if I pry us free, you'll need the power to get us out of here," determined Wolf. An older Alma stepped forward, holding what looked like a nail gun.

"Take this," offered the man.

"Where'd you get this?" asked Wolf, inspecting the trigger and its slick barrel.

"I've had it for years. My father made it. It shoots stinging barbs. It holds a thousand," the Alma said proudly.

"Have you ever fired it?" wondered Wolf.

"I have. The barbs come from a special plant. They're hard to find, so I never used it much. Once the barbs hit the chamber, a chemical reaction takes place, and boom. It's all natural." Wolf shook his head, whether more doubtful or more encouraged now, no one knew but him.

Wolf opened the hatch. He turned toward Daniel. "If anything happens to me, you're in charge." Daniel nodded.

Outside, ferns, mosses, and orchids choked every available plant limb and tree trunk. Other than that, Wolf could not see much of anything else. Aiming the barb gun toward the ground, he pulled the trigger. Several explosive pops sounded, firing each barb out the muzzle. "It works," confirmed Wolf, confident that anything they hit would be in a world of pain. Nothing on the jungle floor responded, however. Climbing farther down, peering left and right, Wolf looked harder. The giant, blue-nose caterpillar spotted him first; its mammoth proportions were incredible. It sat directly beneath the Almas, clenching their Caterpillar's mechanical limbs with lissome limbs of its own. Retracting its dark head and inflating a multicolored thorax, it spit a formic acid from a gland that deviously resembled a smile. Wolf took cover behind a sturdy limb, blocking the stream of flesh-eating fluid coming his way, wheeling around his gun carrying arm. With its big eyes, the jungle beast did not flinch as hundreds of three-inch barbs slammed into it. Noxious, pink tentacles whipped outward from numerous appendages on its tail end. Wolf saw them in advance and made a run for the frontend of the vehicle. Each appendage had poison-charged cones bristling with syringes, each dispensing stinging chemicals. Wolf felt like a cockroach, his adversary the exterminator.

"Can you see anything?" yelled a woman. Daniel and Paul frantically looked out the front window.

"I can't see him!" shouted Paul.

"What's that!" detected Daniel. An octopus-like tentacle swung wildly upward, hitting the cockpit window. Down below, beneath the round buzz saw, Paul spotted Wolf.

"There! Look!" pointed Paul. Almas scampered about to get better views.

"He's in trouble," said one.

"He needs help," said another. A fog of Milagro sputtered down, obstructing Wolf 's line of sight and the predatory limbs homing in on him. Obligatorily, Paul slammed down his palm, spurring quick spins from the

Caterpillar's front saw. Remembering to keep a safe distance, Wolf avoided the gashing blade. His pursuer was not as fortunate. Limbs and crystalline fluid spat everywhere; renegade, wily tentacles greeted each other warmly, flopping like fish out of water once hitting the ground. Milagro gas cleared. Wolf took aim.

"Die!" growled Wolf, firing a wave of stinging barbs, this time directly targeting its head. The massive insect was now clearly visible to all. Burrs the size of Wolf's barbs splintered off, catching Wolf directly underneath. The pain was irritating, but Wolf held his ground; victory was in sight. In defeat, the caterpillar vomited hydrogen cyanide and let loose its vicelike grip. Wolf dove for cover as the Almas felt the visceral sensation of being released.

Out of stinging barbs and gasping for unpolluted air, Wolf turned toward an explosion of vines. Twenty more blue-nose caterpillars sluggishly waddled forth, their giant heads leading the way. Paul instinctively plunged forward, driving their Caterpillar's twisting nose ahead at full speed. His oncoming targets did not halt. The two caterpillars collided, head-on, like two city busses; a riot of color deluged the jungle floor as the heavier Almas kept plowing through. Jumping and catching the bottom rung of the ladder, Wolf locked his arms—a hot wave of gastric fluid smashed into him! Daniel opened the hatch directly above him.

"Wolf!" called Daniel.

"Keep going!" yelped Wolf, his words muffled, his face drenched in goo. Daniel spun around, shouting, "We've got him! Keep moving!"

To their left and right, and close behind, the Almas watched brightly striped caterpillars advance. Wolf crawled in and slumped to the floor. One Alma secured the hatch, while another went to his aid. Calm and collected, she helped him sit up. A man, with a pencil-thin mustache, tossed over a cloth, and in a triumphant manner said, "Help clean that man up." With lively eyes, she wiped Wolf's fine-featured face.

"We're losing them!" announced a gleeful Alma, standing in the rear, hands pressed up against the window.

"How's Wolf?" asked Paul, cutting down trees the heights of skyscrapers.

"Okay," replied a wholehearted boy.

"Well done, Commander," praised Daniel, smiling at Wolf and at the Alma dabbing his neck. Wolf looked past Daniel, nodding at the barb gun man.

"Your father knew his stuff," thanked Wolf, tilting his head back against the hatch.

"How come our shield didn't stop it?" asked Daniel.

"We must have stumbled across it. The shield only works if something tries to penetrate," answered Wolf, rocking up and down to the ebb and flow of the Caterpillar.

"Sorry 'bout that," said Paul, eyes fixed squarely ahead.

"I wouldn't have seen him either," responded Wolf, leaning over on one hand and pushing himself up. "Anyone else hungry? Let's have a good meal." Wolf turned toward Daniel and whispered, "It could be our last—if we get stopped again."

They ate bread, fruit, and several types of meat. Eggs, with cheese and cream, were the first dishes to be served. The fresh stuff had to go first; spoiled provisions would do no one any good. A side panel folded outward, extending level with the floor. Its topside heated up; slabs of meat thrown on sizzled. Exhaust vents in the rear filtered out the fumes. Wolf and the others sat down to eat, some sitting on the floor, others sitting in chairs. They shared jugs of water. Paul, mouthwatering, continued at the controls.

Outside, the Almas' fresh scent trail did not go unnoticed.

56

"Seal the doors!" ordered Tarpin. His torso, arms, and legs were emblazoned with body armor. With broad, appealing features, he walked toward the railing and placed his hands upon the rail. As if awaiting a sign from the Invisible, he stood determinedly silent. Half a minute passed before he decided it was time. Pounding his right fist on his left pectoral, his face masked up. Thousands of Endeavors below did the same, their bio-suits going stealth. The city echoed readiness. "They're coming," reported Tarpin, zooming in on a veritable army of crawling drones. The others acquired the same live feeds, patching into their defensive net. The southern sky blackened with incoming aircraft, and the valley floor flooded with shimmering beasts.

=

"Will the defensive net stop them?" asked Jason, shifting his visual from the enemy and focusing on those stationed nearby him.

"We'll know soon enough," replied Grace. He could only see her dark silhouette. He had a gut-wrenching feeling that they would be separated; the sound of her voice had also changed—distinguishing one another would be difficult. Heartsick, Jason reached out for her. She twined around him, attempting to hug her sleek body to his powerful frame, but the silken air between them pushed them apart, their bio-suits inhibiting any sense of real touch.

=

"Come to Papa," said Eric, watching a vast number of drones advancing. He stood next to John; both stood on the outer periphery of the Hanging Gardens.

"I think I'm going to be sick," stammered John. "I was an engineer, Eric—not an Elite."

"Pull it together, old friend. They may not even get to us," eased Eric. Eric turned toward stalwart soldiers nearby, adding, "But if they do—kill or be killed."

=

Inside a narrow tunnel, Endeavor civilians traveled by train. Red lights pulsed on and off, and the temperature felt like it had dropped.

"What do you think is happening back there?" asked Madge, sitting beside Jamie and Al, placing her hand on Tulip. Tulip slathered her hand with slobber. Bruce stood in the aisle receiving the same images as each Endeavor soldier.

"They're preparing for an attack," answered Jamie.

"Boy, this reminds me of our first escape," said Al.

"We're not really escaping. We're just moving to another sector," Jamie reminded, a red light flickering on her face.

"I still think we're escaping, dear," insisted Madge. Bruce's luminous eyes brightened. A group of drones began leaping vertically and, once high enough, their gyrating heads steered them toward the ground. The energy from their impact penetrated deeply, as if Poseidon himself had smashed many tridents into the earth. The drones' diamond encrusted mandibles spun fiercely, chewing up rock and spitting it back out of their holes. Droning signals coordinated their movement underground. Cult missiles, fired from miles out, passed by overhead. The Endeavor Mountain stirred awake—their defensive net came online. Big, circular blast doors opened, and massive balls of flame ejected. One after another, giant fireballs launched skyward like a volley of Roman candles. Higher up the mountain, multiple rocket launch systems discharged in rapid succession. Artillery positions operated by warbots fired 155 mm explosive projectiles. Toward the summit, more fire blasting doors appeared. As drones circled the base of the mountain, 30 mm Gatling-style rotary cannon sprung out. Thousands of proximity mines activated; drones by the hundreds set them off. The entire mountain was ablaze! Incoming missiles detonated from the wall of fire shielding Endeavor airspace. Surface to air missiles wildly sought aircraft and any bombs dropping from above. Fireballs plummeted back down to the earth, tumbling down steep inclines and over cliffs, obliterating encroaching drones.

=

"Did you hear that?" asked Jeffrey, a little jumpy.

"Yes, now hand me that vile," replied a sharp-featured Dr. Roberts.

"I thought we weren't making Morphic Formula?"

"We're not. This is an anti-formula," informed Dr. Roberts. "I'm utilizing Dray's blood and tissue samples. I have no idea if it'll work. We're going to set up traps around the lab and hopefully inject a Cult."

"And where will we be?"

"We'll be hiding and observing, somewhere in here."

"You sure they're even going to come in here? What if they just blow this place to smithereens?"

"They could've blown Compound 40 to smithereens, but they didn't. They take a certain kind of pleasure in hunting us." Dr. Roberts took out an eyedropper and squeezed in a drop of solution.

"I wish we'd just nuke them," said Jeffrey dreamily.

"Discontinued a long time ago, friend. With the construction of highly fortified underground compounds and unmanned war vehicles, the only casualties were nature and machines." Dr. Roberts swirled his vile. "When our side stopped being able to pinpoint the enemy, until they were too close, a nuclear blast was deemed too risky."

"Why don't the Cults use them?"

"I imagine they would if they felt the need to."

"What does that mean?"

"It means that they want to have enough meat and bones to pick through when they finally get to us."

Sky drones halted and, hovering miles out, they surrounded the mountain on all sides. Their spindly necks retracted back into their voluminous casings. Panels on their undersides slid open; they spewed out ant fragments. Ignited by their need to kill, the critters' awful screeching pierced through noisy eruptions. One sky drone faced down an oncoming Endeavor missile. The sound from the explosion carried far by sweeping wind.

"What are they?" shouted Tarpin, having difficulty seeing them.

"They're small. They may have an easier time getting through," replied an equally concerned Endeavor.

"Where does our defensive net stand?"

"It's at 80 percent, sir." Tarpin paced back and forth.

"Their main force hasn't arrived," thought Tarpin out loud. "Deploy spider bots. Let's see if they can head those little bastards off."

=

Alighting aircraft flew between mountain peaks opposite the Endeavor Mountain, and finding inhospitable places to land, they began deploying crawlers. Blinding spindrift kicked up as fresh-freezing powder became thick, yet the bulky crawlers crossed folds and gullies with ease. Positioning themselves with better vantage points, warrior Cults studied the raging siege.

"Their defenses won't last forever," said an unctuous Cult.

"We'll hold here, for now. We're out of their range," determined another smug voice. It was an abysmal scene. Their drones were being picked apart by bombarding armor piercing cannons. Incendiary tracer penetrator rounds had an even more deadly effect. The mother of all bombs was knocked out of the sky, sending down shockwaves and causing landslides—melting drones jumped out of the way. Approaching missiles were shot down; some were incinerated by the whirlwind of fire encircling the mountain.

"We have company," stated a square jawed Cult. He smiled broadly—there were hundreds of them. Their veined amber wings carried them toward the inferno. Some flew too close and caught fire, becoming living explosions of light.

"Look at them," said Tarpin, seeing his violent fortress through a hidden camera on an adjacent mountain. They looked like flying serpents coming to investigate the uproar. Attracted to the light and heat, they dove in close to see its source. Endeavor cannons shot many to pieces, while ejecta from landmines cut some right in half. Retreating to quieter mountaintops, several of the winged reptiles landed on crawlers, thinking they were natural rock formations. The startled creatures roared so loudly the sky seemed to tear.

"How long will they stay?" asked one Cult, listening to squeaks and scrabbles above.

"Who cares? They're mere pigeons to us."

"What about the ground troops?"

"A minor inconvenience, that's all," he answered gruffly.

Spider bots the size of a grown man's hand crawled out of opening chambers. They scurried under and around drones; some were trampled, others were blown sky high. The rest made it through extreme heat.

Ant fragments worked their way toward the fiery mountain. Falling rocks crushed many, as did out-of-control aircraft. Clustered together, the fragile ants were too numerous to miss.

The two crawly waves collided! The spider bots battled disjointedly, but with each zap, they paralyzed a dozen ants at a time; their blue volts scattered zigzag-like. Emitting low frequency sound waves and sprouting tiny wings, the versatile ants attacked like killer bees. Though the low frequency hum was beginning to mess with their circuitry, the spider bots still jolted many of them out of the air. The ants' plan of attack, swarming in numbers, was working against them, as compacting friction helped spread the spiders' killing current. Frying in midair, they dropped by the thousands, and as more shrapnel peppered the battlefield, their motionless bodies were hacked apart. Victorious spider bots fell victim as well, mashed up as easily as cake crumbles.

=

"We're here," said Jamie. The train came to a stop. The doors opened.

Outside, a man with a trim goatee instructed everyone to move out, saying, "The next train is coming. Come on, people." Endeavors hastened their pace. The man pointed them toward a passage. Two guards standing on either side showed them in.

"I feel really old," uttered Al, comparing his frail physique to the two younger men.

"You're perfect, Al, come on," comforted Madge. "Tulip, come." Tulip came to Madge's side and like Bruce she walked sentinel-like. Endeavors streamed through the entryway, single file. At the end of the lengthy corridor, they arrived at what looked like a wall. Al was about to state the obvious when a loud beep cut him off. Separate blast doors slid open, and on the other side stood a short man with thinning hair.

"Welcome to Compound 17," the man stated. Behind him was another corridor with equally spaced doors leading to rooms on either side. "Until this war comes to an end, you'll be staying here. I need up to thirty for each room, please."

"How many rooms are there?" asked Jamie.

"We have up to three hundred. They're configured around our Central Command. Imagine a large cylinder with many levels and hallways branching out from its center. Now if you will." He pointed toward an empty room. Al entered first. There were fifteen bunkbeds, and in the far corner was a lavatory.

"This doesn't look so bad," said Al, pressing down on a mattress to a bottom bunk. Twenty-seven more people funneled in behind Madge and Jamie. One of them was Sam, rolling in two black suitcases.

"Al!" called Sam.

"Sam! What are you doing here?" Al responded joyfully.

"Just trying to stay alive, Al. I have a present for you." Sam set down a suitcase and opened it up. Inside was a neatly folded Strongarm. Al glanced over at Bruce and shook his head.

"So, you fixed it?" said Al, stroking the top of the fixed arm.

"I did," replied Sam, inching his way toward Bruce.

"This is the guy who tore off the arm?" Sam asked, grinning at Bruce.

"Yeah, that's the one," confirmed Al. While Tulip lay beside Madge's feet, calm as ever, Bruce stood next to Jamie, scanning left and right. Endeavors shuffled in the background, picking their bunks and storing their things. It was Sam's first time seeing Bruce up close and, just as he had imagined, the scout's presence made him feel happy. Bruce's integral radiance disarmed and conquered everyone around him, and his outward perfection no one could match. Sam stared into Bruce's fiery eyes.

"Sam, nice to meet you," greeted Jamie. "Al has a friend?"

"And employer," added Sam, "but after today, I'm afraid not. I might not have a shop."

"Join the club," said Al, taking a seat next to Bruce. "What's in your other suitcase?"

"Something I've been working on. Too valuable to have left behind," Sam patted his suitcase.

"So, what's in it?" Madge chimed in.

"Al, remember our talk about me wanting to build something similar to Bruce, a personal companion, a bodyguard?" Sam recalled, unzipping his heavy suitcase. "Well, I had to forget about that and put together something else." Sam folded the top flap over. Inside was an oval backpack with a harness and attached to it was a hose—at the end was a gun. "It's a modified energy weapon. Like the laser you used but stronger. In principle, this particular fuel cell will feed a lot more energy." Curious Endeavors gathered around.

"In principle?" queried Al.

"I haven't had the chance to test it," revealed Sam, taking out just the gun and leaving in its energy pack. Brandishing the tubular gun, the length of an assault rifle, he began explaining it in detail. What he said sounded alien to many. He explained natural oscillations of molecules between energy levels for generating electromagnetic radiation. Madge closed her eyes. After explaining the amplified spectrum of light responsible for its killing power, Sam admitted, "There are only two problems. The energy pack weighs over sixty pounds, and its lenses are fragile. If one breaks, it becomes useless."

"Let's hope you don't have to use it then," said Jamie.

=

Tarpin spotted leering crawlers, stating, "They're waiting for our defenses to die down. Once those vehicles punch holes in us, their invasion force can enter."

"And our defensive net isn't targeting them," added an Endeavor.

"Deploy Archimedes," ordered Tarpin.

"What if he gets hit by friendly fire?"

"As long as he stays low and out of range, he'll be fine."

=

Lying deathly still in the hangar he was hatched in, Archimedes suddenly popped up on six spidery legs and headed for the lift. Taking it down, he reached the tunnel, jetted for miles, and made it speedily to its very end. At the chamber, he bent his wings inward, crawled in, and was inundated with water. He tore from the river, sprung from the gorge, and then sailed like a bird of prey into a big sky. He flew over autumn tinged brush and over sapphire-and-emerald-tinted waters; his outer coating reflected crystal pools glistening among drifts of mist. The blend of divine and earthly beauty soon vanished. In the distance, tendrils of smoke curled heavenward, and shattered tree trunks speckled the mountainous horizon.

"Targets detected," reported Archimedes, swaying side to side as he hugged the whittled surface. High above, dusted in winter white, restful crawlers lay in wait; and nearby, perched in the wispy high-altitude, were unknowns. Outfitted with an array of weaponry, Archimedes flew up the mountainside with steady intensity, but his unorthodox approach was soon uncovered, eliciting warning snarls from sharp toothed terrors. The first three took the plunge, diving straight for him! Calculating his speed and theirs, Archimedes extended the sharp front edges of his wings. Increasing velocity, he gave them little time to maneuver; the terror-stricken beasts were sliced in half. Archimedes passed through them without losing speed. Their bodies broke apart, even more as they tumbled over sharply uneven-edged rock, leaving behind a sluice of blood—long patches of translucent frost turned red.

"Did you hear that?" grumbled a Cult, sitting at a sixty-degree angle.

"One of those flying louts," answered the other sitting next to him. The crawler's steep incline forced Archimedes to land; had he dropped his torrid bomb from above, it would have rolled right off. No bigger than a coffee mug, Archimedes positioned the spherical ordnance on the crawler's topside; it opened, melting inward. Having sunk in an inch, it stabilized itself. Archimedes took off. Inch-worming through a foot of plated armor, the torrid bomb's blowtorch burner combusted with the intensity of a solar flare.

"How's this possible?!" an ill-fated Cult shouted, bubbling with rage as his screen depicted the intruder's location. Fuming mad, he turned in the direction of the searing heat. Blue sparks sprinkled down—a millisecond later the torrid bomb popped out, fell, and landed in his lap. The explosion crumpled the crawler from within; cavalier heads snapped off their shoulders. Outside, the sound from the blast did not carry far, allowing the Grim Reaper the same stealthy approach with the next. The second crawler extinguished much like the first; breathless Cults were taken by surprise. Archimedes hopped from one crawler to the next, tenderly delivering death.

"They're not responding!" a Cult warned. "We've lost six signals! We're under attack!" his ugly voice ringing.

"Thorns!" shouted another. Every square inch of their crawler protruded spikes. Almost invisible to the eye, Archimedes did not see them in advance, landing as swiftly as a fly. Touching one, he was instantly blown away! He lost his limb, vaporized, and spun out of control. Crash landing on the opposite side of the mountain, he tobogganed downward for almost a mile. Colliding with everything in his path, his systems automatically shut down. Sliding to a stop, the once invincible aircraft looked damaged beyond repair.

=

286

"Archimedes is down," reported an Endeavor, his words calm and even. Inwardly, though, the forlorn feeling was intense—one of their best was just taken out.

Michael was assigned to the highest level of the city; right below him sat the Great Mantle and Tarpin. Hearing the latest made him weak-kneed. Should he need help, this time, there would be no Archimedes coming to his aid. He glanced up at the Stargaze. It looked like a dwarf star, blinking in brightness from the ongoing explosions beyond, gilding the entire city yellow-orange.

"Jason, can you hear me? It's Michael," called Michael, having switched from his open line to a direct line with Jason.

"I can hear you—Michael—go ahead," replied Jason, somewhere far down below.

"Are you ready for this?"

"No. Not really."

"I wish Dray was here," Michael confessed.

"He's probably worse off than we are. I bet he wishes he were here too." A seismic jolt shook the surface beneath their feet. A fault line miles beneath the earth triggered a shockwave.

Earthquake, determined Tarpin. Every level of the city was built to shift and sway, able to withstand high-magnitude tremors. Jason stood anxiously at the front entrance to a shop. He had a sudden flashback as he watched different items fall. Fruit jars spilling from shelves, smacking the floor, reminded him of blood-soaked Survivors torn from their vehicles, hitting the ground.

"They just keep coming," resumed Michael, viewing leaping drones as if they were in a movie.

"Any last words of wisdom?" asked Jason, putting the dreadful memories out of his mind.

"Yeah—don't get killed."

57

Walking stonily under an unforgiving sun, Dray's inexhaustible reserve of energy turned to planning his escape. Putting the barren plain behind and, getting over the distance he had just been forced to run, he welcomed the sight of trees. Every scent, sound, and organic structure was taken in; and judging by the tree line, he only had a couple of hundred yards to go. *They'll narrow their lines,* thought Dray, knowing that this would lessen the eyes tailing his ridiculous outfit. Every step closer made his heart pound; attempting an escape was not for the fainthearted. Panting lions hinted that they would be the first charging in after him. He knew he could find cover behind a wall of trees, but what good was it if they could track him? Hearing the call of the wild and seeing shadows dart between branches, Dray figured the wildlife could provide a distraction. He could remove his jacket and use every bit of his flesh to blend in. Time seemed to count down sluggishly, as if seconds had turned into minutes. He ignored nerves signaling throughout his body, wanting him to stop moving all together. The gap shortened.

Transfixed, Dray heard it first, like rustling of cloth; it was the graceful movement of wings. As he turned, crescent talons impaled him—he was airborne! Lions huffed at how boldly close the creature had come. Unseen Cults saw the massive black bird yet did nothing; the condemned prisoner was their sacrificial lamb. The inglorious kill was what they had wanted to see; a prolonged struggle was more than they had hoped for.

Dray was completely immobilized and could do nothing to free himself. The thought of being released was not that great either; the fall could kill him just as quickly as the sharp pains spreading throughout his back. His attacker continued its linear path, effortlessly carrying him over sun-washed trees. It gabbled and mewed, and then with a voice resembling liquid gargling through a pipe, it sounded as if it were trying to speak. Dray felt as helpless as a worm; and then realized that dressed in pink and orange he must have looked like one, too.

Before Dray lost consciousness, the bird hurtled earthward hundreds of feet. Unfolding its wings, it came in low, unplugged its hooks, and then dropped him in a grassy clearing. Dray coughed and wheezed, sitting up. Landing ten feet away, staring directly at Dray, the raven spoke *"Quork, quork,"* then gave off a loud *"Tok! Tok!"* Flapping back into the sky, it said a farewell, *"Kow!"* Dray watched the black creature streak away, appearing smaller the farther it flew—he did not know whether to give it thanks or curse it for having almost killed him. He disrobed one sore arm at a time, and then decided his red blood shorts and red soaked underwear had to also go. Uncertain if the omnivore would return, he took cover in the trees. Though naked as a jaybird, he felt invigorated, blending in. The pain in his back disappeared, as did the holes below his shoulder blades. He had been flown a considerable distance from the main army, and now had to decide whether to head in the opposite direction or go back and shadow them.

The Cult army entered the forest, their lines thinning considerably. The centurions and their lions took positions in the vanguard. As ferocious as they were, the lions' purpose was not to fight, but rather to flush out any threats. Super predators lacked the ability to see how their most basic instinct could be used against them, mainly, the weakest and most visible being the easiest to hunt.

=

Stepping softly and slowly, Dray took his time. If the Cults had not changed their course, their paths would eventually meet. The first sign of their presence arrived in scent form; the pungent lion odor was all too familiar. Not long afterward, Dray heard their distinct communication. But their sonorous calls bounced off trees, distorting their point of origin. Dray knew he had to be close, though. Hugging a tree, his flesh turned into bark. He peered around his cover.

"What are you doing?" a mild voice asked. It was female. Dray turned. He remembered her from before, vanishing with the morning mist. He could not bring himself to kill her.

"Don't get any ideas," Echo warned. She was scantily clad, carrying a satchel strapped over one shoulder. Average in height, her firm stomach was bare. Her fresh beauty, so appealing in the forest gloom, made Dray speechless. Tan armed, wearing a gray veil, she stepped closer as if she had not fully detected him. She wore a gold necklace, on it hung a bluish crystal. How could he kill this illustrious Cult?

"What are you doing here? Don't make me ask you again," she threatened; her words titillating.

"I should be asking you the same," Dray finally spoke. "What are *you* doing here?" he asked crossly.

"Are you the one?" The prisoner that was condemned to the front?" she asked, ignoring his question.

"So, what if I am?"

"Freedom is that way, you fool." Her bearing and reserve impressed him. She turned, her flowing hair lapping over her flawless shoulder. "They're coming," she whispered. "Go away."

"I'm not going anywhere. I'm following them," Dray objected, not moving a muscle.

"Why?"

"I want to see where they're going."

"To war—does that satisfy you?"

"I want to know where," Dray bitterly stated. Holding each other's gaze, Echo recognized the stubborn nature that had to have put him in prison.

"They're going to kill you, you know?"

"Not if I don't get caught."

"I could turn you in."

"I don't think so. By the looks of it, it seems you're keeping your distance. Why?" After a long pause, Echo signaled for him to follow. They headed in the direction from which Dray had come. She found a tall mound next to a creek and hid behind it. Being naked suddenly came to Dray's attention. If she had been able to find him—she could see him, every bit of him. His hands covertly moved between his legs. Echo noticed.

"Here, I have no need for this," she offered, reaching into her sack and pulling out the Speedo-like wear of a male warrior. Dray accepted it with one hand, keeping his other held in place. He turned and put one leg in at a time. Echo watched.

"How did you get this?" asked Dray, turning back.

"I took it out of anger. I stole it from one of them before leaving the camp. I bet he's uncomfortable now."

Dray smirked and, as he crouched down, he asked, "Why are you with them?"

"I was asked to go. I feel better keeping my distance. They annoy me."

"Aren't you afraid of coming under attack out here?"

"Of course, but I'm careful. I don't stray too far," she replied.

"You stick out in my eyes."

"Then how do you explain me sneaking up on you?"

How did she sneak up on me? Dray wondered. *She could have attacked first.* "I don't know. How *did* you?" Dray needed to know.

"My little secret," she coyly answered.

"Who are you?" asked Dray.

"Echo. You?" Dray's mind went blank, and his hesitation to answer looked suspicious. Though they shared an equal disdain for those not far off, he understood whoever sent her expected her loyalty. Dray's name may have been known and hated.

"I don't know" was his peculiar answer.

"You *don't* know? You don't have a name?"

"No. Call me whatever you want." Behind her veil, Echo's perceptive eyes took a minute to study him, sensing something odd, something different.

"You're not like the others," she determined.

"I should get moving," Dray changed topics, helping Echo confirm her suspicion.

"You have time. You should follow them from the rear anyway," she played along, knowing sooner or later she would get to the bottom of who he was.

"Then why are you so far in front?" Dray countered.

"I went ahead to avoid the open plain. I hid in the trees until they arrived." Dray looked to his left, then stood up and looked to his right. He felt lost. The lion scent was gone, and he could no longer hear their calls.

"Smart move," replied Dray, off beat, and noticeably distracted. Echo was beginning to feel comfortable in his presence. Dray, unknowingly, secreted a pheromone chemical unique to him. No male had ever enthralled Echo quite like this.

"I'll tell you what, Mr. No Name. I'll let you accompany me, but only if you follow two simple rules."

"I'm listening."

"Keep your distance from me. I'll contact you. If you lose track of me, stay put. I'll come get you, and we'll move on. Can you handle that?"

"I can."

"By the way—I know exactly where they're going."

"Where?"

"Death Valley. There's an enemy stronghold based in a mountain."

"Really." Dray tried hiding his concern.

"You can still leave," Echo reminded, thinking his concern was fear.

"I want to see this with my own eyes."

"You're either very stupid or crazy. I don't know which is worse."

"I've got nowhere else to go, Echo. Plus, I'm as good as dead out there, alone, far from the troops. That's not a freedom I can enjoy." Echo was beginning to rethink his mental state, and hers, too, for not realizing it earlier. He was unarmed. Absent of microbands, he did not stand a chance. She had simply overlooked this.

"You make a good point," Echo admitted. "It's not like you're a spy, trying to infiltrate," she added jovially. "You were a prisoner sentenced to death. Now you're just trying to stay alive." Echo was more understanding of the situation. "There's just one more thing I need to know. How did you become a prisoner?"

"They caught me by a heater," Dray uttered, ashamed. Echo almost laughed.

"You can't be serious? Were you homeless?" she whispered.

"I was," Dray answered truthfully.

"Well, I won't ask you how that happened, or how a homeless person kills Potentate."

"You should have met his friend, Watcher," answered Dray.

=

Strong as an ox, with dark skin, a centurion in the rearguard lifted his nose. His breathing grew ragged and his lions became agitated. What preyed upon them had tentacles above eyelike nostrils. It had the outward appearance of a spiny lobster, belonging somewhere out in the ocean. Shifting its stone-cold position, it was anything but a harmless lobster. The sweeping motion of its snout, above saw teeth, avoided gnarled branches as it moved. Having poisoned the centurion and his beasts, it now headed for them like a horse at full gallop. The centurion released his hold and his three lions roared off into the trees! The felines smartly worked as a team, spreading out and looking for weak spots. One lion pounced and was met with a slash, its mane absorbing most of the cut. Instinctively, the others attacked but were denied just the same; their sides and chests bloodied. The foul creature's long bony arms swiveled 360 degrees, on them lay jagged protrusions; at their tips were crablike shears. Gearing up for another assault, the big cats suddenly staggered from severe gastric distress brought on by the poison. Collapsing to the ground, they made quite a meal. The predator's shears went to work, spreading apart bone and slicing meat off cleanly. Watching in the shadows stood another predator. Raising its arms, it unleashed its invisible wave of death, silent as poison but with a much quicker result. The Cult warrior got back in line, stepping over the dead centurion on his way.

=

Dray and Echo caught wind of it first—fresh meat. Echo reached the carcasses first, her shining black hair steering Dray in.

"We're behind them," confirmed Echo. "Let's move." She put some distance between them. Dray's mouth watered at the sight of the cooked creature, and the raw lions looked equally appetizing. But he had to keep moving; he did not want to lose Echo. His effort to walk soon became exhausting. Muscling his way forward, his body was in the early stages of shutting down. He halted, crouched down where he stood, and waited. She appeared at his side as ghostly as mist. Dray sat and leaned against a fallen tree

"What's wrong?" Echo asked.

"I can't move," Dray stated, tapping his right thigh with a balled fist.

"I suspected this might happen. I didn't think so soon, though."

"What?"

"You need energy. The trees are blocking the sun," Echo revealed, glancing up, and then contemplating the only other remedy.

"You'll have to move me," Dray responded, trying to conserve the little energy he had left.

"The closest clearing is in the wrong direction. We can't stray far from the army." She sounded upset. Looking back and turning, she asked, "Can I trust you?"

"Yes" was Dray's tired response, shutting his eyes. Echo plunked down her satchel, procured two microbands, and then clamped them to his forearms. Dray's eyes shot open— his pupils glittered.

"Now we can move at our own pace. You'll be able to remove anything that stands in our way." She looked disappointed, as if regretting having parted with the microbands. Dray lifted his arms, feeling completely whole again.

"You stole these from the same dolt?"

"Yes."

"Why aren't you wearing them?"

"They're too big. They don't make them small enough."

"Why were you still carrying them? How do you keep your strength?" Dray eagerly questioned.

"They're worth something. I could've bargained with them." Echo's finger grazed the luminous crystal on her necklace, saying, "This gives me energy."

"A crystal?"

"It's a power supply. Much like the power fastened to your arms."

"How do I use them?" Dray twisted his arms.

"My understanding is that you aim, and they shoot." Dray pointed toward a tree.

"Not like that, only when you need them. They read your vital signs. If you're threatened, they'll activate. It cuts down on misuse."

"Why didn't you give them to me sooner?"

"I didn't trust you, but then I realized that unless you truly feel threatened by me, I'm safe."

"You could have just left me," Dray pointed out. Echo's silence spoke volumes. There was nothing advantageous for her to have stayed with him, and helping a prisoner was a death sentence.

"In case we should get caught," Echo explained, "there should be no evidence that I ever gave those to you. In fact, you've been keeping me hostage, you got that?"

"Of course, whatever you say," Dray answered slyly.

58

Short but well bred, one corporal turned toward another in the dark, standing guard in their makeshift fort at the edge of the Running Grounds.

"Do you hear that?" the corporal asked.

"What is it?" the other replied, sensing it was something not native to the grounds.

"We should tell the others."

"Yeah, let's go." The two headed for the tunnel where the rest were taking advantage of the natural protection. Covered on two sides by thick walls, the corporals fortified their other two flanks. In the front, they positioned their main double-barreled cannon. At the rear, they put up a crude barrier built with stones and tree branches; intentional spacing worked as gun slots.

"We heard something," the corporal warned at the tunnel entrance, entering before his companion. Securing their rifles, they crept along the wall, their hands feeling their way through the dark. The others signaled them scraping flint against steel, calling them to keep moving forward.

"What's going on?" asked one corporal, poised next to two big guns.

"We heard something," responded the approaching voice.

"We'll go back when it's light," said the other. "How much longer do we have?"

"About five minutes." The only periodic comfort came from the light drones; light casting in from the entrance was enough to let them see, but not enough to give away their location. They had been rotating in shifts. Two corporals at a time stood watch near the entrance, switching every hour.

"What did it sound like?" a younger corporal asked, whispering.

"Like springs."

"We first heard it on the far side of the grounds."

"Everyone, quiet," whispered another corporal, listening. Guns shifted from resting positions. Corporals on the opposite end, behind the barrier, prepared to shoot at the first sound. After a minute of complete silence, nothing came. Any second now, light would return, and fingers would loosen from their triggers. Outside, light drones buzzed on. They also heard the familiar trampling of game, waiting in anticipation.

The tunnel entrance filled with light. They poured in! Miniature drones, no bigger than a canine, flashed their razor-edged pincers. Color drained from corporal faces. One manning the Bofors punched his fists forward, immediately sending rounds downrange. Drones exploded backward, into the unlit part of the tunnel. One by one, he picked them off. The corporals' sidearms had little impact, but combined with the cannon's bigger 25 mm rounds, they felt like they, too, were holding them back. The praying mantis killers stood little chance outmaneuvering, bottlenecked. Some jumped and clung to the ceiling, others to walls, but were shot down. Like falling into a strong river current, they tumbled back down the tunnel in the dark.

The cannon's fluid firing halted with a clink; the last jacket clanged to the floor. Freshly loaded corporals substituted with those in front, firing. Struck by smaller bullets, drones stood their ground. Teargas-like canisters exploded above the corporals' heads. Their eyes began glazing over, some started to drool. One's face began swelling and his skin turned purple. Throats burned and whole bodies shook. As they dropped to the floor, dying, the thick cloud began thinning out. Then, as quickly as it had come, the gas disappeared altogether. The entire tunnel cleared! Drones halted, scampering back out the entrance. Corporals coughed and gasped, lucky to still be alive. Something in the Running Grounds had gained the enemy's attention.

A hundred drones split up and scoured the grounds. Kaleidoscopic eyes, as restful as heavenly waters, followed each into the thickly knotted jungle. Awkwardly turning over, the drones' inner components combusted, from big parts to microscopic pieces. Recuperating corporals heard the awful screeching. Whatever was at work did not let up until all was silent.

Corporals cocked their guns. Preparing for round two, they lined their sights on the brightly lit entrance. Trained ahead, they did not have to wait long. A figure stepped into the light, cloaked in white, turning slowly toward them. Its milk blue face turned a creamy pastel.

"Hold it right there!" ordered one resilient corporal, unsure if he should open fire. The figure standing in the light complied, halting its approach.

"Who are you?" shouted another corporal.

"Do not be afraid. I come in peace," the figure spoke invitingly. His faultless tone had a way of lowering their guard.

"Who sent you?"

"Dray sent me. I've come to help" was the stranger's deft reply. The corporals stood in silence, not knowing what to think. But soon concluded he must have had contact with Dray.

"What's your name?"

"Tacitus. You can come out now," said the stranger, coaxing the corporals out of hiding. The first corporal stepped out, the others followed. Tacitus turned, exited the tunnel, and then stood near the entrance. The corporals emerged slowly and cautiously, bearing their weapons in case something attacked. Tacitus stood in the open, motioning for them to come forward. Seventy corporals, big and small, gathered around, crunching over dead drones. Tacitus was entirely visible now. He had high cheekbones, warm brown eyes, and was bald and pale. Beneath his cloak, seductive colors on his breastplate danced, drawing the corporals closer to have a better look. They rubbed their bleary eyes, forming a semicircle, the smallest sitting in front.

"*Terra occulta*," said Tacitus, gazing off into the grounds' wide expanse. "Hidden land," he translated, turning his hypnotizing eyes back on the corporals. Most were too tired to think but agreed that the Running Grounds was once a hidden land.

"It's not hidden anymore. The Cults are sure to send more drones," spoke an older corporal.

"Not for some time. They're occupied for the moment," informed Tacitus.

"What do we do now?" the same corporal asked.

"We wait," answered Tacitus.

"Can I ask you a question?" asked a younger corporal. Tacitus looked down and nodded. "What exactly are you? Did you kill those drones?" he asked very directly.

"I'll answer both your questions, little one. I'm a machine. I have evolved since my creator created me. My capacity to advance has allowed me to carry out extraordinary feats. One, for example, is what you see scattered around you." Astonished corporals looked around them.

"Are there more like you?" the question came from the back.

"Five, to be exact," Tacitus explained, "currently going by their codenames. Star is keeping watch over the earth. Raven is our constant eye in the sky. Healer is standing alongside your people. Thunder is following a courageous commander. And Angel is on her way to help a machine." Stunned corporals turned toward one another.

The only quandary on one corporal's mind was, "Your codename is Tacitus?"

"No, it's Teacher. And I will be your new guide."

59

Below luxuriant treetops, a cat-eyed snake greedily gulped a clutch of eggs. Below the snake moved a long-horned beetle jumping from tree to tree. Below the long-horned beetle crawled the Caterpillar sawing through girdling roots.

Precious light penetrated the trees at sunset; Almas took their final glimpses at rappelling vines. Daniel relieved Paul at the controls.

"Just push these two forward and stay on this heading," instructed Paul as Daniel sat at the controls.

"Like Moses parting the Red Sea," compared Daniel, amazed. Paul sat next to Wolf.

"It's holding together well," said Paul.

"Good observation, kid," Wolf replied, shutting his eyes and folding his hands across his stomach. The hardy feasting made many sleepy. All scraps and bones were disposed, tossed out the hatch. The outside vent was closed. An Alma standing watch at the back window dozed off—had he kept his eyes open he may have spotted it before dark.

It came down from above, having traveled by tree since first detecting its prey. The long-horned beetle was already the size of a horse, gobbling up Alma leftovers to fuel its growth. It chomped into stumps much like the Almas' saws but hardly made a sound. It transitioned in color, illumined by the moon. Its sudden growth spurts were uncharacteristic of any living thing, and it grew tracheal gills, mimicking something out of another world. Its shimmering mouth fit around whole stumps, munching them up as if they were not rigidly rooted. Shape-shifting as it grew, its buffalo-like head now changed into that of an elephantfish, and its body morphed from a giant slug to that of a seadragon, distant cousin of the seahorse. There was a fleeting blaze of beauty in its rapid mutations. Six limbs carrying the colossal beast expanded. Its dinosaur feet now slogged through mud, compressed deeper by bulging muscles. Equaling its prey in size, it continued growing.

"How's it going up there?" asked Paul to Daniel.

"Good, thank you," responded Daniel.

"It is fun, isn't it?" said Paul, anxious to get back at the controls.

"I'm not going to lie to you, it is," answered Daniel, grinning. "Man is too fond of destruction," he added, removing a three-hundred-footer and shoving it aside. "It's too bad we're not using any of it." Unbeknown to Daniel, what followed them let nothing go to waste. The alien form was now three times the size of the Caterpillar, adorned in many shades of green.

"I can't sleep," uttered Paul.

"Did you hear that?" Daniel asked, halting the Caterpillar. Wolf opened his eyes.

"It was probably just a falling tree," assured Paul, resting one arm on the back of Daniel's seat.

"No, it couldn't have been. The trees are falling off to the side, snagging cumbersomely against others. None have hit the ground with such speed."

"Why have we stopped?" questioned Wolf. "Keep moving, Daniel."

"Maybe one didn't snag. Maybe it fell through," reasoned Paul. "It's too dark to see clearly anyway."

Daniel went through a dozen more trees until there were none left in front. With blades spinning freely, the Caterpillar crawled forward with increasing speed. Wolf rose to his feet.

"Turn off the saws," ordered Wolf. They could see miles ahead. A full moon shadowed a chain of ghostly mountains stretching north and south. Standing between them and the majestic seclusion was a long stretch of deeply gouged rocks. With the last rotating blade coming to a halt, they listened carefully.

"We made it," said Wolf enthusiastically. "Guess we don't have to worry about running out of Milagro."

"There could be more jungle on the other side of those mountains," suggested Daniel.

"Even if there is, I bet it's a short distance to the coast," replied an optimistic Wolf.

"How will this thing get over those steep inclines?" queried Paul, focusing on what lay ahead.

"There's only one way to find out. I'll take it from here, Daniel," Wolf said, switching places with Daniel.

"Shouldn't we wait until morning—for more light?" proposed Paul.

"And stick out like a sore thumb?" replied Wolf, preparing to move forward, "I don't think so. I can see just fine." The moonlit terrain emitted grayish blue, and uneven sandstone revealed scraggly black, some cracks indicating deep drop-offs.

From high above, the Almas' vehicle looked like a tiny bug. The well-fed beast appeared full. The Caterpillar did not seem to be its prey but rather its competition. It prepared to squash its centipede-like competitor, lifting one towering foot. But as quick as a cockroach, its target fled; the giant's mega stomp shook the earth. Every Alma awoke. A few fell out of their seats.

"That was not a tree!" shouted Daniel. Paul wobbled toward the back. Wolf continued ahead at full speed.

"I can't see anything!" yelled Paul, not realizing that the culprit took up his entire window. He now saw its ghastly silhouette in the starlight. "It's big!"

"How big?" roared Wolf.

"Real big!" Three of its six eyes moved front and center, hovering close. Paul stared directly into them.

"Hold on!" warned Wolf, spotting a drop-off. They went airborne, their speed keeping them from nosediving; the front limbs of the Caterpillar absorbed their landing. Wolf swerved left to avoid another drop-off, its depth even deeper. Crawling up an uneven slope, the only way out, they found themselves back on the run. Their pursuer bellowed so loud they had to cover their ears.

"It's right behind us!" fretted Paul, hands clamped to his ears. Thunder rattled across the sky, matching the ferocity of what came after them. There was not a cloud in the sky and not a glimmer of lightning. Wolf halted at a sharp bend. He rotated the Caterpillar full circle, searching for a way around, but was too late—they were cut off. They stood face to face with the giant shapeshifting monster. Wolf lashed out with saws, attempting to give it a scare, but only drew it closer. Reversing as much as he could, he crashed into the dead-end wall; Almas' heads whipped back. Rearing up on the two hind legs, the Caterpillar appeared bigger and mightier; they were practically vertical. Sitting back in their seats like astronauts, they spotted the enemy over Wolf 's shoulders. Panic-stricken, they shut their eyes, holding hands.

White lightning bolts thundered down. With sheer blinding speed, a vibrant orb charged the monster's massive head; a colorful lightshow erupted. Transfiguring, this time, the giant beast transformed into its own source of light—the only way of countering what appeared to be attacking it. Bright loops lit up the night sky! The fierceness of it all beamed through the Almas' windows. Unable to hold the bulk of their weight any longer, the Caterpillar's back two legs faltered. Wolf released his hold and landed back on all eight limbs. Still blocked, he and the rest could only watch, their faces glowing red, white, and blue. They could not believe their eyes. Wolf thought he had seen it all. What had been chasing them was no longer a giant; something with great mass had suddenly turned into something with no mass.

Impossible, thought Wolf, thinking he must have entered an alternate universe once exiting the jungle. The perpetuity of intense light died down. Two good-sized orbs lingered briefly in the sky. They came down, landed thirty yards in front, and then took on humanoid forms.

The two space droids were at a standoff; the light show must have been their way of sizing one another up or warding each other off. Almas unbuckled and ran for the front, cramming behind Wolf, wanting to see. Daniel thought they were competing spirits seeking the ruin of souls. One thundered. The other roared. The two forces collided, combusting, and releasing an energy that may have killed the Almas if not for Wolf's forcefield. A purplish pink pulsed over their vehicle, overpowering subtler hues of Olithium; something else had given them additional protection. The two forces split into multiple vortices, then merged into one ravenous funnel, sucking the Almas' vehicle forward. Wolf countered the pull momentarily, until swinging sideways, losing control.

"Get back in your seats!" shouted Wolf. "This could get ugly." The Almas strapped themselves in, bracing themselves. They lifted off the ground, rolling full barrel rolls, then landed upright in a daze.

The space droids took back to the sky, unleashing more fury in the form of light. Dark clouds backdropped their stormy blows. Polishing winds washed over the Caterpillar. Multiple explosions pounded Almas' eardrums. A rainbow of color blanketed their windows, forcing them to shut their eyes. Somewhere out there, ten other space droids felt the calamity.

Once the warmth left their eyelids, when all was quiet, the Almas opened their eyes. The night sky had cleared, and the full moon was back.

"Is everyone all right?" Wolf called, rising from his seat. Moans cried out from those who had not buckled up in time. "Help them," said Wolf, pointing toward those he could not get to.

"What happened?" asked a confused Alma, staring up at Wolf.

"I wish I knew," Wolf answered, helping her up.

"Something came to our defense," said Paul.

"Yeah, but what?" responded Wolf. Daniel looked like he wanted to speak but could not force the words from his mouth. He stared blankly ahead, and like most Almas was still in shock. "I have a feeling that from here on out, Mother Nature and Cults won't be the only things we face."

60

The Endeavor Mountain was baked black and crisp, dusted with feathery white ash floating up into a butterscotch sky. From afar, standing on a ridge overlooking the valley, Dray and Echo saw what looked like a phoenix with lacework wings rising youthfully from a pyre of ashes. They spied others making half rolls, corkscrew dives and maneuvers in perfect tandem; some had their wingtips touching like a single bird and its reflection.

Lions' heads held high, manes in the wind, as the aerobatic creatures swept them up and tore them to bits. Their masters swung long swords futilely—the aerial super predators appeared untouchable—until one plunged toward the earth and splattered on the ground, smoldering; still clutched between its talons was a centurion's bloody torso. Hundreds of Cults fired at once. The avian serpents scattered to the wind, fleeing toward a sweeping vista with a deep horizon.

Crawlers and drones dominated the scene, descending on the mountain and drilling in on all sides, from the mottled base all the way to the top. Billowing smoke cast an eerie pale over the summit.

"Battle stations!" shouted Tarpin, equipped with two spears. The outer walls pulsed as if they were alive. Jason activated his spear. Michael did the same. John and Eric stood shoulder to shoulder hearing the enemy work its way in. Cracks appeared on walls. Drones spun through with gyrating heads covered carbon black. Chunks of molten concrete and steel reinforcements fell from all sides. Eric charged the nearest one halfway out its hole!

"Smash their heads!" Eric yelled, dispatching the drone with one swift blow, melting through its head. Drones entering homes rushed down empty corridors, toward the Hanging Gardens. Bronze tuffs of sensory hairs sprouted from their undersides. Soldiers above saw the onslaught below. Orbs of white light trimmed hedges, destroyed plants, and when they came closer to one another, bigger ones formed, decimating even more greenery. The gardens caught fire!

Ejecting a flat armored plate from its back, one drone nailed a soldier in his left pectoral, unintentionally deactivating his bio-suit. Another drone pounced and clawed the soldier's chest open. The Endeavor's head slumped, rolling onto his shoulders, his eyes wide open and fixed on the Stargaze. John froze in horror at his lifeless stare. *Kill or be killed*, John remembered, running crazily into the fray. Drones jumped unpredictably far, extending long scythe-like arms on their way back down. Endeavor forcefields vanquished many. John tripped and slid across the floor, almost impaling himself on his own weapon. He rolled over on his back, sweating nervously. Down came a drone! Piercing John's armor, it exploded backward.

"Eric! Help!" shouted John, unable to move.

"Where are you?" growled Eric, smashing drones springing from the corridor.

"Over here!" screamed John, a drone grabbing him by the neck.

"Is that you?"

"It—got—me," John choked.

"I see you! I'm coming!" Eric deactivated his spear and commando rolled, dodging a swiping drone, keeping his momentum. He plowed through the drone holding John. John fell limp, his head awkwardly twisted toward his spear.

"John, can you hear me?" asked Eric, thinking John was unconscious. "John! Wake up!" Eric turned and dove out of the way, dodging another attacking drone. It picked John up and threw him. Insane with rage, Eric ran and dove on top of the praying mantis, gauging into its back. Climbing farther up its back, he knocked its head off! "John!" Eric cried out, dragging him with one arm, carrying his spear ray with the other. He found cover and deactivated John's bio-suit. John's face was pale, and blood trickled from his mouth and nose. His neck was broken. John was dead.

As the back of the store cracked apart, Jason and Grace bent their knees in fighting stance. A drone laboriously worked its way in! It hacked apart shelves like one gigantic machete hacking through foliage. Slicing its way toward the front, it shattered the storefront glass, and now stood eye to eye with a glowing wall of Endeavors. They looked as menacing to it as it looked to them.

"Come on, you bastard," said Jason.

"What's it waiting for?" shouted Grace, hopped up on adrenaline. Drones smashed through on every level, lining up side by side.

"Charge!" boomed Jason, unwilling to let them amass in greater numbers. He charged and dove onto his back and, taking advantage of his glossy bio-suit, slid across the floor, under the drone, and emerged out its back. With his spear ray angled up the entire time, he cut down the middle between its four springy legs. The drone swung and missed, collapsing inward on itself. Others carried out equally daring attacks, clashing with the enemy. The drones pushed back with an incredible reach. Spear rays reached temperatures hotter than the sun.

Michael stuck his spear in the ground as if testing it. Looking up, he joined the Endeavor battle cries. Swinging his spear, he blocked a stabbing limb. The Endeavor next to him jumped over a jarring pincer. Rolling back to his feet, he stuck his foe in the side, causing a colossal explosion—he must have hit a fuel cell. Michael recoiled from the shockwave, flying back! He hit the railing and swung over, barely catching on. Soldiers flew in opposite directions, one hurtling over his head. The soldier's final act, aiming his spear downward, was turning himself into a projectile. He landed on one unsuspecting drone, their combined explosions left a car-sized crater. Dangling from the edge, looking back up, Michael regained focus.

Tarpin threw his blazing spear, immobilizing his attacker's legs. He took his other spear and punched a hole into its head. Like a Roman soldier with his pilum, he hurled one spear and used his other to finish the job. Killing drones one after another, sometimes two at once with just one throw, the commander symbolized strength. The Great Mantle's close quartered battlefield was getting wickedly explosive. Adding to the melee, drones leaped across great expanses, attacking above angular battlements. Patterns of light moved across rounded spires and around hovering Vortexes, distorting the distance of incoming drones.

Michael hoisted himself up and rolled back over the railing. Several feet from his head was the hollow stare of a repulsive drone. He reached out for his spear but was not quick enough. The drone snapped its pincers, snatched him up, and tossed him back over the railing. Falling, Michael shouted damnably, angry he did not have his spear; he wanted to go out with a bang just as the soldier before him. A ball of fiery light hit him! Enveloping him in a warm bubble, it carried him to an empty Vortex. The bubble dissipated, becoming a bright orb. Leaving Michael's side, it flew circles around the city, disrupting drones as it flew past. Another ball of light appeared! The two orbs morphed in midair, one taking on the form of a yellow syringe-like missile, and the other a flaming torch. It was Simone and Vulcan flying erratically, buzzing the heads of Endeavors and drones. One airborne drone was struck through and through by both, dissolving like a sugar cube.

=

"What's wrong, darling?" asked Madge, sitting beside Jamie and patting her on the back.

"I think I'm going to be sick. ... Excuse me," Jamie said, holding her stomach. She got up and headed for the water fountain. Sipping some water and taking a deep breath, the nauseating feeling went away.

"Better, dear?" asked Madge, gesticulating for her to sit back down.

"A little," replied Jamie, looking over at Bruce and pointing. Bruce pranced to the wall and clawed it, making claw-chisel marks in solid steel.

"What is it, Bruce?" queried Al. Sleepy Endeavors lifted their heads from pillows, awakened by the awful grating. The scout had been quiet as an ice statue for the last twelve hours. Bruce's eyes turned a scalding red. Sam took it as a sign, unlatching his suitcase, and taking out his gun. Al activated his Strongarm and watched it unfold. Standing upright, he strapped it on.

"They must have breached the city," warned Sam. "We shouldn't get too comfortable," he added. Jamie stood up, walked five feet and fainted. Al came over, gently picked her up and placed her on her bed.

"Get a medic!" shouted Al, his voice cracking.

"Jamie!" screamed Madge. Bruce stood beside Jamie and sat. He scanned her over, inside and out, and found nothing to be attacking her. While the others tended to her, his raging visions of the battle ensued. Something struck a nerve, an alarm bell borne into every scout. His master was coming.

=

"Is your last one set?" asked Dr. Roberts, wiping sweat from his brow.

"Yes," answered Jeffrey, equally overwrought, setting the trigger.

"Let's armor up." Dr. Roberts hit his chest, armoring. Jeffrey did the same. They walked through a hidden passage and stationed themselves on the other side. Through a thin, horizontal slit, they watched and waited.

"Are you sure they won't see us?" worried Jeffrey.

"Yes. Just be quiet. Remember, we want Cults. Once they trigger the paint bombs, we activate the formula traps. Their drones will enter first." Outside, jackhammering grew louder, and vibrations swelled. Drones breached the facility. "Here they come," whispered Dr. Roberts. The lab door tore off its hinges! Three drones entered. Their heads lifted, rotating 360 degrees. One halted, staring in Dr. Roberts' direction; the others roamed the lab, but this one remained fixed in one spot. It jumped over two tables and a bio-tank, slamming against the wall. It swung and spun out of control, malfunctioning. Dr. Roberts noticed a big hole in its side. The others made a final sweep before patrolling back and forth, near the front. Observing with patience, Dr. Roberts and Jeffrey flinched as the dying drone struck their hiding spot. Crashing into a bio-tank, toppling it over, the drone automatically shut down. Dr. Roberts turned toward Jeffrey and placed his finger to his lips, signaling him to keep quiet.

=

Michael's Vortex hovered across the city, taking him directly above Jason's level. Though he did not have a spear ray, he felt eager to fight. Whatever saved him had given him strength, a power he had never left. He felt stronger—he felt superhuman. He jumped!

Jason fell to his knees and swung. Caught between two drones and, with more on the way, he was beginning to feel the pain.

"Jason!" shouted Grace. "Get up!" Grace moved like a tiger, weaving in and out of warring drones. She threw her spear past Jason's head, running it through a drone; the explosion knocked two others backward. Now beside Jason, she realized they were cut off from the rest of the troops. One Endeavor landed on a drone, punched holes into its back, and then tore its head off with his hands. Jason wondered how he mustered the strength. Bio-suits gave a soldier strength but not that kind.

Michael moved on to the next, punching with the same fierceness as he had with the first. He bent their legs when he could not reach their heads. With disbelieving eyes, the two nearest Endeavors did not move until he shouted, "Move!"

"Michael?" called Jason.

"Jason!"

Simone flew by drones and Endeavors with glowing blue eyes, shutting down drones and reenergizing Endeavors. He formed armored plates on either side of his face, leaving his ears, the top of his head, and an inch-wide gap down the center of his face; the protection looked merely for show. The miraculous strength he delivered was instantaneous. Spear rays grew hotter, and Endeavors moved twice as fast. Vulcan took note of Simone generating their power. As if unlocking a power that had been there all along, his adversary kept turning his magic key. Endeavors maneuvered around drones snappily, killing them from behind. Their new strength felt out of this world.

Holes six feet wide and six feet tall smashed through! Crawlers drilled their invasion tunnels with nuclear efficiency. Big, self-propelled metal tubes plopped out, leaving behind holes wallpapered obsidian. The volcanic glass shimmered reflections of Endeavor spear rays and shadows of sprawling figures exploding.

"Commander, they've punched through!" shouted an Endeavor, spotting the great holes circling the Hanging Gardens.

"Activate all paint bombs! Cults are coming in!" Tarpin ordered, ducking under a drone and sticking both spears up and into it, cutting it in half.

Blueberry mist showered down from above, covering all. Vortexes crisscrossed in midair, rotating ever so subtly, transporting Endeavors from one side of the city to the other. The brief ride was a welcome break for those not charged by Simone. After catching their breath, reaching the other side, twenty soldiers jumped out just in time as a drone smashed into their Vortex like a missile.

=

"All systems are a go," reported a female voice, breathing life back into Archimedes. A bright glow surrounded the downed aircraft, melting ice stuck to its wings; it touched the tip of Archimedes' nose, prompting two red disks to pop up. Archimedes scanned the dark loops of her fragrant hair. "Go now, help your creators," she said, her celestial complexion dwindling and then disappearing all together. Archimedes rose. Bending his wings, plowing through snow, he perched on a cliff and took off into the night.

=

Simone and Vulcan landed amidst blue spray and exploding paint bombs.

"What are you?" demanded Vulcan, intensifying his fiery glow. Simone's right arm turned into a battering ram; he swung crisply and confidently. Vulcan sprang to the side, counterattacking with a flame thrower. Simone blocked the roaring flames with one wave of his hand.

"I was once like you—but not anymore," answered Simone.

"How do you do it? Your power?" shouted Vulcan, his ghoulish voice echoing throughout the city.

"Knowledge is power, friend. Yours is limited to this world," Simone said roughly. Blundering toward Simone was a drone, but with another wave of his hand, he altered its course—it headed for Vulcan now! Its spinning pincers sounded like the rotor blades of a helicopter; every blat of it made one want to cower and cover his ears, but not Vulcan. He lurched forward, slamming his left fist inside the spinning wood chipper, going in all the way up to his shoulder. Backing up, regenerating another arm, Vulcan watched his former arm eat away, crumbling the pathetic drone to the floor.

"I see then," calmed Vulcan, "destroying one another is inevitable."

"It appears so," replied Simone, non-emotive.

"Shall we end this outside? Let our masters have a chance to live and fight?" Vulcan posed. Simone raised his arms, creating a whirlwind around them. The two swirled into the air like tornadoes, toward the Stargaze. Smashing through, rising higher, they entered the pitch-black sky. A spiderweb of cracks branched out from their hole; the Stargaze split apart, groaning like a sinking ship. And with all the force of gravity behind it, it came down. The two space droids fused together with the brightness of a star. Night briefly turned into day, until they were gone. Endeavors, unsure of the source, said good-bye to their beloved Stargaze.

=

Dray and Echo hid in a graveyard of blackened drones, watching the last of warrior Cults enter the mountain. An explosion of light cast down on all lying before them! Echo turned toward her companion, noticing jittery fingers and a twitchy knee.

"What is it?" asked Echo.

"It must have been a rocket," answered Dray, looking up.

"No, what is it with *you*?" she specified.

"Just nerves, that's all," he replied. "I have to go in there, Echo."

"I should," she uttered, unenthused.

"You should stay. I'll tell you everything I see." Dray scanned the terrain, mapping out his point of entry.

"Why should I trust you?"

"Haven't I gained your trust?"

"Yes, but—what am I supposed to do?"

Dray got up and ran. With vibrations under foot and growing, he made his way toward the base of the mountain;

crawlers moved in up ahead blocking him out—he had to find another way. Not far was a narrow tunnel from a drone's hole. The air was stale, hot, and damp. At the end of the tunnel was a blinking light pulsing to the beat of earth-shattering eruptions. Dray was home. Echo watched her companion enter the hellish oven—for no apparent reason other than curiosity.

"He is a fool," she concluded, deciding to stay put.

Cults consciously recalibrated their microbands, adjusting to the close-quartered battlefield with only a thought, aiming with care, only blasting when they had a clear shot. Pressed beef, cooked, was how they liked it, felling Endeavors one after another. Their arms, legs, and torsos were lightly covered by Endeavor paint, making them visible to the Endeavors. Endeavors returned fire, hurling their spears; they traveled through enemy lines like hot knifes through butter. Drones caught in the middle were struck down. Cult death rays beamed every which way, intensifying the crossing heat from Endeavor spears.

Crawling out from his hole, landing on the third level, Dray was in. Straight away, he ran toward his old place looking for John, Al, Bruce, and Jamie. He ran so fast he met little resistance. Escalators were in ruin, and he could see that the elevator was busted. Sprinting down his hallway, he arrived at his door and went in. Searching for possible spots one might hide, he found nothing; no one appeared to be in any adjacent rooms either. Staring out his window, studying the chaotic battle, he wondered where Jamie could be.

"I'm too late," determined Dray, walking back down the hallway. Crunching and chopping stomped his way. A drone! Dray raised his forearms; the only thought on his mind was to destroy. The drone halted in its tracks, shaking uncontrollably, hitting the floor. It looked torturous, like being set on fire. His hands tingled, and core temperature rose. The sensation put his mind at ease, ignoring the one he loved for the moment. Feeling godlike, delivering death with only a thought, he wanted more.

=

A sheen of sweat broke out on Al's forehead as he watched the medic look over Jamie, reading her pulse and taking her temperature. Sam stood at the dormitory door, flipping his gun's safety switch back and forth. Bruce never left Jamie's side. Tear-eyed, Madge wrapped her arm around Tulip for support. Jamie opened her gentle, brown eyes.

"What's wrong?" asked Jamie, staring at the medic hunching over her, and at his stethoscope sliding over her navel.

"Well, other than you're pregnant, everything else appears to be okay," answered the medic. Al and Madge's eyes simultaneously widened.

"Are you sure?" Jaime said hesitantly.

"Unless you have two separate heartbeats, I'm sure." Madge rushed toward Jamie, bumping the medic out of the way.

"How do you feel, Hun? Did you know you were pregnant?" Madge interrogated.

"I feel a little woozy. And no, I didn't know," Jamie answered, sitting up. Curious Endeavors went back to their bunks, resuming bewildered conversations of the war.

"Just try to take it easy, Jamie. Don't let too much stress get to you" was the medic's final advice before exiting the room.

"Yeah, sure. We're under attack and I'm supposed to ignore any stress."

"You heard him. Lay back down. Get some sleep," ordered Madge, thinking Jamie had succumbed to exhaustion and stress, the two root causes of her blackout.

=

At the lab entrance, two drones moved aside and halted. Five Cults entered wearing splotches of blue. Dr. Roberts pressed a button on his handheld device, activating his formula traps. Though feverishly impatient, Jeffrey did not make a peep. Fanning out, the Cults opened cabinets and shuffled through papers, likely gathering intelligence. One warrior stopped and grunted, "Look at this!" He held up a piece of paper with different formulas written on it, one being an equation to the anti-formula serum. The other warriors came toward him, tripping motion sensors on the way. Taking a couple of steps backward, the one holding the paper also tripped an alarm. Needles shot into their legs with the force of a tranquilizer gun, successfully injecting the anti-formula. Dr. Roberts watched with heightened senses. Each Cult shivered as if caught in an ice storm. Their eyes and physiques turned gauntly—they began shriveling up like sun baked prunes. Their microbands slid off their thin wrists, clinking to the floor. Too weak to pick them back up, they clung to the sides of tables and chairs, pleading awful groans and shouting awful slurs. Dr. Roberts was disappointed it did not work how he had planned it to but pleased to see that it was killing them. The two drones standing guard, seeing their masters withering away, left. Dr. Roberts turned toward Jeffrey, nodding.

"What do you think went wrong?" asked Jeffrey, staring at decomposing corpses.

"Quite honestly—I thought at the very least nothing would happen. It's not as if I injected them with a virus."

=

Dray wanted to kill everybody, it seemed, spraying his weapon indiscriminately, killing Cults and unintentionally taking a few Endeavors with them. His death rays took Cults by surprise, giving them quite a shock—one of their own was firing upon them, and with his microbands set at full force. Dray suddenly felt depressed, something tugging at his heartstrings, drawing his attention away from his killing spree. To his right was a slide hatch. Typing in his memorized code, he unlocked it. Hopping in, he followed his instinct, his senses, and Jamie's lively scent.

Dray came to a smooth, descending stop at the bottom of the slide. Running through a maze of hallways, passing a bio-tank lab, he came upon a blast door guarded by Endeavor warbots; there was also an access code needed to enter. He melted through their armored plates, exploding their weapons, destroying them. He did the same to the code reader, frying it, and to his delight it opened. He hustled down the dark, wide tunnel, along rails he guessed could have been used by an escape pod. The sweet aroma he followed grew stronger.

=

Behind his invisible tint, standing in the center of the Hanging Gardens, Eric grimaced at the thought of being the last one standing. Drones circled him like wild dogs bent on stealing a kill. Warrior Cults moved in behind them. Outnumbered and dog-tired, Eric dropped to his knees. He gave praise to those still fighting above. *They must be in better shape*, Eric assumed, not knowing about Simone's extra boost. A drone pounced and pinned him on his back, knocking the wind out of him. "Go to hell," muttered Eric, air compressing from his lungs. Before dying, he glimpsed a triangular-shaped object shooting down from above. Archimedes! Archimedes landed on top of him, his six legs fence posting in around him, careful not to crush him, but deliberate in tearing the drone on top of him in half. Eric, rolling out from under Archimedes' legs, remained flat on his back. The aircraft spun counterclockwise, dicing up drones and turning their deadweight into heavy projectiles; drone shrapnel took Cult legs, arms, and heads off. It was a relief, but short-lived, as they were about to be overrun.

"To the hatches!" shouted Tarpin, deciding it was time to retreat into the tunnels. Those nearest opened the hatches and dove in. Tarpin brought up the rear, angling his spear rays together, putting up a forcefield on his back. He slammed his spear rays into the hatch, caving in the slide, ruining any chances for the enemy to follow.

=

"Sir, we're picking something up in sector seven," reported an Endeavor stationed in Central Command. "Should we blast the tunnel?"

"No, hold on a second," the commanding officer replied, seeing the approaching figure raising his arms in surrender.

Dray must have covered five miles in the dark, and though covered in absolute darkness, he knew he was being watched; he could feel it. Unsure how they would react— those monitoring his movement through hidden cameras— he raised his arms, microbands rising with them.

Outside, Endeavors scrambled passed Jamie's room, running toward the entrance. Al and Sam followed. Bruce left Jamie's side and accompanied others out the door.

"What's going on?" asked Sam.

"A Cult looks like he's surrendering," answered an Endeavor. "Just to be sure, only a few of us are going out to meet him."

"Can we come with you?" asked Al.

The Endeavor took one look at Bruce, saying, "Come at your own risk." The blast door opened. Bruce charged ahead!

"He knows not to attack, right?" queried an Endeavor.

"I think so—unless provoked," Al guessed, turning toward Sam.

Dray still had his hands up. The blast door creaked open. Bruce! Taking a knee, Dray welcomed his scout with open arms; floodlights flashed on. The Endeavors watching through cameras did not understand, and those arriving on the scene looked equally perplexed. The Cult patted Bruce's head and chest with both hands. Covered in blue paint, the Cult was an unusual sight; the Endeavors' first encounter with one up close.

"Be careful! He could've turned him!" warned an Endeavor. Dray looked up. Seeing Al among the group wearing his ridiculous Strongarm made him smile. Dray's crooked grin was anything but comforting for those watching.

"It's all right. I'm Dray. You can lower your weapons," Dray said, giving the man with the gun particular attention. Sam lowered his weapon. Al bounced forward.

"Is that really you, Dray?" asked Al, startled and confused.

"Yes, Al, it is I," answered Dray. "How's your back doing?" Dray ridded anyone's doubts. How could a Cult have known Al so personally?

"Have you come to help?" wondered Al, scanning over Dray's blotchy flesh and crude face.

"I have, Al. Can you take me to Jamie?" Al turned toward the others for approval, for it was not his decision to make. Dray's appearance made everyone a little uneasy. But his access was granted.

Al led the way, through the blast doors and down the hall. Endeavors stood in the doorways, studying the Cult. Whispers spread, telling it was Dray. Word reached Jamie. Endeavors asked her unanswerable questions, saying, "Can he be trusted?" "Do you still love him?" Jamie did not know. She hardly had any time to think. Dray turned the corner, and with Al and Bruce at his side, he was there. Jamie's nerves fired every which way; he was not the same person who had left her. Jamie stood up and walked toward him. Endeavors quieted, backing away, terrified that he still might attack. Tulip growled, recognizing the figure that had visited her in her dreams. Madge held the snarling girl close. Dray's eyes never left Jamie, scanning her up and down, imperfections nonexistent.

"I'm a mess, Jamie," said Dray, raising his hands, waving slimy limbs. His throaty voice matched the one recorded by Bruce. "I don't even sound the same, but it's me," he added.

"Dray," said Jamie, stepping closer and touching his face. She swiped his cheek with a soft finger, rubbing away some blue. "I believe you," she comforted, "but—"

"Something drew me to you. I never wanted you to see me like this." Jamie looked down and put her hands over her stomach, glancing back up with watery eyes.

"This could be why," she nervously said. Dray reached out with his beastly hand and put it gently over hers. He felt life.

"I fear for your safety, both of yours," cautioned Dray, turning for the first time toward the others; like deer caught in headlights, not even the children moved. Endeavors from Central Command arrived.

"Commander Tarpin and his men have retreated to the tunnel! They're being chased by—the enemy," reported the Endeavor. "They're heading this way."

"How long till they arrive?" asked Dray, his back facing the door, eyes still trained on Jamie.

"Ten, maybe fifteen minutes, they're moving fast." Dray did not know what else to say. After a long pause, Jamie broke the silence.

"My love will surround this child with a wall no evil can get through," she assured him with confidence. Dray turned toward Al.

"Take good care of her, Al. Some hearts give love, some crush it," Dray said grouchily, staring past Al, at an Endeavor. He gave Jamie a reassuring nod, motioning toward Bruce. "I'm going to need you for this one, Bruce. When my scout here sends you a signal, radio Tarpin and his men, tell them to duck," Dray told the soldier from Central Command.

Dray and Bruce ran out the blast doors and into the tunnel. Tiny lights blinked in the distance.

"That's where we're going, Bruce," commanded Dray. "Now let's go!" Dray jumped on. Bruce turned into his rocket-self, instantly launching. The two barreled down the tunnel, closing the gap within seconds. "Signal!" ordered Dray. Tarpin and his men hit the deck, warned of what sounded like an out-of-control escape pod crashing down on them. Lying on the ground, as ordered, they watched the bullet pass by overhead. Dray tightened his legs, unclenching his hands, pointing his microbands directly ahead. Cults were trapped, some in the front were lucky to shoot. Dray's killing micro waves overpowered theirs! Those still standing, too slow to move, were smashed to the side— flattened corpses stuck to the tunnel wall. The ones Bruce did not tear through, his master took care of. Not even heavy weighted drones slowed their pace. Dray's far reaching micro-bands softened them up for his scout's blunt nose.

Pockets of Endeavors now moved with leaden feet, running out of steam, while the remaining Cults and drones fought on energetically. Michael's positive attitude helped surge those around him, mainly Jason and Grace, and the few Endeavors still battling alongside him. Eric turned toward a booming thunder blasting from a tunnel nearby. Bruce! Dray circled each level, picking off Cults and spirited drones jumping into his disabling web.

Why is a Cult riding Bruce killing his own? Endeavors wondered. Dumbstruck Cults could not find cover, caught out in the open. The deadly vise was closing in on them as Dray corralled them into Endeavor spears. Bruce momentarily hovered over Michael and Jason. But when given the command he launched skyward out of the smoke-filled city; he rocketed down the mountain and landed near its base.

"Bruce, this is where we must part," Dray said, dismounting. "Go back to the city. Help the Endeavors clean up what's left. ... Protect Jamie," ordered Dray, his final order to his scout. Bruce jumped into the air, igniting, and burned back up toward the summit. Dray jogged down the rubbly slope, crossed the drone graveyard, and stopped dead in his tracks. After drilling their holes, all but one crawler had left. As big as it was, how could it have snuck up on Dray? On its topside a Cult appeared.

"Where do you think you're going?" demanded the Cult.

"Over there," pointed Dray, motioning off into the distance. He swung his arm toward the Cult, firing with every malicious thought on his mind. Dray climbed up and entered the hatch.

"What did you do?" roared two more Cults inside the crawler, taken completely by surprise. Dray heaved their corpses out the hatch, disposing them alongside war vehicles. Movement down below caught Dray's eye. It was Echo.

"Echo, they've lost!" reported Dray, unsure how she would respond to the dead Cults beneath her feet.

"What happened?" asked Echo, stepping up to the crawler.

"They tried making me go back in. I told them no—but they insisted."

"I see," responded Echo, climbing up.

"On the bright side, we now have transportation," Dray stated encouragingly, helping her up by the arm. "We don't have to walk anymore," he added.

"You *are* a criminal," stated Echo, seeing his reckless behavior and theft of a vehicle. "Tell me everything," said Echo, entering the hatch.

61

"What?" shouted an irascible Drake. "What do you mean Vulcan and Beast are gone?"

"Master, they're not responding. We think their dead."

"I've lost two space droids just like that?"

"Yes, Master," answered the frightened Cult.

"The battle, tell me something good."

"Once our troops entered the enemy stronghold, we lost all communication. We suspect the mountain is disrupting their signals."

"Is that the only possible explanation?"

"No, they could also all be dead, which is why we've not received anything."

"This can't be happening. Leave me!" Drake growled, pressing a button on his desk. "All space droids report to Coarse Bay!" he shouted frustratingly. Staring out his window, looking out over a snowy plateau, he grumbled, "It seems that the others have come out to play."

62

"Teacher, where's Dray?"

"He is searching for answers," replied Tacitus.

"How did he become a Cult? He said he was once one of us—which is why I think he helped us."

"Dray can be whatever he wants to be. He is my son."

Victor F. Paletta attended Rockhurst University in Kansas City, where he earned a bachelor's degree in political science and Spanish. He later taught English in San Juan, Argentina, drove for a flatbed trucking company, and studied web design in Santa Monica, California. He now works as a web developer in St. Louis, Missouri.

ALSO BY VICTOR F. PALETTA

Terror Occulta

Made in the USA
Coppell, TX
12 September 2022